WHISKEY SCARS

WHISKEY SCARS

KRISTI COPELAND

Twisted Tales Publishing 2024

Whiskey Scars

Twisted Tales Publishing 2024

Edited by: Carrie D Krause – www.GetCarriedAwayEditing.com

Cover by: JODIELOCKS Design

ISBN (ebook): 979-8-9889645-4-4

ISBN (paperback): 979-8-9889645-5-1

For information contact :

https://kristicopelandwriter.com/

For “Ant” Cathy:

You believed in me from day one; for that I will be forever grateful. Thank you for being my best cheerleader!

CONTENTS

Chapter 1

Fall 2008

COLD METAL FILLED the palm of my hand as if the Glock had been designed with this moment in mind. Time stood still as a midnight thunderstorm surged outside the thin double-wide trailer's walls. Hail pounded the roof, and with a flash, the power went out.

My index finger squeezed the trigger of the 9mm for what seemed like days. Lightning flashed again, and I let the hammer drop. Thunder absorbed the gunshot as it rolled through the atmosphere. In the brief moment of light, I caught a glimpse of the 12-gauge shotgun in his hand.

One hot shell bounced on the linoleum floor and rolled under a ripped and stained rocking chair. Hatred mixed with a healthy dose of excitement overcame me. My heart surged blood through my veins; I swear my heartbeat reached my ears. Heat ran up my neck to my cheeks; the 9mm remained heavy in my grip. I never thought I would be in this position again, with a smoking gun in my hand. It seemed strange how the shortest moments in time felt like an eternity.

My brain didn't register that I had fired the shot until after he slumped to the floor and the life drained from his eyes. Blood trickled down his forehead, between his eyes, and pooled on his chest. I stared at his lifeless body until the lit cigarette between his fingers burned out.

I couldn't find any sympathy for the way this man lived his life. Dirty dishes covered the counter and garbage overflowed in the container beside the refrigerator. A metal rod with an "M"—the same shape as the imprint on her neck—sat on the stove. Such a poor excuse for a human being.

This piece of shit didn't try to explain why he left his woman to walk home in the middle of a thunderstorm. He didn't ask why I was there, just reached for his weapon. It was almost as if he knew. And why wouldn't he expect someone to rescue her at some point?

Confused, I wondered why he didn't even bother to beg for his life. Maybe that's normal; my dad didn't, either.

In that split second, I was back in Moose Pass; it all came back to me. I was a scared fourteen-year-old boy praying to a God that may or may not exist. That time was different, though. I wasn't able to save the woman and the man I shot was my dad. I really didn't have a choice nine years ago, not like I did tonight.

My dad beat my mom bloody so many times I lost count. He finally took it too far that night and put a bullet in my only protector. When she stopped breathing, my world officially came to an end. He killed my mom and when he came for me, I had no choice but to end his life.

Every night, my reality turned upside down in the same nightmare: the barn doors swung open with a strong gust of wind. One glance at my mom's body lying in the hay, then the sight of my dad crumpled, a pile of skin and clothes, and I knew what I had done.

I don't remember pulling the trigger after my dad killed my mom, but I sure as hell did the night I picked up a scared, defeated girl. None of us men were much worth saving, but at least I had never hit a lady.

This loser didn't deserve her. I didn't try to hide the gun or the crime I had committed. I understood exactly what I was doing and exactly what it meant for my future. I also understood exactly what it meant for her future. Even though I may never be free again, she finally would be.

The storm ended for the small town of Talkeetna, Alaska, at the same time as it did for the girl in my truck. Both of our lives would never be the same. Somehow, I knew in my heart I had made the right choice, even if it was the worst thing I'd ever done.

There was no point in trying to run. I placed my pistol on the hood of my truck, then sat on the porch smoking one of his cigarettes and waited for the cops to come.

Neighbors must have called the police because they arrived a few minutes after I walked out the door. She didn't get out of the truck, just stared at me through the windshield as cold metal cuffs enclosed my wrists. I swear she mouthed, "Thank you."

If I could have talked to her, I would have told her there was no need to thank me. When I saw the look on her face and the bruises on her neck, I knew I had to do something.

Chapter 2

Kennedy, age fourteen-February 2002

"KENNEDY AMBER Smith!" My mother's high-pitched voice rang through our single-wide trailer. I had pissed her off again. Not that it was anything new. She yelled at me through the open door as if it were closed. Loud enough that it caused me to jump out of bed and frantically search for something to wear.

"You're late for school. Again. Girl, when will you ever get it together? Why can't you be more like Megan?" Words spilled from her mouth, but all I heard was, "Blah, blah, blah." It was always the same with her; she constantly complained about stupid, insignificant things. At least with her out of sight, I could roll my eyes without getting slapped.

I didn't have my own alarm clock and my big sister, Megan, who I shared a room with, always refused to wake me up for school. The way she figured, I was old enough to get up on my own. Being fourteen sucked; too old to be treated like a kid, too young to be treated as an adult. The everlasting in-between.

Our mom hardly ever bothered to get out of bed to see us off to school, so it startled me even more that her voice bounced off the walls. She didn't have anywhere to be that early, so she usually stayed in her room while Megan and I helped the younger kids get ready. It's not like she had a real job like everyone else's parents. She earned her money from whoever she let spend the night in her bed. She called it "entertaining", but I knew what she was doing, and it made me sick. Since she was up, it was probably one of her regular guys.

I must have been tired, I slept so hard I didn't even hear them through the thin walls. I looked out my bedroom window to see who had parked their car in the driveway overnight. It was my way of preparing for which face to put on.

We rarely interacted with any of the men; the regulars were the exception. I was nice to Issac—white F-150—because he was nice to me. If his night fell on a weekend, he would make pancakes for all of us kids the next morning.

Mike was a jerk—black minivan—I refused to even look at him. He had no patience for smaller kids. One morning, my sister, Emily, hid behind my legs when Mike yelled at her to be quiet. I found my voice, raised it, and advised my mom's friend that he had better not scare my sister again. I didn't expect my mom to slap me across the face for protecting her.

Steve—red Camaro—was okay in the beginning, but anymore, the way he looked at me gave me the creeps. Last week, he winked at me and reached for my arm. I tried to pull away, but his grasp was too strong. He forced me to sit on his lap and whispered in my ear, "you're so pretty, Kennedy. And so young." He tried to kiss my neck, but I wriggled away. I told my mom that he tried to touch me, but she blew me off. Told me to forget it, that I was imagining things.

A newer model silver Camry sat in the driveway buried under a fresh layer of snow, so I knew it wasn't any of them. Of all the men my mom "entertained"—her word, not mine—more than one drove this kind of car, but none ever stayed more than a couple hours.

I found a halfway clean sweatshirt and jeans in the dirty laundry basket and pulled them on, ran my fingers through my shoulder-length curly brown hair, and stuffed my feet into bear-foot shaped slippers to ward off the mid-winter cold which permeated the floors.

Even at fourteen, I knew that what my mom did was wrong, but as she explained, how else would we eat? I told her that maybe she should go get a job at Dollar General or as a receptionist at the hospital.

Even a waitress or bartender was something she could be proud of and actually tell people what she did for a living. She wouldn't hear it; told me how I was too young to understand her struggles and I didn't know what she had to put up with—whatever that meant.

If my daddy had stuck around, maybe things would be different. Maybe not, but I liked to think about "what if."

What if he had been a caring person who would fight for his family and his kid?

What if he didn't leave Seward for a college education in Anchorage?

What if he was man enough to break the cycle of his own family tree?

From what Mom told me, his dad left when he was a kid, too. She thought telling me that would help me feel like I wasn't alone. Didn't work. She didn't even bother to give me his last name: Johnson. The only thing he gave me was his genes.

Tom Johnson had been on a vacation with friends in Seward when he met my mom. They hooked up and she got pregnant. He had already enrolled in college and didn't want to be tied down with a kid. Gee, thanks, Dad.

He and Megan's dad had the same MO, though—neither of them cared, they didn't want to have anything to do with us. They walked away from their responsibilities and didn't even bother to pay child support. More information than a fourteen-year-old needed to know, but here we are.

Most of Mom's middle-of-the-night phone calls when she's drunk were to my little brother, Nathan's dad. He was the only one who still answered her calls. The normal conversations began with her begging for money, and ended with her screaming obscenities, then slamming the phone on the counter. Those nights, she'd cry herself to sleep.

In my opinion, Mom is so hard to deal with that she scared our dads away even if they cared at one time, but Megan doesn't agree. She thinks all they're losers and we were just dealt a bad hand. Except Zack. He was the lucky one. His dad got full custody last year after our mom showed her true self in court.

When she came home without Zack, she told us kids about how she chewed out the judge when he asked stupid questions. No one needed to convince him Mom was an unfit mother; she proved it herself.

Mom must have been hungover; her hair was in a rat's nest and her makeup was smudged. A bruise on her neck became more visible with each passing second. Usually, she did her best to be presentable the next morning, to make sure her friend returned for more. She didn't even have the energy to completely close her robe, her black lace bra and panties peeked out through the opening.

A gust of cold air rushed through the front door as the man from last night left. Mom leaned against the kitchen counter and sighed. "That was a rough night, he barely let me sleep. He left a nice tip, but I'm almost too old to entertain like that anymore."

EIGHTH GRADERS were supposed to have best friends and people they could count on when life turned bad. At least, that's what it looked like for everyone but me. I was the only girl in class who didn't have a buddy to study with or eat with. Even in grade school, no one ever wanted to play with me during recess.

Most of the time, I chose to stay inside and read. Next year, in high school, I wouldn't have to worry about being alone. Next year, I'd be able to hide in the library and study as much as I want without anyone knowing any better.

Only a few of my classmates lived in the trailer park and they were part of the smelly kid group. Everyone knew how poor they were and that their family life was depressing. I refused to walk the two miles through spring breakup to school with them because I didn't want anyone to think we were alike.

Thankfully, my mom demanded that all her kids stay clean and taught us to care about how we looked to others. Megan caught a ride with her boyfriend but wouldn't let me tag along. Whenever I asked Mom to drive me, she would shrug and say she didn't have enough gas.

Melted snow mixed with the still-frozen ice patches and I managed to step in almost all the slush. My boots from last year were too small and had cracks in the soles, letting freezing cold water seep through to my socks. At the beginning of last winter, I got smart and shoved my feet into Ziploc bags before pulling on the boots. Even if my feet were cold, at least they would stay dry.

When I finally made it to my locker, I changed into sneakers. Alan Martin, my locker mate, told me every day how smart I was for thinking of the Ziploc solution.

The popular kids ignored me, which was better than getting picked on, like Alan. The boys made fun of his ripped clothes and messy hair every day. He wasn't a good-looking kid, and he didn't get good grades, but maybe someday he'd grow into himself. At least he didn't smell.

Kids of two backgrounds jammed the hallway—the "have its" and the "don't have its." Those who "have it" were gorgeous and rich. They wore all the newest fashions, donned the latest hairstyles, and rode to school in their parents' Hummer or BMW instead of walking or riding the bus. They ran the halls and decided who would be welcomed into their group and who would be forever ostracized.

These same kids thought Megan had it; she knew exactly who to hang out with and what to say so they didn't find out her truth. I had learned some of her tricks, but the fact still remained that I didn't have it. No question. Not even close.

Teachers and my mom's boyfriends always told me I was pretty, but even I knew you couldn't trust what adults say. They'll lie to you just so you don't turn into a mean, uncaring person. Just because they said I was great, didn't mean I was, or ever would be. One day, maybe I would be lucky enough to find a good guy, get married, and move to Florida or California. I've seen plenty of palm trees on TV and wished, with all my might, that someone would get me out of Alaska.

The bell for lunch startled me out of my warm-weather daydream. The days seemed to meld together, each one the same as before. Lunch hour was my favorite time of the day. One server would sneak extra dessert onto my plate if she noticed I was in a mood. Her daughter, Brittany, would be going to Seward High School next year, and she promised I would have a friend waiting for me when I got there.

I always sat at the table closest to the hallway entrance so I could escape if I needed to. One of my weird quirks; I hated to be trapped. Once I finished my cold French fries, I picked up my chocolate milk just to have it batted from my hand. I frowned, ready to kick someone's ass for messing with my food. I searched for the source and found Cody Miller standing over me with a big grin. His buddies laughed and gave high-fives.

Long strands of blonde hair framed his symmetrical facial features. Blue eyes sparkled as he took in my surprise. Not only his gorgeous face, but everything about him checked off the boxes of my description of perfection. His quarterback physique, his straight-A report card brain, and his smooth, deep voice.

"Kennedy, right?" My mouth hung open as he straddled the seat beside me. I could hardly believe he knew my name. Cody sat in the front row of my English class and always turned around to look in my direction, but I thought maybe he was eyeing the new blonde girl with boobs who sat behind me.

My voice shook. "Hey, Cody."

"Want to go to the dance with me Friday night?"

In that moment, all my dreams came true—in an instant, my social status changed for the better. I could visualize graduation, getting married, moving to Florida, and having four kids as if it were written in the stars.

"Okay."

Chapter 3

Jake, age twelve—May 1997

KITTENS CUDDLED with their mother, kneading her stomach as they nursed. Mews and purrs brought a smile to my lips; simple, natural love. Leather and hay mixed with my mom's shampoo scented the stagnant air in the main barn until she opened the double doors facing the pond. A light breeze brought freshness and a calm energy as it flowed past our horse and out the opposite doors.

The barn was the one area of our property where I could hide from my dad when he drank. He hardly ever bothered to wander very far from the house when he had a bottle in his hand. My happy place was in the middle stall; it was also the closest area to the house where I could close both the exterior and interior stall doors to escape the sounds of arguing, breaking dishes, and slamming doors.

The mother cat kept her new babies in a box I put in

the stall just for her. Mom and I played with them for a few minutes each day while we did our chores. White fur covered my favorite new kitten; I named her Peanut because she was the smallest of the litter.

Mom let me name all the critters as they found their way to our property. She said I had the most creative mind of any twelve-year-old she knew. Sometimes I wondered if she even knew any other kids my age.

Soloman, our black gelded Morgan, sensed trouble before other creatures in the barn. From his spot in the first stall, he knickered, stomped, then turned, and ran out the outer door into the pasture. The goats and donkeys followed, throwing dust behind their short bodies. A tall, slow-moving shadow stalled as my dad stood in the middle of the aisle between the tack and feed rooms.

"Susan." His deep voice vibrated through the air and chills ran up my spine.

We stilled, and I stared at Mom through the thick lenses of my new glasses. I questioned with my eyes if I should speak. One quick shake of her head kept me quiet. Her eyes were wide, and she held her breath as he neared. I was sick of being scared.

I promised myself that one day I would be strong enough to be a man and stick up for my mom. She always told me to just do what he said, but she always did, and where did that get her? Hit, bruised, in the hospital time and time again. I was so sick of this being our normal.

"I know you're in here. The doors are open."

Knowing she had no choice but to reveal our location, she closed her eyes and took a deep breath. Somehow, she found the strength to put a sweet tone in her voice. "We're in here." She stood and when I joined her, she pointed to the corner; I sank into the hay, thankful I couldn't see him. Maybe that meant he couldn't see me, either.

With my back against the wall, I pulled my knees to my chest and waited. Whiskey on his breath wafted from the middle of the barn all the way into my stall and stung my nose. I tucked my face between my knees to ward off the smell and pushed back tears. If he knew I was crying, I'd get it, too.

At the same time his hand connected with her face, Mom cried out. Through the partially open stall door, she glanced at me from the floor. Dirt covered her hands and dusted her tear-stained face.

"Don't tell me that rat of a cat had more kittens." His giant hand wrapped around her hair and Mom disappeared from my vision.

"She only had four this time. I'll find homes for them, I promise." Pleading with him, her voice raised an octave.

"What you'll do is what I tell you to do. You're

supposed to be processing chickens for dinner, and what do I find? You wasting time with useless animals."

This time his contact was forceful enough that she landed on her knees in the stall beside me, her eyes sad and wet. Blood trickled from her split lip, down her chin, and dripped into the hay. Every time this happened, she promised she would make it stop, but never could. No matter how many times she tried to be sweet, it ended up in another bloody nose, split lip, or bruised eye.

"You're also supposed to be raising our kid to be a man, not a fat-ass wimp."

I held my breath; I had hoped he would forget about me.

Deep-set eyes the color of coal focused on Mom. Dad's gaze darted from her to me to the box of kittens, then back to Mom. In one swift motion, he raised his hand, closed his fist, and connected with the soft spot on Mom's side. One eye swollen shut, she looked away before she cried out in pain.

"The way you're raising him, locals will think he's a cheechako. Is that what you want? For our neighbors to think your precious Jakey has just arrived in the Great Land? Like he doesn't know how to act or make a life in the Pass?" Flannel covered my dad's enormous frame; his muscles flexed under the material as he picked up my mom and wrapped his hand in her long dark blond hair.

"No, I swear. Everyone knows he's blood." She

whimpered and kicked her feet, trying to reach the ground. "Please let me go."

He carried her to the neighboring stall, which we hadn't cleaned yet and, when he shoved her to the ground, a pile of horse poop softened her fall. "That's not what I'm told."

Riding equipment lined the outside of the stalls; my dad pulled a whip from the wall and swung it. Hard. Hard enough for him to grunt, and for her to scream.

"No, no, Robbie. Please, don't." Her voice was weak and thick with emotion.

There was nothing I could do. If I tried to fight him, he'd beat her worse. And me; he'd do the same thing to me as he did to her. It killed me how she took the full brunt of his fists to save my face and body from breaks and bruises. My mom loves me so much that she's willing to put her life in danger to save me.

One day, I swear, I'll make him stop.

Anger rose in my soul and my chest tightened. A frown pulled my eyebrows into a "V" and tears wetted my cheeks. If I were only big enough, strong enough to fight him. I'd pound him to a pulp and make him sorry. At least once every day I fantasized about what it would feel like to punch him in the face and drop him to his knees. Sometimes more. I would force him to apologize, leave all his money, and walk down our long driveway never to be seen again.

After a brief struggle, the whip sounded different but I couldn't tell why. Over the next several minutes, my mom cried, begged, and screamed before eventually going silent. Only then did my dad relent. He stood tall; between the iron bars which separated the stalls, the sweat dripping from his face seemed normal. I had witnessed the same expression many times, just not after he had beaten my mom into submission. He panted like a tired dog, turned and exited the stall, locking it behind him.

Once I was certain he had left the barn, I went to her. Outside the locked door, a pair of jeans, a shirt, and her muck boots lay in a pile beside her parka. It made sense why the whip sounded different; she was naked. My stomach rolled, and I thought I would be sick. I unlocked the door and squeezed my eyes shut as I pushed her clothes through a crack in the door.

As she dressed, she reassured me. "One day, Jakey, I swear we'll get away from him. I just need to save up enough money first." She took a deep breath, wiped her face, and put on a fake smile. "Right now, though, we need to clean some chickens."

I MOVED THE chicken block outside so the rain could wash away all the mess. This was the absolute worst part of my chores. I hated killing anything—even if it was for food. These poor chickens hadn't done anything to hurt me, yet I had to hurt them. I was forced to end their lives.

Feathers scattered with the crushing blow of the hatchet. Blood spattered my clothes and stained the stump. The first time I cleaned the chickens, I forgot to take off my parka and tried to hide the stains when I went to school. Kids are so cruel when they don't understand. Disturbed at the sight of birds running around, headless, until they finally died, I cringed. More feathers littered the ground as we readied the three dead birds to be plucked.

Lost in a memory, I did the rest of my chores in a daze. It was the best way to keep my mom from having to explain why she let him continue to hit her. When I was younger, Mom had hidden the horrible arguments well. She would make Dad wait until after I was in bed before they went to the barn to fight. I could still hear them, but I never said anything. She covered the bruises on her face with makeup or made excuses when I asked what had happened. Scared to know the truth, I convinced myself not to ask about it.

Mom had always told me how real men did something good for other people. Her dad had saved a man from a fiery car crash when he was younger, got burned himself, but never complained.

"Now, that's my idea of a real man. Someone not

afraid to risk their life to save someone." Her advice was to make my friends and more importantly, strangers, happy; to help them be better people. In turn, I would be a better person; I'd have a purpose.

On my tenth birthday, Mom let the ice cream melt too much and a sticky residue coated a circle on the table. Dad slapped her across the face so hard she dropped to her knees. I guess he thought I was finally old enough to recognize the consequences of not obeying.

I was so surprised that all I could do was stare at her in disbelief. After he went to bed, Mom sat me down and explained that as long as she didn't make him angry, he wouldn't slap her again.

"He's done this before?" I didn't know what to think. She'd always been so happy and kind. It didn't make sense to me how he would hit her in the face for punishment. Over something so stupid. "That doesn't sound like a very good man, to me."

With pursed lips, she nodded. She always promised she would never lie to me. I understood, though, that she also meant she would only tell me the parts of truth which she felt I needed to know.

"He's done it a lot, hasn't he?" My voice cracked.

Her eyes pleaded for me to understand. She tilted her head, then looked away.

Multiple emotions rushed through me, and I didn't

know whether to be sad, angry, or disappointed. I settled on sadness. I wrapped my arms around her and lowered my voice. “Is that why Jasmine died?”

Surprised to hear my sister’s name, Mom’s breath caught. She pulled away from me and looked into my eyes. She didn’t even need to answer. I already knew.

Over the years, Mom talked about Jasmine every now and again. She didn’t say much, but I could sense the despair in her energy when she said her name. My little sister had been born three months early; she died just a week later.

EVERY WEEKEND, Dad would invite a bunch of his friends over for late-night parties. They would make drinks and play cards until I went to bed, then they would go outside. Mom said it was so they wouldn’t wake me up, but sometimes they were loud enough for me to hear every word, sometimes not.

They all used to play football during high school and would sometimes throw a ball around in the yard. One of the guys must have brought it with him because I’d never see it after they left. “Susie, come over here.” Dad’s voice rose to my open window, so I crawled out of bed and over to the window to hear the conversation.

“Why don’t you take the guys for a tour of your precious barn?”

I peeked at them through my bedroom curtains. Two men followed Mom to the barn; she didn't sound happy about showing off our special place. She should have been proud of it, but the tone in Dad's voice had been teasing.

"You'd think with all of us here, she'd do something with that hair." One friend complained. "Why don't you buy her shit to keep her prettied up?"

"Mind your fucking business." Dad hissed and poked him in the chest. "You like her well enough, don't ya?"

The man lowered his head. "Yeah."

"Keep it up and I'll make sure you don't have a turn with her again."

Tom Johnson, the only one of Dad's friends who ever talked to me, strolled over to my dad. He was a good guy, in my eyes. "Hey, Robbie. You doing business tonight?"

"Why the hell do you think I invited everyone over?" Dad smiled and slapped Tom on the shoulder. "Just you wait; I got a good pile of crops for everyone to rummage through."

Disheveled, Mom limped out of the barn. I wondered if someone had accidentally tripped her, the way she favored one hip. Her pretty blue shirt was buttoned crooked, and she ran her hand through her hair, trying to calm the frizzies. She frowned and wiped her eyes; I hated to see her so sad. When she glanced up to my window. I ducked, hoping she didn't see me snooping.

READY TO SNUGGLE my sweet Peanut, I opened the stall door with an ear-to-ear smile. The little fur ball and how she purred when she nuzzled my neck made all the bad stuff go away. It had been a couple of days since we had time to visit, and I wanted to apologize with a treat and a string for the kittens to chase.

Dad followed us into the barn to make sure we didn't waste any time on our chores; he did that sometimes. It annoyed Mom because he didn't trust us to complete our tasks without nit-picking.

The box was gone. Confused, I glanced at my mom and her shoulders sank. Tears filled her eyes, which confused me even more.

"Robbie? Do you know what happened to the kittens?"

My dad responded with one word: "Yep." He smirked at her. She nodded once, signaling that she understood not to put up a fight. A high-pitched, jovial whistle followed my dad through the barn doors and to the house.

"He found them homes already, Jake," she lied.

My heart raced; tears burned my eyes. I didn't

believe him. He lied about everything. I didn't want to cry; I was twelve. Twelve-year-old boys didn't cry.

She read my thoughts. "I'm sure Peanut is with someone who loves her just as much as you do."

Tears fell down my face, and my mom pulled me into one of her warm hugs. She held me for a few beats before she wiped my face dry. "I'm so sorry, honey. I know you wanted to keep her. It just wasn't in the cards."

"Why does he do that? He always ruins everything."

Hay mixed with mud and poop covered the stall floor. Mom pushed the pitchfork into my hand. "I wish more than anything that you could have kept all the kittens. You know your dad—he doesn't think feeding useless animals is smart. I'm sorry, Jakey. Once I have enough money …" Her voice trailed off to the fantasy she kept alive in her mind.

"Why do you let him?" My thought escaped into actual words. For a moment, I didn't think she heard me. I had hoped she didn't hear me. Then and there, I made a promise. "I'll stop him one day, Mom."

Chapter 4

Kennedy, age sixteen–December 2004

BOOKS TOPPLED from my arms to the floor; pages of notebook paper flew across the hallway as impatient kids trampled my homework. I tried to push between everyone to gather my notes, but only caught a few papers before the rest floated out the doors with the crowd. Pandemonium ensued every day after seventh hour; the last place anyone wanted to be after school was inside the school.

"If Cody were here, no one would just walk by and let my notes get destroyed. No one would have the balls to walk all over my papers." I mumbled to myself, and Brittany rolled her eyes. She had tired of hearing Cody's name after about three weeks, but I didn't let that stop me from talking about him at least once every day.

"Look, just because you dated forever before he moved to Anchorage doesn't mean you're destined to be together. You should keep your options open. He's not here." Over her shoulder, she smiled at two seniors who stood against the lockers watching us. This conversation was not new; Troy and Kevin had made it clear weeks ago how much they wanted to date us. "But they are."

I ignored her. "He thinks I'm perfect—he told me so. He loves everything about me, even my voice. I love how he makes me feel and the little things he does for me are so sweet. He's coming back for me after he graduates high school; he promised. We made a pact."

Although Cody did promise to come back for me, it crossed my mind more than once how I could just be another girl. His dad had moved him to Anchorage to finish high school because the captains of his fishing vessels needed help. Since all his Seward boats were doing well on their own, he decided to shift his focus to the larger fleet. Cody said he begged to stay so he could graduate with his friends, but his dad didn't want him to live alone.

"I know, I know." She didn't mean to be condescending, and I knew it. If anything, she was a little envious because she had never had a love as strong as Cody's and mine. Besides, if I didn't hurry, I would be late for my first day of work. She needed to push me out the door, as usual.

"You don't want to let Hannah down—my sister doesn't vouge for just anyone. Let's go get you ready for tonight."

"Cody's my future. We're going to take on the world, I just know it."

A smile spread into a grin. Brittany put her arm around my shoulders and led me past the boys. "You're right. He is."

The only thing that kept me moving was Cody's promise. On his last night in Seward, Cody and I spent an entire night of uninterrupted time together. We drove to the Waterfront Park and watched the northern lights. Blues and greens streaked the sky over Resurrection Bay and gave me chills; I'd seen this phenomenon my entire life, it never got old.

Parked between picnic tables, Cody lowered the tailgate and sat a bottle of liquor between us. We each took a long swig, then engaged in a longer kiss. As he slowed and came up for breath, he reminded me of how wonderful our relationship had been. "I've never wanted to be with anyone forever, Kennedy. You're my match."

It took all I had to not cry. Weakness wasn't a good look for anyone. I leaned into him and offered my love with physical touch. The beauty of the sky couldn't compare to the way Cody made me feel that night. I was his.

Covered with an old blanket in the back of his dad's Escalade, he convinced me to give myself to him and vow not to be with anyone else. Ever. Wrapped in his arms, he whispered how beautiful I was—something only old guys said—and how he wanted us to be together forever. If we had been older, it might have been a proposal, but at the moment, I took it as a promise.

His touch was gentle, his kisses were passionate. We explored each other's bodies until I was about to explode. I didn't know what to expect to happen, but whatever it was, I wanted it.

Positioned between my bent knees, he asked permission. "Will you let me make love to you?"

Scared and excited at the same time, I nodded.

"Tell me you want me." Cody's voice lowered and he held my gaze as he waited for me to respond.

"I want you," I whispered, and he kissed me. I meant it; I wanted to be with him in every way possible.

Intense pressure mixed with anticipation as he pressed into me. I gasped; I thought sex was supposed to feel good, but it didn't. It hurt. Tears leaked and streamed down the side of my face. Cody kissed them away as he moved his hips.

"I love you so much, Kennedy." After a couple minutes, he sped up the rhythm, panted, then groaned in my ear. He filled me completely; I cried out.

"Now you're mine." His tongue tangled with mine. "And I'm yours. Look at me."

Under his weight, I focused on breathing and stared into his eyes.

"Tell me you love me."

"Cody. I love you more than anything in the world." I meant it.

"I'm sorry if I hurt you. I just couldn't help myself. You felt so good." Kisses trailed down my chin to my neck. He rolled off me, still panting. "Don't worry, the first time isn't ever any good for the girl."

I didn't ask him how he knew that; I didn't want to know. We held each other the whole night and promised our love would last through the vast distance. In time, he would come back for me, and we would live happily ever after. I had to believe it. If I didn't, the last frontier would swallow me whole.

DARKNESS concealed booths at the far back of the Next-door bar. Chairs sat upside down on tables, as they waited for the bartender to prepare for a packed Friday night, even though it was only Wednesday. In one corner a large black bear stood on his hind legs with arms stretched out as if he would grab someone as they passed. I shuddered at the thought of those claws piercing my skin.

Fifty years ago, when the bar was new, it may have been an upscale establishment. All these years later, though, with little upkeep, it would be considered a dive. Scented with stale beer and cigarettes, the purpose of this watering hole was clear—to drink. Most of the customers did just that; a lot.

Brittany had told her older sister about my life at home and how we never had any money. If it wasn't for Emily and Nathan, I wouldn't have accepted Hannah's offer to help me make some cash. The twenty-year-old shared her knowledge about other jobs in town. They didn't pay well enough for her to afford rent in the neighboring apartment complex, but since working at Next-door, she had built her savings account enough to buy a new car.

After school, Brittany pulled me into the bathroom, made sure my makeup was on point, and handed me a too-tight shirt from her backpack. "Oh, man. If Cody could see you now. He'd be so proud." An evil grin touched her lips. "And hard."

In thirty minutes, we had put together the perfect outfit, accentuating my thin waist and all my curves in the right places. I walked out of the school looking like a professional businesswoman. Or so I thought.

We hurried to the bar for my interview. Hannah had lied to the owner so he would hire me even though I wasn't old enough to work there. I could easily pass for eighteen but didn't have a fake ID to prove it. No matter: the next thing I knew, I had a job.

Two days later, I arrived early, as Hannah suggested, to loosen up a bit before my shift. I didn't know what that meant until she pointed to the stool beside her at the bar. Two shots of something amber colored sat beside her, she slid one to me and nodded. I'd never tasted diesel fuel, but imagined the flavor was probably close to whatever it was I had swallowed in one gulp. The second shot tasted just as bad, but I forgot all about the flavor when the giggles took over.

"This is Yasmine." Hannah introduced me to a heavy-set lady in her early thirties. She looked like my mom, in a way. "She's another waitress. Between the two of us, we serve a hundred customers a night."

"It's exhausting." Yasmine's pretty smile eased my nerves. "We're so glad you're here to help." She floated into the sea of chairs to deliver drinks to a table of four.

"Come on, I'll show you around."

I followed Hannah to a large private area beyond the restrooms. There, a rack of skimpy clothes and bikinis lined one wall and a sectional couch sat in the other corner with a curtain secured to the ceiling. Dressed in a crop top, short jean shorts, and strappy heels, Hannah slid hangers to the left until she found the perfect outfit for me. "You're covering entirely too much skin."

Only then did I compute how her clothes didn't coincide with the cold day. I tilted my head and squinted. "To serve drinks?"

"Yeah, something like that," she chuckled and

pushed the small pieces of cloth into my hands. "Here. Change."

I surveyed the room then settled my gaze on Hannah. "What, in front of you?"

"Listen, it's not like I haven't seen a naked girl before. You're my sister's best friend. You're fine. Change."

"Naked?"

"No bra. And you can NOT wear granny panties—thongs only, my love."

I held the teeny-tiny clothes at eye level and cringed. I needed the money, so what would it matter if I didn't wear a bra? With a sigh, I undressed. The skimpy outfit made me nervous; I've never really shown any skin in my everyday wardrobe. But they were paying me to dress a certain way, so I had to give it a shot.

Hannah handed me another drink—this time, a fruity concoction—and I downed it in seconds. For the next thirty minutes, we practiced my new sexy walk and toothy smile. Heels were a new addition to my wardrobe, but I only tripped a couple times. Once I mastered my new style, she gave me pointers on how to make the guys want to give a ten or even twenty-dollar tip instead of a single.

"Use your curves, stand too close, smile too wide. If you think you're being too forward, be even more forward. But, whatever you do, don't directly ask for anything. These guys can read women like a book. If you want something from them, hint."

I raised my eyebrows.

"Listen, it's weird at first, I get it. But look at it this way. I just bought a brand-new car with the cash I've made here. Brit told you about my apartment, right? I paid six months up front. In cash. Trust me, this job is worth it. You'll be free in no time. I promise."

Loose, a little dizzy, and ready to mingle, my head buzzed, and my steps met the rhythm of the music on the jukebox. I followed Hannah's lead, smiled, and flirted while taking orders. The first few interactions were uncomfortable, but Hannah reminded me that I could be anyone I wanted to be while I worked. No one knew me.

It took some time to get used to the G-string and I found myself pulling at the hem of my too-short skirt. Men gaped at my body, though. The thought of them wanting me, that I turned them on, was exciting. Invigorating.

All my inhibitions disappeared with the next shot. Just as Hannah suggested, I smiled too large and stood too close. Close enough for the men to take in the scent of my perfume. One of them actually growled as he reached for me. I backed away and waved my index finger at him. When I delivered his drink, he called me a tease. "I'm John. What's your name, sweetheart?"

"Kennedy, but I like sweetheart," I flirted.

When I staggered home that night with two hundred dollars in my pocket, I couldn't hide my smile. Men hitting on me and putting their grimy paws on my ass wasn't nearly as bad as my imagination let me think it would have been. Flirting with the older men had actually been kind of fun; the attention boosted my confidence. As long as they didn't try anything with me, I was just fine. I could do this.

The next night, Hannah told me what I could expect from certain regulars. The men paid her to look pretty and act like they turned her on. She showed me how to do a little dance and take off my clothes in a way that made the men want me. At first, I was hesitant, but I figured if she could do it, I could, too. We did a couple shots and practiced until I looked comfortable.

No one was allowed to touch me; I could touch them, though. If I wanted to. When they sat on the couch, they would sit on their hands to quash the urge. "Sometimes, if I really like a guy, or they're a regular that I dance for all the time, I'll let them grab my ass or touch my boobs. Bigger tips." Hannah winked. "Better car."

So, if someone wanted to be alone, I led them to the couch in the back room and pulled the curtain. Brittany and I spent most of our time watching the latest videos and dancing as if we were in them, so I knew shaking my butt and moving to the music wouldn't be a problem.

It's the taking off my clothes part that bothered me a little. But, honestly, only a little. We were in private, and I could close my eyes and pretend I was alone. Who knew making this kind of cash could be so easy?

LIFE CHANGED ON my seventeenth birthday. After school, I blew out the candle on a store-bought cupcake at home with Nathan and Emily, then walked through a foot of snow to work.

Contentment took over; for the first time in my life, I didn't need to worry about my next meal or if we would have heat through the winter. My mom didn't ask how I could afford to buy new shoes and coats for my siblings or even thank me for the new robe I got her for her birthday.

I bounced through the door an hour before my shift with a skip in my step. My usual drink and two shots were lined up on the bar. Willy, the bartender, poured a third shot. "Happy birthday, Special K." I smiled and threw it back without a second thought. Everyone thought I was nineteen, so I decided I had better act as if I was.

Hannah waited for me in the back room, a gift bag on the makeup table.

"Awe, you shouldn't have." Gifts are one of my favorite things, ever. Gifts and pizza. I peeked in the bag and found something fluffy. Something soft like rabbit fur brushed across my fingertips. I gasped, “You didn’t.”

“I did. You’ve talked about wearing something cashmere for months. Happy birthday. You deserve it.”

Tears stung my eyes as I hugged my friend. “Thank you.” She had officially made my day. No one could ruin my mood.

Until they did.

“Yeah” by Usher blared from the jukebox as I wound my way between tables to pick up the next order at the bar. Each beat matched the sway of my hips, I winked at Willy, and he poured me another Lemon Drop. He laughed at my scrunched face as I sucked the lemon. He laughed harder when I flipped him off.

“Hey, stranger.” I hadn’t seen John in a couple of weeks. At one point he told me all about how his job took him out of town for long periods of time—something about fishing—but I didn’t really care.

He looked me up and down as I placed his regular order—a beer and a shot—on the high-top table. I brushed his arm with my breast, and he groaned under his breath—I smirked. As much as I liked how much money I was making, I enjoyed the responses from the men more.

His friend lifted his chin and smiled; he looked familiar, but I couldn’t place him. Even though he was probably old enough to be my dad, I still flirted.

His white teeth gleamed in the dim light and his dark brown, almost black eyes danced as they roamed over my body. I turned to take his order and "accidentally" rubbed my behind across his hand which rested on his leg. From the look on his face, I instantly understood a large tip was in my future.

"How's my favorite girl, tonight?" A wink accompanied John's slurred words.

"Better now that you're here." I blew him a kiss.

"My boss wanted to see why I smile more on Thursday's, so I decided to show him."

My long hair hung over my shoulders, covering most of my chest. Men loved when I brushed it back to show a tight spaghetti string crop top which barely contained my breasts. Until then, they both hid like scared children. "Nice to meet you."

When men reached for me, but realized that they couldn't touch, I liked it. I liked the way it made me feel to know someone wanted me. John's friend ran his hand from the back of my leg and over my ass on his way to pick up the shot glass. I didn't stop him—it was the best way to get more than a dollar tip.

"Take a load off, gorgeous. Stay a while." John offered a sip of his beer.

"Sorry, sweetie. It's too busy to chat tonight." I glanced toward the back room and raised an eyebrow. John tipped better for drinks when I gave him lap dances, so I led him to believe he wanted to spend his ten minutes behind the curtain. He smiled and stood.

"WHAT SONG DO you want to start with tonight?" I asked as John took his place on the couch.

"Kiss."

My favorite and he knew it. I smiled and provoked him with my swaying hips as I pushed B13 on the personal jukebox. More of my favorites would follow: D02, G16, and A04. Five minutes into our session, I was at the point in my routine where I straddled my customer's knees, bent at the waist, and shoved his face between my exposed perfect C cups.

John's boss entered the room and pulled the curtain back. His radiant smile turned into a devious grin; his eyes darkened the minute he saw my bare ass surrounded by straps of the thong. I swear I heard him growl. Old guys were easy to please.

It's not unusual for friends to want a double dance, but we didn't approve unless Hannah and I went back together. That way we could kind of tag team while keeping each other safe. Everyone knew and abided by these rules. And we only agreed to doubles when Yasmine worked so she could still serve the customers. By the end of my first night, it was clear she stayed in the front room. Tonight, however, Yasmine had called in sick.

I crawled on John's lap, held his gaze, and covered his hands with mine as they squeezed my breasts. I spoke to his boss, "Sorry, hon. One at a time." My sweet tone sang above the beat of the music. It wasn't the first time I had to refuse a double. When he didn't turn around, I strengthened my voice and shrugged. "Bar rules, babe."

Two steps later, the stone-faced older man stood behind me and above John.

I rose on my knees only to find resistance on my hips. John held me in place, never taking his eyes off mine. My stomach turned and in a shaky voice, I begged, "John. Please. Let me go."

"Oh, but we're not done with our songs, K." He lifted one eyebrow.

"You know we're only allowed one at a time back here. Please. Let me go." I tried to wriggle out of his grip; he slapped my ass hard, and I stilled.

"Don't tell me you never break the rules. How old are you, again?" The way he stared into my eyes told me he knew I was too young to work at the bar. "You wouldn't want your boss to find out your real age, now, would you? Little girl."

Stunned, I relented. John held me in place and unzipped his pants.

Too scared to move, I remained still as he forced

himself inside me. “No.” Tears streamed down my face as dizziness flooded through me. As he had sex with my body, I felt like I was in the middle of a dream—more like a nightmare.

When he finished, he pushed me away and his boss wrapped an arm around my waist.

“Stop. Please.” It came out as a whisper; they didn’t hear me. If they did, they would have listened. Wouldn’t they? “Stop.” The words were audible the second time.

John’s evil grin gave me chills. “You know you love it.” He squeezed my breasts, hard this time. I whimpered. “She’s all yours, Gus.”

Stubble from a day-old beard scratched my cheek as Gus held me tight against him. “Baby, if you know what’s best, you’ll hush.”

Numb, I found myself bent over the arm of the couch with an old guy ramming me from behind. Pain flooded my entire body. I cried and begged them to stop. The more I spoke, the louder I got; I had found my voice and just wanted to escape.

“Relax, now. I don’t want to have to get rough with you.” Gus forced me onto the couch and smiled, suddenly ugly. “Now gimme some sugar.”

I knew if I fought them, it would only get worse. I hushed and eventually they finished.

Tears smeared my makeup. I forced myself to stop crying and cleaned myself up. In a fog, I dressed in slow motion, not believing what had just happened. Hannah had told me sex wasn't allowed, just dancing. She said it was okay. I believed her.

I didn't do a very good job straightening my hair and I'm pretty sure my shirt was inside out, but I couldn't care. Money littered the jukebox table, and I pushed it in my purse; what I had just endured, you better believe I would take the bills.

I told Willy I wasn't feeling well as I rushed out the front door; he was oblivious. His conversation with one of his fishing buddies was evidently more important than me. Besides, business had died down and Hannah could handle the rest of the night alone. She had been on the opposite side of the room getting close with some guys in one of the booths, so she didn't see me leave. I didn't realize I had left my gift until after I made it home.

If other customers had a clue of what happened while Hannah or I disappeared, they didn't let on. Of course, Willy was in on it; when someone asked how to get one of us alone, he set up the connection. He had always been kind and seemed to care. After what happened though, I wondered if Willy knew exactly what went on behind the curtain.

Before my seventeenth birthday, I only danced for the customers. Some of them wanted more, they had been clear, but Hannah had given me the best tips on how to turn them down and keep them interested at the same time. Now it seemed obvious she had been in the same position before. I wondered if she had ever been raped.

Chapter 5

Jake, age fourteen—May 1999

DURING SPRING thaws, mud holes popped up in random areas of the far back pasture. Legend has it that our land was once part of a glacial path and could be unstable, which was probably the reason Dad had been able to pick up so much acreage at what he called a "steal."

Unbeknownst to me, one of these mud holes appeared along the fence line, and before I could turn the John Deere, it practically swallowed Dad's new tractor. Three quarters of the front tires and most of the frame were under the heavy muck.

I swore into the wind before I turned the engine off, hopped down from the platform, and surveyed the situation. As I kicked the ground with each step, I figured how the bucket could be used to pull the tractor out. Relieved that my dad wouldn't have to know about this, and I would avoid another bruised rib, I climbed back into the seat and turned the key.

Nothing.

Shit. I hadn't checked the gas level before I left the barn.

Dad had bragged how he spent more money on this piece of brand-new equipment than both of our cars, combined. I called bullshit under my breath; new equipment wouldn't have so many dents and scratches. Even so, my new job was to clear brush along the fence line and to mend any breaks before we brought the reindeer home.

Before he handed me the keys, he grabbed my arm in his fist, lifted me enough so only my tiptoes reached the linoleum floor, and touched his nose to mine. Through the whiskey on his breath, the warning was clear: if I broke his tractor, he would break me.

The closest barn was nearly a mile walk through woods, around a pond, and across two more pastures. I had plenty of time to think. Visions of how hard Dad would hit me raced through my mind.

I always tried to brace myself for the blows far before his fists connected. If I ducked at the right time, he would miss, which would just piss him off more. If I turned, though, he would at least get my shoulder or the middle of my back, which was better than my eye.

I pushed away the bad present and dreamed of a better life after graduation. More than anything, I wanted to be an archeologist. Glaciers and volcanoes both frightened and fascinated me. Fire and ice, good and evil, content and angry; just like my life. Mom and Dad and the way they lived together and hated each other confused me. I thought people were supposed to love each other and help make the other's life worth living. Television shows sold a complete line of crap. No one's life was that good. Was it?

Why couldn't it be, though? The day I decided to open my eyes and really see—observe—their marriage was the day I promised myself to cherish that special woman I knew I would find one day.

Sally Mae Jones made my heart skip a beat every time those dark eyes flickered with mischievousness. There was no reason she shouldn't want to fall in love with me and accept my proposal. I'm a nice guy, pretty good looking, I have some handy-man skills from fixing stuff around here. I'm smart—my grades should allow me to get into the University of Alaska; I didn't care if I went to Anchorage or Fairbanks, either one would do just fine.

Some girls let their boyfriends kiss them under the bleachers. I wondered what it would be like to kiss Sally Mae. My best friend—my only friend—Scott Harrison said it was like nothing else he'd ever experienced. Once he did it, he wanted to keep doing it and nothing else could make him stop thinking about how he could make it happen again.

Scott moved to Alaska in fifth grade when his mom divorced his dad. I never asked why, didn't care. He sat next to me in the back row and every day we found reasons to giggle about some skinny girl or geeky boy.

We laughed in class; something I had to be careful about at home. I asked my mom if he could come over to see Soloman, but she said no. That's it, just no. No reason. All the other guys in my class ignored me, so it was nice to have a friend.

Summer loitered right around the corner; wildflowers and pine scented the air and temperatures soared to sixty degrees. The walk to the barn would have been enjoyable with the mountain range set behind the house like you would see in a magazine, and puffy clouds which stretched to the heavens, if I lived someone else's life.

Sunshine warmed my face enough to bring a smile to my lips; it was the little things that made me happy. A moose caught my eye in the distance, and I paused to watch it graze. Majestic, yet common, in my eyes they were the most beautiful animal in all of Alaska—maybe anywhere.

If I kept my grades up, I should be able to get money for college. That's what Mom said. Then I'd be able to get away from my dad. I would make a good career for myself and buy my mom a house where she could stop worrying about her every move.

I knew better than to daydream; it made me lose focus of what was in front of me. Tangled in the barbed wire, my already-torn overalls ripped even more as I shimmied between the fences. Mom wouldn't notice—because she had other things to worry about—but Dad would. Anything for him to find a reason to kick my ass. Again.

Maybe every old guy hit their kids to keep them in line—so they wouldn't grow up to be weak—and I shouldn't whine about the pain in my body after I made a mistake. But maybe not. Scott never complained about his dad getting rough with him.

Every now and then, I decided not everyone was raised with a fist in their side and if I ever had kids, I would hug them instead. My mom confirmed my suspicions when she told me to keep our family matters to myself; no one wanted to hear about my hardships. For the life of me, I would never understand how she could keep letting him treat us worse than he treated the animals. At least he fed them regularly.

Expensive toys found their way into the barn and driveway even though Dad complained non-stop about how much he spent to keep the farm running. He deserved to live a better life and Mom and me were an expense he despised.

When he left the house, he dressed in the best-looking clothes, and drove a Hummer, which I think was pretty pricey. In comparison, our refrigerator rarely held more than a gallon of spoiled milk, some cheese, and a case of beer. Sometimes there were hotdogs, but condiments like ketchup and mustard were nonexistent.

Because Dad ate dinner at work every night, there was no need for him to spend money on food. All our meals came from the meat and vegetables from our farm. Last year, Mom and I lost so much weight we had to wear clothes a size smaller than our normal wardrobe.

I offered to help with money by taking a mowing job or helping neighbors around the yard, but she discouraged the effort. Dad wouldn't like other people to know we needed money. He didn't want his reputation ruined. Architects made a good living—from what he said—and he wouldn't want anyone to know that his family needed a job because he couldn't make smart financial decisions.

Twenty minutes later, I reached the barn and located the gas can. It was about half full, which should have been enough to get the job done.

"Where's my tractor?"

Shit. I stopped in my tracks and held my breath. Nonchalance was not one of my superpowers, but I turned and almost smiled anyway. I pushed my glasses to the top of my nose. "Just need a little more gas to get her back to the barn." My voice always shook when I lied. It was a trait I wished I could control. Dad knew me well enough and had heard me try to lie in the past. Even though I told a half-truth, he could still tell I wasn't wholly honest.

He stepped closer and hovered over my head, his voice low. "Where. Is. My. Tractor?" His large hand clasped my bicep and I winced. He squeezed tighter and smirked at my pain. "Now, fat-ass."

"In the back pasture. Just ran out of gas, is all."

"Is that all?" His voice raised and his eyes squinted. I tried to step back, but he held me still. "Tore up your clothes, too? What don't you understand about respect, son?" Spitting out the unusual term of endearment, my cheek caught the liquid, and I knew better than to wipe it away. A sour odor oozed from his pores; he'd been drinking, as usual.

My muscles tightened in anticipation of his hand striking me.

"I spend my hard-earned money to keep you in the best clothes just for you to rip them apart. No respect."

I turned my head as he raised his hand. With my arm glued to his palm, the blow would certainly leave a mark on my chin.

"Robbie?"

Shit, shit, shit. I would always rather take a beating instead of watching my dad hit my mom. It broke my heart that I couldn't save either one of us from turning black and blue. When she rushed into the barn, I knew his focus would turn to her.

"Leave us be, Susie. This doesn't have anything to do with you."

"He's just a kid, Robbie. Let him go, huh?"

His eyes turned dark, and he released me with a shove. I stumbled backwards until the wall stopped my motion. With my mom in his sights, he reached under his shirttail and backed away. For a minute I actually thought he would leave us alone. I relaxed for about two seconds before he brandished a small handgun.

BLOOD POURED from her head into my lap as I held her lifeless body. Thick and warm, the fluid ran between my fingers, staining my jeans and shoes. In a fog, the scene before me was simply unbelievable. I tried to wrap my mind around what had just happened.

Not in a million years would I be able to come to terms with how my dad killed my mom. He pulled a gun from his waistband, pointed it at her, and mumbled something under his breath. An explosion came from the weapon, then my mom sank to the ground. It all happened so fast.

Her dirty blonde hair flowed around my legs as her empty eyes stared up into mine. She couldn't be gone—just couldn't. Absolutely no way could I believe she was dead, I needed her here to show me how to live a good life. She promised she would never leave me.

"Mom, now's not a good time to fall asleep. I need you." I shook her and begged her to wake up. "Please. Mom."

She turned her head—or did it turn because I shook her so hard? The exit wound became visible, and my stomach churned. Bits of sticky substance filled my hand. Bile rose up my throat when I realized it was her brain. I shuddered and just wanted to run away, but I knew if I showed fear or weakness, my dad would capitalize on his power.

"Shame suicide is so rampant in these small towns." My dad's voice reverberated off the heavy wood pillars. "Some people just don't know how to handle life in the Pass."

A puff of air beside my leg caused me to glance at the straw; he had tossed the gun. The same one he had just used to murder my mom. It was almost a tease; he knew me well enough to know that I would never find the gumption to use the firearm.

The first time he tried to teach me how to use it during target practice, I shook my head and backed away. Dad just shrugged and said, "If you want to be a pussy your entire life, fine. Suit yourself. Maybe one day you'll listen to my advice and be a man."

I hated using his guns when he made me hunt elk or

bear.

"How sad that a mother would kill herself in front of her chubby little son. She found it impossible to be happy with all the things her husband provided. A beautiful piece of land, all the animals and tools needed to live freely—just like she begged me to give her when we got married." He chuckled and crossed his arms. "Well, being a momma's boy, I guess you have nothing left to live for, either. Why don't you hurry up and kill yourself? Come on, now, just get it over with."

Something snapped inside me. I literally felt reality shift.

Careful not to disturb Mom, I lifted her head, scooted from under its heaviness, and rested her on a pile of straw. "Shh … it's okay. I'll take care of everything. I'll take care of you." *Why couldn't I save you?*

I reached for the discarded weapon, stood, and aimed. Dad watched my every move; right up until the moment I pulled the trigger.

Chapter 6

Kennedy, age seventeen-April 2005

COVERED IN FISH guts, Cody sauntered down the dock toward the bench where I was sitting with his dinner. Even the slimy layer of goo on his jeans didn't dampen the heat in my chest. His bangs fell into his face and covered one eye. He smiled and I melted.

He expressed how he wasn't thrilled to spend his Spring Break week on a boat, but he was happy to see me. In no time, we had fallen right back into our routine. We spent every possible second together, which wasn't nearly as much time as we wanted with both of us working now.

His dad's fleet of fishing boats produced much of the seafood for Seward's restaurants and grocery stores. Cody's dad had spent the better part of a year getting his three Anchorage crews under control so they would be able to continue supplying fresh fish to the city and its residents.

Although Cody wasn't allowed to go out with the captains on long trips until he graduated, his dad let him work the dock for experience with the fish and customers. Cody's favorite crew worked on Miss Vera, named after his mother who had passed away three years ago. A freak accident, Cody said but wouldn't elaborate.

King Crab season dominated Alaska in April and the Miller fleet capitalized on the expertise of their captains. However, one ship focused on non-shellfish. Cody began his work career, not his full-time life-long career, but just work in the Cook Inlet fishing for Pacific Cod.

"What'd you bring for me?" Behind long bangs, Cody winked at me. His smile gave me goosebumps.

Anxious to please my man, I had ordered food from a local restaurant. Mason's Café by the Bay—Cody unloaded the majority of the catch for this restaurant—they had the best gourmet fish tacos around.

"Mason's specialty. Only the best for you, babe." I pointed to the styrofoam carton on the bench beside me and leaned forward. I didn't care if he smelled like raw tuna, I closed my eyes, ready for a thank you in the form of a heated kiss.

"Really?"

His tone startled me, and my eyes popped open. He was upset. Oh, no.

"You couldn't think of anything more original than

something my dad caught this morning?" He knocked the carton of fish tacos to the ground, stepped on them, and walked away.

"Cody, wait." Through my tears, I couldn't convince him to turn around. I disappointed him; I would just die if he left me for good.

All through the night, I left him voicemails begging him to forgive me for being stupid. My best guess was he ignored me as punishment. I couldn't prove it, but why else would he not talk to me?

Early the next morning, I showed up at his door with a homemade triple chocolate brownie mousse stack cake; the recipe pulled from Southern Living magazine. I knew he had to have cooled off by then, but I didn't expect him to be so hungover. When he answered the door, a plum of marijuana smoke surrounded him and alcohol lingered on his breath.

"Hey." I tilted my head and smiled real pretty. The glass container between our chests held my present. "I made this for you." I didn't know what he would do, but in my fantasy, he pulled me to him and kissed me like he would never be mad at me again. Reality didn't quite live up to the expectation, though.

With one eyebrow lifted, he pursed his lips and yanked the dessert from my hands. "What is it?" Backing into the foyer, he lifted his chin.

I had quickly learned that this was where I needed

to apologize. "Baby, I'm so sorry about the fish tacos. I wasn't thinking. I know better; I should have made you a fresh pan of lasagna. Can you forgive me?"

"I asked what this was, not for your dumb-ass apology."

"Oh." I exhaled the single syllable and tried not to let emotion take over. I blinked back the tears. "It's a brownie mousse cake."

He squinted and wrinkled his nose. "What on earth would make you think I would like something with the word moose in it? Like, seriously? You're naming a dessert after a smelly beast? Besides, it's either a brownie or a cake—not both. God, I swear, sometimes you're so fucking stupid."

My mom's best baking dish came with a plastic lid; Cody opened it, sniffed, and gagged. "Gross." The next thing I knew, it was in the trash.

I didn't mean to gasp; I was just so afraid that I wouldn't be able to show him how much I loved him.

"What's your problem?" He pulled me to him and kissed me hard.

Blood seeped from the inside of my lip. Oh, thank God. He will forgive me.

"You need to prove your love. If you're truly sorry—show me." He twisted my hair around his hand and kissed me again. Using his body, he pushed me through the living room, and we toppled to the couch.

Excited, I wrapped my arms around his neck and my legs around his waist. I moaned when he yanked my hair.

Confused—or maybe curious—he pulled away.

"You like when I pull your hair?"

"A little." My breathing labored, I flirted.

TANGLED IN half-discarded clothes, our hair matted and sweaty from shared passion, Cody rolled off me. He settled beside me and nuzzled my neck. "I couldn't hold back; I was so turned on. The way you screamed when I pulled your hair—that just got me."

Even though my head hurt, and he had been too rough, I smiled, relieved that I had pleased my man. The weight of his arm across my stomach made me feel safe. Secure. Loved.

"You're so perfect. I can't imagine there is anyone else like you in the vast state of Alaska. You're not like all the others."

Unsure of what he meant by *all* the others, I squinted but didn't interrupt his compliments. It felt so good to be cherished. Besides, it's not like he's sinister. He interpreted my reaction as acceptance.

"I mean it. You're the exact right height, not too tall. You could stand to lose a few pounds but I'm willing to help work it off." The passionate kiss made me lose my breath. "Your smile, your eyes." Kisses landed on my lips, then each eye.

On one elbow, Cody stared into my eyes and frowned. His voice was almost a whisper, "You promised to wait for me." It was unlike him to pout.

My heart rate increased, and my temperature rose. "I did wait for you." *How did he know?*

"You don't need to lie to me, Kennedy. We were apart for a long time. It makes sense that you would break our pact. I didn't, though, so I'm a little disappointed."

"Cody …"

"I know you slept with someone else, Kennedy. Don't lie." His eyes darkened.

"I …" Tears told my truth. "Didn't. I promise."

"Then how do you know to tighten yourself around me just before I'm ready for release?" His eye twitched and he squinted. "Only a slut who sleeps around knows that trick." He stood and threw my shirt at my face. "Get out. I'm done with you."

"Wait! I can explain." I shimmied my jeans the rest of the way up my thighs, pulled my shirt over my head, and ran to catch up with him.

As he headed up the stairs to his bedroom, he slowed and turned.

My head and shoulders slammed into the wall as he wrapped his hand around my neck.

"Well, explain."

"I was raped."

"Bullshit." He squeezed; lack of air made me dizzy.

HEADACHES WERE rare before I started working at the bar. Since then, they were more common than I liked. My head pounded harder than any other time in the past. Pain radiated from behind my eyelids and wrapped around my throat.

When I opened my eyes and turned my head, I remembered being held by the neck against the wall in the stairway.

A wet spot under my hair brought back the memory of being dropped and hitting my head on the banister. I reached up to feel the sticky blood which ran from my temple to my ear. My shirt covered my top half, but I wasn't wearing my jeans. *Where did they go?*

Cody stirred beside me. "Hey there, sleepyhead. I'm sorry if I hurt you. I didn't mean it; you drive me so freaking crazy I can't stop my brain. When I think about someone else touching you, I lose it. I just love you so much, my princess."

He leaned up on one elbow and kissed my nose as lightly as if his lips were a feather. "Forgive me?" The tone of his voice made me shiver; he almost sang the words.

I smiled and ignored the pounding in my head. "I love you, my prince."

In one swift move, he straddled me and ripped my shirt open.

Surprised, I tried to pull away. With one hand, he grasped both of my wrists and held them above my head. His weight on my hips prevented me from escaping, no matter how hard I squirmed. He rubbed himself against me and I tried to move away from him.

"Don't bother trying to get loose. I have you right where I want you." Teeth marks remained after he bit my breast; he broke the skin. "You like the pain, admit it."

"No, I don't. Please stop."

"I can tell from your body what turns you on." He pulled down my panties in one painful tug, then flipped me over and shoved himself inside me. "Ah, you're so wet. You do like getting fucked."

"No. I don't like this," I cried, hoping to get to his heart. Hoping that seeing me in pain would make him stop. It didn't. I could feel him all the way to my stomach; I begged him to stop. "Cody. Please. You're hurting me."

Since he was too heavy and strong for me to push away, I gave up and laid there. I took what he wanted to give me, just like that first time at the bar.

SEWARD HIGH School students slammed lockers and gathered outside classroom doors until the next bell. The metal clang ran in my ears and their voices carried through the hallway. With only a few minutes between classes, most students rushed to change books and chat with friends. Others found their significant other and engaged in a passionate make-out session.

Sore from Cody's antics the previous day, I winced with each step and prayed that I had applied enough makeup to cover the bruises. Even my hair hurt.

On my way from English class to my locker, I stopped in the bathroom for a breather and to make sure my façade hadn't failed. The mirror reflected the face of a defeated teenager; sad and confused. Wrinkles covered my forehead from long-term frowning, so I opened my eyes wide and forced myself to stretch them out.

Mondays sucked.

After fourth hour, Brittany showed up at my locker, as usual. She noticed the bruises around my throat; I guess twenty-four hours wasn't enough time for skin to forget. "Oh, my God. Who did this to you?" She reached out and touched the sensitive area on my neck.

"One of the guys got a little rough at the bar." I avoided her gaze and whispered the lie.

She raised an eyebrow; she knew that's not what

happened. I silently thanked her for not pushing for details. "How'd you do on the Chem exam?" Changing the subject, she led the way to our next class. My worst: Geometry.

Honestly, who cared how to measure the circumference of a circle? When would I use that in the real world?

"Okay, I guess. I got a B. You?"

"You got a B?" Her voice raised an octave and I shrugged. "Wow, a B? I studied for days and barely passed. How do you do it? School, work, Cody, and still pull all As and Bs. Girl, you're a freak of nature." She nudged me with her shoulder and smiled. "Wanna hang out before work? The diner for pie?"

I smiled and nodded, knowing I would stand her up again. Cody didn't like Brittany. He said she was bad news; she wasn't smart or pretty enough for me to hang around. She didn't care what others thought and according to Cody, that kind of attitude would never get her to the lower forty-eight. In his eyes, everyone who was anyone would get the hell out of Alaska to have a successful life.

The feeling was mutual. Brittany said Cody was too controlling and he was as proud as a peacock. A college psychology major should be mature enough to not care so much about what brand of clothes his friends wear or what kind of car they drive. She said I was just a pawn in his game. According to her, his way to keep me was by giving me what my mom couldn't.

Both of them were right. Brittany didn't care what other people thought, and Cody could take care of me. Unfortunately, she would just have to understand that there would be time for our friendship later. For now, Cody needed me, and I needed him.

DUCK FARTS, THE Alaska State drink, gave me courage to strut half-naked around the bar like I owned the place. After the first two, my vision fogged, and I spoke with a slur.

My expression after downing the shot entertained the guys. Someone ordered one for me at least once a night and the entire bar laughed when I grimaced.

Most Wednesday nights—when he wasn't working—John arrived at the bar religiously at nine o'clock. He said it was his night to play with the boys. A good cover for his wife, but most of the time was spent with me behind the curtain.

Tonight, he spent the first half-hour playing pool and slamming Jack & Coke's with his friends. I also spent this time slamming drinks to prepare for my session with him. At ten-thirty, he lifted his chin. I nodded to Hannah and led John to the back room.

Some days he only had time for a quick dance or

two but most of the time he expected more. After the night he and his friend introduced me to the Seward way of earning hundreds of dollars in just an hour, sex became his go-to.

His drink sat on two one-hundred-dollar bills and my entire body tightened. I anticipated the pain; John was never gentle. Loud music covered my cries when he pushed and pulled and grabbed too hard. He interpreted my whimpers as moans of pleasure which turned him on.

His rough ways took a toll on my body. My insides hurt enough for me to seek out a stronger source for pain relief than generic aspirin.

Hannah introduced me to Oxycodone when I asked her advice. One pill muffled the pain and relaxed me long enough to complete my shift. And then some. After I discovered the pills, my tips tripled.

I applied makeup to cover my tear-streaked cheeks before I returned to the floor. Hannah raised her eyebrows when she caught my eye. Not wanting her to worry about me, I offered a fake smile. *I can handle this. I have to—how else will I survive?*

Visions of Cody's face entered my mind and my smile turned genuine. My future would be bright, I just had to bide my time.

The day that John and Gus raped me, something in my way of thinking changed. I knew that what they did was wrong, and I hated them for stealing a part of my identity. They killed my trust in men. However, my body reacted each time someone touched me. More often than not, the dances turned into more.

Four more men paid for dances that night, the local grocery store owner, Mr. Ripple, being one of them. In the past, he would only come in every once in a while, but for the previous five nights, I had noticed him staring at me from a booth in the corner.

Each time I followed him to the back room, he had laid a twenty on the table before he sat on the couch. Uncomfortable at first, he always walked away with a smile.

It was the same routine each time, but he didn't seem to mind. With the help of the Oxy, I was able to enhance his show. My body moved almost without thought—definitely without inhibition. My favorite songs played on the jukebox, and I danced like no one was watching. If the men didn't touch me, I touched myself, earning more of a tip each time I moaned.

Mr. Ripple decided he wanted extra attention for the first time, mid-dance. He placed the cash on the table and lowered his chin. Shy or turned on, I couldn't tell until he unzipped, then it was clear.

My toothy smile, and more innocent-than-not tone appealed to him. "Sure thing, Mr. Ripple." I stood on the couch and straddled him as I shimmied out of my thong. The beat of the music spoke to me, and I moved to the rhythm.

His hands roamed up my legs and over my ass. Still unsure how much he could touch, his fingers fluttered over my breasts. It almost tickled. I leaned my head back and moaned while lowering myself onto his lap.

He closed his eyes and put his face between my breasts. I rocked my hips and he exploded. First timers usually didn't last long.

As I walked home, I counted the eight hundred dollars and pushed it into my purse. The more money I needed, the more I convinced myself what I was doing was okay. Besides, the pills made it pretty enjoyable. I didn't not like how I felt in those moments.

BACON SPATTERED on the stove, so I stopped and checked my hair in the hallway mirror. Mom never cooked unless someone had stayed over. I was right; a man sat at the small table mostly facing away from me, a mug of coffee in his hand. His mussed brown hair hung beyond his collar, and he smelled of cigarette smoke.

"Come here, Lisa. Gimme some sugar."

I froze. It was him. *How could that be? How is he here?*

Mom sauntered the four steps from the stove to the table, her robe hung open exposing her bra. Her date from last night tilted his head back and wrapped his arms around her waist as she stepped between his legs.

I knew I shouldn't be watching, but I needed to know if it was really him. She grabbed the back of his head and shoved his face into her chest. He moaned from between her breasts and smacked her ass.

"Gross," I huffed. Honestly, I didn't realize I said it out loud until Mom jerked her head in my direction.

"Mind your business, little missy." She didn't bother to cover herself—never did.

"Gus, you'll have to ignore my daughter."

My stomach turned at the sound of his name on my mom's lips and I thought I might throw up.

Chapter 7

Jake, age fourteen—May 1999

ALMOST AS IF I woke from a dream, the heft of the gun in my hand startled me. I wondered how the weapon ended up in my grasp and I dropped it; the thud echoed in the silence of the barn. *What the hell just happened?* The hay beneath my mom's head had turned a deep brown as it absorbed her blood. Lifeless, she stared up into the rafters. *He killed her. Wait—she's … dead?*

"No!" My legs gave out and I dropped to my knees beside her. Her head was as heavy as a bowling ball, but I gathered her in my lap anyway. Expecting her eyes to flutter as she regained consciousness, I shook her and called her name.

She didn't respond. "Mom?" The word dripped off my lips while tears ran down my cheeks. "I'm so sorry, Mom." Then, I remembered what had happened and I turned to find my dad in a crumpled pile only a few feet away.

On autopilot, my body seemed to move without

instruction. I floated across the floor; my movements so smooth it was as if I had walked on air. I found myself standing beside the pile of flesh that used to be my dad.

His face had been frozen forever in an expression of surprise. He no longer gave off the air of anger or intimidation. For the first time, I saw him as a person. Just a man. I almost regretted my action; the man lying on the ground looked like someone I could have loved.

Thoughts of the past few years twisted through my mind. Mom taught me everything I needed to know about caring for our animals and the land. Also how to live off it; how to allow it to provide substance. *Was there a reason for that?* I wondered if she had a premonition of this day.

My dad would stand on the porch with a drink in his hand—usually whiskey—and watch us work. The only thing he helped with was clearing trees with the tractor. I learned early how to use a chainsaw so I could clean up after him; he never did anything with his hands.

I could still hear him call me lazy because I had gained weight over the winter. First thing in the spring, he forced Mom to work me harder so I wouldn't embarrass him. He even restricted our food; both of us. Mom didn't need to lose any weight, but she lost a lot anyway. More than me.

Lost in my thoughts, it took some time to wrap my head around the fact that my dad had killed my mom.

Maybe my mind had tried to protect me. Complacency turned to anger, and I leaned my head back. The scream started low and grew in strength and passion. I paused, took a breath, studied the bodies on the ground, and released all my emotion.

My body shook and heat rose from my chest to the crown of my head. I paced the short distance between my mom and dad. *Who would do that? What kind of sick person kills someone?*

Realization hit me and I stopped. “Oh,” I mumbled. I had just killed someone, too. “Shit.”

I squatted beside my dad, covered my face with my hands, and sobbed. “Why did you make me do that? What did I ever do to you? Now I’m no better than you. I’ve turned into my father.”

I had no way of knowing what would come next. My stomach lurched and if I had eaten anything for lunch, it would have come back up. The recognition of how my life had just changed took over. *I’m fourteen. What am I supposed to do, now?*

Sun shined through the cracks of the ceiling and walls. How did the worst day of my life have to be such a beautiful day? “I guess I’m supposed to call 9-1-1. But why? They’re both dead. No one can help them. Or me. I’m screwed. If I call the cops, I’ll go straight to jail.”

I tilted my head back and stared at the roof. Surely, I would be damned for what I had done. With outstretched arms, I called to the Gods. "If you're going to take me, do it now." I prayed for lightning to strike me dead, so I wouldn't have to endure whatever the universe had in store for me.

Prison didn't sound like an ideal way to spend the rest of my life. I enjoyed spending time outdoors, on the tractor, and with the animals. It's the killing of those animals that got to me. And the bruises from my dad. I shrugged, "Don't need to worry about that anymore." God probably would have answered my prayers if it wasn't such a nice day.

My heart rate increased, and I found it difficult to think. I took off my glasses, rubbed my eyes, and placed my glasses back on my face. A glimpse of my mom took my breath away. She looked so peaceful. Her head rested in the hay; blood highlighted her hair like a halo. Even though I closed my eyes, the vision of her didn't disappear. I shook my head and turned away.

Sobs escaped my throat as I remembered my dad pulling the trigger. My mom crumpled to the ground as if she fell asleep where she stood. "What the hell just happened? This can't be real."

A breeze brushed the hair away from my face and I turned to find the source. *None of the doors are open, so how did the wind reach me?*

"I can't do this alone. I need help. Who can help me? Where can I go?" Talking to myself, I paced the length of the barn. Clearly, I couldn't help Mom, but I knew I couldn't stay put. I had to tell someone what happened. If I didn't, someone from Dad's work would miss him and come looking for him—*or would they?*

My eyes danced around the barn at miscellaneous inanimate objects. "Mom doesn't have any friends, neither do I, really. School's out for the summer, so no one will miss me.

Maybe I *can* do this by myself. Maybe I don't need any help." Shovels and rakes hung on the side of the tack room. Beside them, hatchets and tools used to process the chickens shined. We made sure all our equipment stayed clean.

Visions of raising and processing pigs and chickens, tending vegetables and mending fences raced through my mind. "I *can* do this; I have already done it—I've been practicing for this moment over the past year. I just didn't know it."

Dad raised me to be mindful and smart about the land. He taught me how to fix most everything on the ranch. Lucky for me, I took advantage of his desire to be lazy. His plan was for me to do all the maintenance so he could fluff off and party all day. He told me so.

Mom taught me how to raise the animals and examine them to make sure they stayed healthy. We built a fully functional vegetable garden two summers ago. Mom wrote down all the best dates to plant and harvest. She kept a notebook in the junk drawer with all kinds of tips and proof of success from previous years.

Four cookbooks stacked in a small cupboard held all our recipes for creating healthy meals. Dad made sure Mom made him only the meals he had previously agreed were not only tasty but would also keep his current physique. His appearance was very important to him; only poor people were fat and dressed in clothes from low-end stores.

A sense of accomplishment washed over me, and I made the weirdest decision of my life. "I can live here without them. I don't need anyone but myself. And maybe Soloman. He's good company." I opened the barn doors and the scene in front of me seemed to have changed vastly after the reality set in of my new life.

Snow hung on the peaks of the mountains at the back of our property. Dad had called it Mother Goose Glacier, but my teacher said he was wrong. She told the class there wasn't a glacier near enough to Moose Pass that we could see it with our own eyes. The snow-capped mountain was just another peak along the Kenai mountain range.

The blue sky of Alaska was like nowhere else in the world. Not that I would know; I've never been anywhere else. Mom used to tell me, though, and I believed her.

Tall green trees only grew so far up the steep rocky terrain before it was impossible for them to survive.

Livestock ambled beside our pond in the valley. Would they know what had happened?

"Dammit. Why do we have to live so far from everything? And everyone." I tilted my head and smirked. "Wait. That could be good for me. A benefit." In the past, Dad's choice of words annoyed me; I silently thanked him for the education.

I inhaled long enough to fill my lungs with the clean mountain air. On the exhale, I let my shoulders release the tension I had been holding. Calm bursts of air moved the branches on trees which lined the driveway.

The split-rail fence separated them from the driveway and kept the cows in the north pasture. Sunshine, warm on my face, made me smile. Birds chirped as if today had been a repeat of the day before.

Am I the only one who knows why it's different? So completely different.

I decided to survey my land—*my* property—to determine how to start my new life. Desperation rose in my chest, making it hard to breathe. Mom's face appeared in front of me as I walked in the center of the half-mile-long driveway.

This time, though, her eyes were bright, and she grinned. I became numb, unable to feel my feet, my knees buckled. I tried so hard not to cry. I didn't want to be a baby, like my dad called me when I got upset. I failed. *Figures.*

Tears streamed down my face, and I couldn't control it. I loved my mom so much and now she was gone. Sadness turned to anger when I watched my dad pull the trigger. Again. The vision repeated when I closed my eyes. He pulled the trigger again and again, almost like a CD skipped. Or the movie *Groundhog's Day*.

"If Jasmine were here, I bet she'd know what to do. She would have been just like Mom—smart and calm. A planner. I should have paid more attention when Mom taught me things instead of getting distracted by kittens. Jasmine should have lived. I'm sorry, Mom. I wish I could have saved her. And you. I let you both down." Talking to myself wasn't helping. It just made me feel worse.

A rustling within the woods along the driveway sent a chill up my spine. I stopped to listen; if a grunt or growl broke the silence, I knew I was in trouble. Bears would start to hunt soon.

I need to close up the barn.

Darkness came quickly in these hills.

MY DAD'S EXPRESSION hadn't changed from the previous night. I'm not sure why I had expected it to. He looked up at me from a four-foot-deep hole in the far back pasture. The property line was clearly marked by a fence made from barbed wire; I couldn't get further from the house if I tried.

It's funny the things that ran through my mind when I was tipping the bucket to drop a pile of dirt on my dead dad's body. "What do I need to be able to live here alone? He just had the fuel tank filled, so I should have enough gas for a while.

The guy from the feed mill just delivered a grain supply for the animals that should last until winter. There's plenty of meat in the freezer and canned vegetables. I'll tend the garden and pull eggs. But …" The only uncertainty revolved around money. "How will I pay for the house and the electric bill?"

The more dirt I pushed over Dad's body, the more I realized I should have buried his face first. He watched my every move; I'm sure he had a better way of completing this chore. Always did. A sort of satisfaction blew across me with the warm breeze as I pushed the last of the dirt into the hole, covering his face. A finality.

As an afterthought, I made a short cross out of sticks and placed it at the head of his grave. I knew I should say some last words, pay my respects, so to speak, but nothing nice came to mind. I spoke the only positive words I could come up with.

"You'll never hurt Mom again. You'll never hit either one of us again. I'll never hear your voice again. You'll never call me a fat-ass or say mean things to

Mom. For that, I am thankful. Goodbye and good riddance." I shrugged. The universe won't miss my dad any more than I would. The time he had on this earth was wasted; he could have made much better choices.

Sun warmed the back of my neck on the ride back to the barn. A numbness replaced the tension in my shoulders as clouds formed. The scent of the coming rain blew in with the wind and I knew I didn't have much time. I pushed the tractor faster and reached the backyard in record time.

While I had tossed and turned the previous night, I thought about the best place for Mom to stay. We had plenty of areas on the farm where she and I shared special memories. The barn, however, was off-limits for obvious reasons.

The pines beside the pond wouldn't be a good area, either. I wanted to be able to visit her on a whim and get to her relatively quickly. An area of the land climbed the side of the mountain where Mom and I would go to rest after a summer swim. The overlook offered breathtaking views, but it was too far away.

As I drifted off to sleep, it came to me. There's a spot under the oak tree on the edge of the backyard. It was her favorite place to rest on a hot summer day. She would lay out an old blanket and we would share a pitcher of iced tea and talk about school or what needed to be done with the farm critters. It was visible from the porch and close enough to the house I could visit often.

After I spit on Dad's grave, I did my best to avoid the bumps and potholes on the way to the house. When I stopped at the area I had chosen for Mom, I climbed off the tractor, then froze. I couldn't move. It seemed like an hour before my legs gave out and I sank to the ground.

"I can't do it. I can't throw dirt on your face like I just did to … him. Can I?" No, I shook my head. But I had to bury her; she wasn't alive anymore and I needed to give her a proper farewell. A respectful transition to the afterlife. If there was such a thing.

"I'm sorry, Mom. I should have been man enough to protect you." I closed my eyes, lowered my chin, and winced at the memory of the gunshot. The first one. The one which took her away from me. "Will you help me? One last time? Give me the strength to do this."

I manipulated the bucket controls and maneuvered the tractor to pile the dirt on either side of a hole. When I couldn't dig any deeper, and couldn't cry any more, I powered down the tractor at the edge of the steps leading to the porch and wiped my face with the bottom of my shirt.

Following my plan, I found everything I could think of to keep my mom comfortable in the afterlife: her favorite quilt made by her momma, a pillow, a locket given to her by her grandmother, the photo album of our life, and her bible. I placed the items in the bucket and drove the tractor to the barn.

For the second time that day, sweat rolled down my temple, sopped up by the collar of my shirt. Heavier than she looked, it took longer than I expected to lift her into the bucket and place her just so. With her head on the pillow, I secured the locket around her neck, covered her in the quilt and laid the photo album and bible on her chest.

Unlike the previous time I placed one of my parents in the ground, I said a prayer to a God I wasn't sure existed, then lowered Mom gently into her final resting place. She looked so peaceful with her head on the pillow.

I wanted to make sure she wouldn't get cold in the harsh Alaska winter, so I pulled the quilt to her shoulders. At the last minute, I decided not to add the photo album to her grave so I could hold onto the memories we shared.

"He'll never hurt you again, Mom. I kept my promise." I pushed the last of the dirt into the hole and regretted not covering her face with the blanket. *I hope she doesn't choke on the dirt.*

Chapter 8

Kennedy, age seventeen-October 2005

COWBOY BOOTS decorated with enough bling to blind me caught my eye in the Main Street Boutique window display. “Those would be perfect for the dance next week.” I pulled Brittany back three steps and dragged her through the door of the store.

A Help Wanted sign sat propped against the wall and I had an epiphany. The cute clothes in the window were enough reason to ask Brittany to fill out an application—the discount would be great for us both.

“But I don’t need a job.”

My best friend had forgotten how persuasive I could be. “But I need those boots.” I lifted one eyebrow and waited for her to sigh and roll her eyes. That’s how I knew she was under my spell.

Like a good girl, she took the sign from the front window and asked to speak with the manager. Just like that, the store owner hired her on the spot.

She opened last month and needed someone with good fashion sense to help her run the store. I nudged her shoulder and she asked, "When do I start?"

They agreed her employee discount could be used immediately, with the understanding that if she quit within ninety days, the amount of the discount would be taken from her last check.

Four one-hundred-dollar bills laid flat on the table and Brittany's eyes widened. She waited until we exited the store before probing. "How do you have enough cash to pay for all this? Does minimum wage really stretch that far?" She frowned, thinking. "What about your brother and sisters? Are they okay?"

"They are. They're better than they've ever been. I'm able to buy them whatever they need. Honestly, whatever they want." The money I made at the bar boosted my confidence. People didn't laugh at my hair and clothes anymore and I wanted that for Brittany, too.

I walked out with those boots, a dress, two pairs of jeans, and a shirt. Brittany made out on the deal, too. I insisted she let me buy her a new dress for the upcoming Halloween dance.

Now that Cody had left me, again, for college, I was so sad. If I didn't have Brittany, I just might want to die. I almost felt like I needed to buy her friendship; my recent MO had been to ghost her.

Downtown Seward bustled with residents who visited the fall festival; we took the bags to my mom's car and stuffed them in the trunk. "What next?"

"Are you hungry?" Let's get some food. Something non-Alaskan."

Food trucks radiated scents of meat and grease from Main Street. One advertised Texas Barbeque and smelled of sweet sauce; my stomach growled.

"Not really. Let's go see what cool art people are selling."

Disappointed, I trailed after Brittany. As many times as I've bailed on her, I felt that I owed her a good day.

Vendor tents lined the four alleys and for the first time in Seward, a psychic had been invited to attend. A purple tent with a crystal ball logo stood out amongst the mostly white, mundane set-ups of local artists. The large two-compartment structure appealed to me.

"Oh, look. A psychic." Brittany grabbed my arm and pulled me to the tent. "I need to know what my future holds. Will I stay in Seward or move back to Anchorage after graduation? Will I get accepted to a college or need to beg on the street corner?" She laughed at her own uncertainty.

We entered the tent and rang the bell, as instructed. A short, pudgy, wrinkled woman appeared and smiled. "Well, girls. Good afternoon. Welcome to my lair. I am Madame Ester." A frown wrinkled her face even more. "You've been in a funk for some time, my dear."

Not sure what to think—anyone can be in a funk at any given time, right?—I glanced at Brittany. "Me?" She had pointed to me, but I needed to be sure.

"Not to worry, dear. Your one true love will come back to you, soon. You'll marry him, one day."

Thrilled, I bounced behind Brittany as we passed through an opening into a private space. We sat around a small table covered with a purple cloth. Madame Ester reached across the table and gazed into Brittany's eyes. "Dear, let me read your palm."

GEOMETRY SUCKED. Just sucked. Mrs. Wilson adjusted the chalk to write the volume formulas on the board. Her voice grated on my nerves worse than fingers on a chalkboard. Nasally and high-pitched, she sounded like Lisa Simpson. I giggled as a picture formed in my mind of her with a saxophone dancing across the classroom.

"Miss Smith, I'm happy you're in such a fantastic mood. Do you have something to share with the class?"

I had been in a fantastic mood ever since Madame Ester read my palm. The part about me being careful, though, impeded my giddiness for about a minute.

She warned me how she saw someone angry in my life. At that moment, a vision of Cody with his hands around my neck appeared. I pushed it aside and focused on the positive. He would come back for me. I would marry him, someday.

"Nope." I leaned back in my chair, confident that she wouldn't call on me.

"Well, then, why don't you come up to the board and solve the second problem on page two-fifty-six?"

Dammit. I knew better than to talk back or resist. Last semester, a kid refused to work on a problem, and she gave him detention. She insisted on her students actually learning, not skating through with little effort.

Heat rose up my neck as I grabbed the piece of chalk between my fingers. I pursed my lips and copied the problem from the book. Surely some of this training had been lodged in my memory, somewhere.

I searched and tried to remember anything but being under pressure caused me to freeze. If I didn't even try, she would give me extra problems and possibly make me stay after school. I had to work, so that couldn't happen today.

With my eyes closed, I thought about Cody and our future. I wouldn't need Geometry to be his wife and the mother of his kids. However, I did need to do well in this class. I opened my eyes and saw that the answer to the question had already been written. My subconscious obviously understood this stupid class.

"Very good, Kennedy. I knew you had it in you." Mrs. Wilson winked, then whispered, "Nice boots," as I passed.

MUFFLED MUSIC reached my ears as we passed by a set of double doors. Students filled the hallway as they waited to check in their coats. Brittany handed hers to the attendant, but I decided to keep my jacket on. "We Belong Together" played over the speakers, I could tell by the beat, but was not able to make out the words.

God, I hope all the songs aren't this lame tonight.

Halloween decorations hung from the ceiling, bopping kids on the head as they bounced off each other and, literally, off the walls. Ghosts, witches, and black cat posters covered the front of the glass cases, which contained football and basketball trophies.

My new boots hurt my feet, but I didn't care. They were cute as hell. Brittany talked me into pairing an old-school jean skirt with a white tank top and a leather jacket to complete the ensemble. I liked it; I felt sexy.

Brittany wore the classic "little black dress" I had bought for her. It clung to her curves and she continuously pulled on the hem which barely reached mid-thigh. The long, stuffed tail and perky ears attached to a headband completed the sexy cat costume. I drew on whiskers with eyeliner just before we left her house.

"Cool it, Brit. If you keep yanking on the material, it will stretch out."

"But it's too short." Brittany pulled on the hem, again, and squirmed.

"It's sexy as hell," I said.

I lifted my chin as I turned to investigate a sound behind me. Warm hands covered my eyes, and someone whispered in my ear, "Guess who?" His breath on my neck made me shiver.

Cody wasn't due back from college until Christmas. I could barely contain my excitement but wanted to play it cool. Obviously, there was only one possibility of who it was; I was in a playful mood, though. “Brian?”

“No.” He chuckled.

“Justin?”

“No.” He huffed and tightened his grip.

I wondered how far I could take the joke and said, “Sam. It must be Sam.” I couldn't help myself. I knew it was Cody, but he didn't know I knew.

Brittany snickered in the background.

“What the hell, how many names are you going to go through?” Cody released my head and turned me around by my shoulders. Looking down, he searched my face. The second my lips twitched into a grin, his hands went to my hips, and he pulled me to him. My arms naturally rested over his shoulders.

“God, I missed you.” He lowered his head, hesitated for a split second before he pressed his lips to mine. It seemed like the soft, sweet kisses lasted for hours, but it only took seconds before Brittany rudely interrupted.

“Dude, get a room.”

She had admitted earlier in the day how she felt like the third wheel. I assured her she wasn’t, but she kinda was. I secretly hoped one of the cute guys would ask her to dance so she wouldn’t feel like she didn’t belong.

I hip-checked Cody. “I knew it was you the whole time. I don't even know a Sam.”

"Yeah, whatever." He wrapped his arm around my shoulders and squeezed a little too hard. An adorable smirk crossed his lips.

"You taste like Cinnamon. Got anymore?" Cody raised one eyebrow, knowing I had gotten into some Fireball.

"Right here." I patted the pocket of my leather jacket.

I followed Brittany through the doors to the cafeteria and a strong guitar riff of "Animals" pumped through the speakers loud enough to make me think my heart was beating at the exact same pace.

That's better.

Nickelback was a huge improvement over Miriah Carey. In my opinion, anyway. Each step I took somehow matched the beat of the bass drum and my hips swayed just a little more than normal. In a couple beats, I was full-out dancing.

We made it halfway across the cafeteria before I reached for Brittany. She turned toward me and took Cody's place. He released me and nudged us toward the dance floor before joining the rest of the boyfriends along the wall.

Annoyed at the short hem, Brittany tugged on her dress between the steps. As I reached into my inside pocket, her eyes widened like she had just seen a monster. She shook her head in a panic as I pulled out the pint.

I lifted one eyebrow and took a quick shot. Brown curls flew from around Brittany's face as she glanced over her shoulder to be sure none of the chaperons or teachers watched. She smiled as she reached for the bottle, excited by the danger.

The button of Oxy we primed ourselves with before being dropped off at the dance, mixed with the whiskey had worked its magic. Brittany and I danced like we had in her bedroom so many times. Honestly, we really didn't care if anyone paid attention to us. Except for boys. We always danced for them.

We were in our element. Wide smiles spread across our faces as our hips swayed and we moved closer to each other. Our eyes locked and something changed—sizzled.

I put my hand around the back of her neck and pulled her face close to mine. Never in my life would I have thought about kissing my best friend—until now. She didn't stop me when I covered her mouth with mine.

Before I knew it, Cody slid behind me, covered my hips with his hands, and whispered in my ear. "Invite her to come over after the dance. I want to watch."

THE NEXT MORNING, I wondered why my insides were sore, as if I had worked the night before. Too much to drink contributed to my pounding headache and spinning sensation. I breathed steadily so I wouldn't get sick. If I moved, Cody would wake.

I reminded myself how we had gone to the Halloween dance and Cody had unexpectedly showed up. His dad had been out of town, so I spent the night. *But what happened in between?*

The memory caused me to gasp. I instantly wished I would have kept quiet and held my breath as Cody turned over. Cody, Brittany, and I starred in a wild after party. After too much whiskey and another Oxy, we relaxed. Maybe a little too much. Cody led us up the stairs and into his bedroom. Closing my eyes to fully grasp the scene, I replayed the night in my mind.

Cody had picked up Brittany and threw her on the bed. As she laughed and wriggled to the center of the mattress, he threw a long plastic pink toy on the bed. He wrapped his arm around my waist and held me tight while he kissed me with a passion usually reserved for long nights. He pulled my tank top over my head, my braless breasts freed, then he kissed my neck. "You know what to do with that?"

I shook my head and smiled, groggy. "If you don't wanna show me, I could probably figure it out."

"I bet you could, you slut." His hands roamed under my skirt to ensure I hadn't worn any panties—just like he liked. "Good girl," he reached between my legs, touched me, groaned, and bit my lip, then shoved me to the bed. “Leave the boots on.”

Brittany had already picked up the toy and licked her lips while she stared at it. I had only ever heard about using dildos from Hannah; I’d never actually seen one in the wild before.

Cody assured us that it would heighten our pleasure and explained how to play. “Lay back and relax, Brittany. Bend your knees and spread your legs. More. That’s right.”

The little black dress gathered above her hips; she closed her eyes and rubbed the dildo on herself. “It’s too big.”

“Take it a little bit at a time. Kennedy, you do it for her.” He backed away, moaned, and rubbed himself; his eyes turned dark with passion. “Mmm. Yeah, like that.”

We quickly learned how to maneuver the toy to make one another squirm and eagerly tried new positions at Cody’s urging. It was hot that he wanted to watch; the experience was made even better by his commentary, his demands. I thoroughly enjoyed my time with Brittany, especially when she kissed me. We had a connection that couldn’t be denied; when she touched me, I felt things no man had been able to ignite. Cody included.

He joined in at the end of the night. While Brittany pushed the toy inside me and begged for me to touch her in return, Cody stood behind her and dropped his pants. I had made her ready for him and she gladly took him, gasping as he slid inside. Her focus turned to my boyfriend, and she stopped playing with me while he fucked her.

To my surprise, he ordered me off the bed. At his command, she did things to him that I had only done at work. Overcome with jealousy, I couldn't tell if it was because of Brittany doing things to Cody or vice versa.

I tried to turn away, but he forced me to watch as he took her in every orifice. The longer he played, the rougher he got; he made her cry when he finished, but she was so messed up she didn't seem to care.

I remembered the end of the night in bits and pieces, like a bad eighties movie. After Brittany fell asleep, he fed me more liquor and took my hand.

"Follow me."

I reached for my clothes, but he stopped me, wrapped one arm around my waist, and whispered in my ear. "Just the boots."

Thrilled to have our own private time to enjoy each other, I bounced behind Cody uninhibited. Down the stairs, through the living room past the stuffed wolf Cody had killed on his first hunt, through the sliding doors to the back patio.

A hot tub's jets rumbled, and I smiled. I'd never been in a hot tub before, but Hannah said they were amazing. Cold air took my breath away and made me shiver. Hot water called to me, and I trotted toward the giant tub.

Before I reached my destination, Cody grabbed my hair. Shivers overtook me, but he refused to let go. "I'm freezing. Let's get in."

My head snapped to the side exposing my neck. Not expecting the pain, I cried out when he bit me like a vampire.

"No woman of mine is going to be a hooker. A whore, that's all you are."

"Cody …"

He turned me around and slapped me across the face hard enough to knock me off balance. I screamed and tripped over the steps. My head hit the side of the hot tub and split open, blood seeped through my hair down my scalp.

Dizzy, I tried to stand. "Why are you mad at me? What did I do wrong? Tonight was so much fun." I desperately wanted to please my one true love and thought by doing whatever he wanted, he would be kind and appreciative. I was wrong.

He removed my boots and threw them in the hot tub. I knew they would be ruined by the water, so I lunged to reach them before they sank. Cody grabbed me by the feet, I fell to the ground, and he dragged me across the concrete slab.

Scratches covered my chest and stomach and I

screamed, "Ow, Cody. Stop. You're hurting me. What are you doing?"

"You think that hurt?" Twisting my legs, he rolled me over. He had grown excited by inflicting pain and shoved himself inside me. "Maybe if I pleasure you enough, you'll stop screwing other guys."

I acted as if it felt good, at first, hoping he would just stop. It worked with the guys at the bar; made them finish quicker. Cody was different, though. He wasn't turned on unless he hurt me. When he slapped me across my face, I shrieked, and blood trickled from my lip. That worked.

He finished fast and leaned over me, sweaty and panting. "I'm sorry, K." Soft kisses covered my shoulder. "I just get so crazy when I think about other men touching you. I can't do this anymore. I can't stand by and accept that I'm not the only one you love. You're going to quit your job."

Tears mixed with dried blood on my cheek. I tried to rub it clean. "But my family needs the money. My brother and sisters …"

"Are not your responsibility." He stood over me. "Your mom can support them. You're going to quit tomorrow, or you'll never see me again."

Chapter 9

Jake, age fifteen—August 2000

THE TRACTOR sputtered to a stop in the middle of the trail. Smoke rolled from the exhaust pipes as it stammered to life, then stalled again. "Shit. I must be out of gas." At least once a week, I took soiled straw and wood chips from the stalls out to the far back of the property where I kept the compost pile. I made sure to steer clear of Dad's grave so he couldn't tell me all the things I had done wrong.

Remnants of his voice flittered in the air around my head. "What's wrong with you, fat-ass? Just because you eat like a hog doesn't mean you can feed the chickens that much scratch."

Sometimes the nit-picking made me mad, other times I just rolled my eyes. "Are you stupid or something? Don't you remember anything I taught you? You need to pull the eggs early in the morning instead of just before lunch."

I talked out loud more often than not; no one else was around, might as well have conversations with myself. The only other voices I heard were from the news anchors on channel four.

Late at night, I would fall asleep to the eleven o'clock news while waiting for the weather report for the next day. It had been an easy summer; temperatures hovered between sixty and seventy during the day and dropped to forty at night. After a fully frozen winter, it had been nice to work outside without a parka.

Without my mom's cooking expertise, I didn't eat as much as I had in the past. My dad's insults about how fat I was rang true in my head every time I looked in the mirror.

Working the farm alone allowed my muscles to expand and my excess fat to disappear. Before my mom died, I stood a respectable five foot eight. At the end of the summer, I had to duck to see the top of my head in the mirror on the bathroom vanity.

Every day after my chores were done, I visited Mom in the backyard. I brought her a glass of iced tea with a slice of lemon, just how she likes it—liked it. Until I ran out of lemons.

We talked about ways to keep weeds from popping up in the garden and how to get rid of the infestation of snails. If my tomatoes were going to produce as much as I needed for canning, they must stay healthy. We discussed the best number of chicks to allow to hatch versus how many chickens to freeze. Everything I tried to do on my own failed. Reluctant to keep with her old ways, eventually I gave in. Mom was always right.

Even though I never got any concrete answers, I still felt better after confiding in her. She had always been a good listener. “I'm not sure I'll ever be able to come to terms with what I've done. I can’t stop thinking about pulling the trigger. On the other hand, it was him or me. Wasn’t it? It had been self-defense.

“What happens when someone finds out, though? I can’t hide in plain sight forever. School starts soon and I’ll need to register. At some point, the bank is going to come, right? They’ll want to take the house. I don’t know how to pay any of the bills. Even though you used to talk about getting delinquency notices, I don’t know how to make a payment.”

I had overheard Mom and Dad fight about money; she never understood why he refused to pay the bills on time when he made more than most people in Alaska. They would fight about where his money went. She even accused him of having women on the side. After the first time she yelled at him, I heard a thud and their arguing stopped.

“I miss having someone my age to hang out with and wish I could invite Scott over. But I know I wouldn’t be able to keep my stupid mouth shut. I’d end up showing him everything and risk the cops finding out."

Every few days I would thumb through the photos in the album I saved. "I love this picture of us. Even if Dad did take it. Your hugs are the best—were." I sighed. "I felt so safe when you put your arms around me and squeezed. I'm sorry I used to complain that it was too tight; I just didn't want Dad to think I was soft."

I flipped the page and smiled. My mom had been so pretty in her youth.

"This one is great, too. Soloman loved you." Dad bought the horse the year they moved to the farm. He said he had to give her something to keep her busy. Otherwise, she constantly begged to go here or there, and he didn't have the time or money.

"He's getting used to riding beside the river. Doesn't spook like he did at first. You're right, by the way, bareback is a totally different experience. We're both getting used to that, too."

Birds chirped in the tree above where Mom rested in her grave. A slight breeze cooled my tired body. I tilted my head back and soaked in the sunshine. The warmth made me drowsy.

Just as I was about to doze off, Mom whispered, "Be careful," then brushed the hair from my eyes. I smiled, happy to feel her touch. Or was that just the wind?

At the end of our conversation, I poured her tea

around the base of the roses I planted near her tree. The plant had grown to over three feet tall in just two months. The blooms made a perfect centerpiece for the table; I picked one stem every night and put it in a vase with fresh water.

On my walk to the house, I hoped there would be enough sunlight to have dinner on the back porch with Mom. At the end of the summer, the sun began to set earlier every night. Winter was coming and I needed to start preparing.

RED AND BLUE lights flashed from the middle of the driveway. The SUV door closed, and a police officer strolled to the front door. He took his time getting to the steps, gazing from left to right, surveying the yard around the house.

With one hand rested on his pistol he seemed to be on guard, as if someone had tipped him off to the killer who lived on this property.

From my vantage point behind the closed barn door, I watched him through a crack where the trim had rotted away after last year's wet winter. He climbed the stairs and turned in a circle, investigating the open space between trees along the driveway.

Once his gaze landed on the barn, he stopped. I couldn't make out his facial features through the falling dusk, but I swear he smiled.

Even though I had been certain I was incognito, I still flattened against the wall, out of sight. Metal garbage cans lined the wall beside me, and buckets hung from the rafters. Careful to lace my way between them without making a sound, I held my breath.

Thoughts rambled around my head and exited in the form of questions to the universe. *Why is he here? Who called the police? Do they know what I did?* I shook the absurd ideas away. *No, that's impossible. Isn't it?*

The screen door to the house opened with a squeak—I made a mental note to bring the WD-40 in from the pumphouse—then he raised his hand to knock on the door. When no one answered, of course, he backed away and let the door slam behind him.

Not expecting the sound, which resembles a gunshot, I jumped. Buckets clanked together above my head, and I tripped into the garbage cans. Angry that I made such a ruckus, I cursed under my breath and kicked the stall door. Chickens stirred; their clucking added to the noise.

"Shit." I shimmied to the stall, closed the door with a thud, and huddled in one corner. The same corner where I hid when my dad hit my mom. My view was blocked by walls; I had no idea if or when the cop would enter the barn.

Did he hear all the noise I made? My heart beat

faster at the unknown. *Where was he? Is he coming to get me? Does he know what I did?* Adrenaline pumped through my veins, and I grew hot.

The officer must have heard the commotion; he pushed the sliding barn door open and called into the darkness. “Jake Knight? Are you in there?”

Shit. He knows my name. Of course he does, jackass. Why else would he be here? He knows you’re a murderer.

“Son, come on out. I just want to ask you a couple questions. I tried to reach your parents, but no one has seen them all summer. Just looking for some answers.”

He knows. I lifted up on my toes just enough to peer over the stall wall into the large open area of the barn. The police officer had pulled his pistol and held it at arm’s length in front of him. Slow, methodical steps told me he was on guard, expecting me to attack.

Rusted latches held the stall door to the pasture closed. The last time Soloman used this stall was almost three months ago. Lots of things have changed since my parents died. The barn had quickly become off-limits to the animals; if I couldn’t enter it to care for them, neither would they.

My hands shook as I twisted and jimmied the latch. The more it rattled, the more I panicked. Finally, it clanked open. I pushed my way through the small opening and ran into the night.

A shot rang out from behind me. My shoulder erupted with pain, and I screamed. A second shot sounded just before the outside of my thigh burned. I was hit. I had always wondered what it would feel like to be shot. It hurt more than I imagined. All the animals my dad had killed while hunting must have gone through the same experience.

Trees provided cover as I ran toward the road. Even though bears were often spotted in the area, they were my last concern with the officer on site.

The Pass, as locals called this area of the Kenai Peninsula, offered many reasons to stay on alert, including cougars, moose, and giant mosquitos. Being chased by the cops was not on the list. Until now.

I had a choice to make: either run next door to the Madison place where they had an underground bunker I could lock myself inside or hide in the woods. Choice two didn't seem feasible, so I decided to go to the Madison property. It would take at least thirty minutes to go the back way.

Last time I went to scope out the hiding place, because the police showing up was an absolute concern, the bridge had fallen into the riverbed. It was possible to climb into the ravine, but with such short notice I didn't think to grab any climbing equipment; I might not have made it out on the other side. Therefore, I had to take the road.

Weeds had grown tall over the trails; I hadn't taken care of them like Dad would have demanded if he had been around. When I slacked on any of the chores, like clearing the underbrush, he would remind me how useless I was. *If I make it out of this, I'll clear the trails over the weekend, I promise.* I hated it when my dad was right.

Once I reached the main road, the pavement slapped the bottom of my shoes with every extended step. Only another half mile until the curve before the Madison's.

It didn't take long to lose my breath; I wasn't in the best shape, even though I had lost twenty pounds over the summer. Stamina was never my strong point. Throbbing in my thigh caused me to limp. Running with one arm holding the other became awkward and slowed me down.

The headlights in the distance started out bright but dimmed as the vehicle approached. I tripped as I slid down the hill into the ditch and fell to my knees. If I stood, the vehicle might see me. I could use the time to catch my breath. *Did they see me already? Should I try to flag them down? What would I tell them? Would they know who I am?*

As the vehicle approached, I could make out that it wasn't a car, but it wasn't a truck either. It was more of a conversion-style van, almost like an ice cream truck. I positioned myself behind the largest tree I could find in case the headlights would reflect off me and give away my location.

It could be a tourist. How would I explain my situation to someone who doesn't know anything about the area? Alaska is an entirely different world from the lower forty-eight, from what Mom and Dad say—I mean, used to say. Strangers would probably ask way too many questions about why I am running along the road and where I'm going this late at night. I can't let that happen.

Then, it hit me: *What if it's a mountain man? Or men?* Mom always warned me about the creepy mountain men in the area and how they are a little wild. I could still hear her voice. I frowned at the memory. "Be careful, Jakey. Not all of them are bad guys, but you never know who you can trust."

I couldn't decide if it would be safe to stand and wait for the vehicle or if I should continue to allow the forest to hide me.

When Dad had his parties, his friends would tell stories of hunting expeditions with the mountain men. They had spent time in their dark world and reported back to civilization. It's possible the person in this car could know my family. Hell, he could have even been to our house before.

At the last minute, I decided to make myself visible.

So, I climbed out of the woods, up the side of the ditch to the middle of the road.

Tires squealed on the pavement as the truck slid from one side of the road to the other, correcting itself before skidding to a stop mere inches from my body. Bottles rattled and shattered within the vehicle, adding to the noisiest incident I've witnessed in months.

Blinded by the lights and frozen from the thought of being destroyed by the impact, I crossed my arms across my face and closed my eyes. This is it. I will finally be able to hug you again, Mom. I've waited so long.

It felt like an hour before I heard a woman's voice—not my mom—asking if I was okay. The radio blared from inside the van, a heavy beat with a raspy voice filled the air. Then, the woman's voice was louder than the music. She ran in front of the van and grabbed me by the shoulders. I screamed in pain.

"Oh, my God! I'm sorry. Did I hurt you? Are you okay?" Her hands rolled lightly over my face and arms. If she applied too much pressure, I might scream again.

"What are you doing out here? I almost hit you! Oh my God, you scared the crap outta me!" The blood on my shirt got her attention and she gasped. "You are hurt. We need to get you to a hospital. Honey, what's your name?" She took a step back and studied my face.

Too scared to admit who I was, I remained silent. If she knew what I had done, I would go directly to jail. I made up a fake persona in a split second. "Tom." I spoke the first totally generic name I could think of. Tom Johnson was someone I wanted to be like when I got older, even though I knew almost nothing about him.

When I just stared at her, not knowing what to say or where to start, she put her hands on either side of my face and forced me to focus on her voice. "What happened to you? Are you hurt?"

I nodded just enough for her to understand that I meant yes. The gunshot wound in my shoulder hurt worse than the one in my leg. The second bullet must have just grazed me, like when I hunted for the first time with Dad. He never let me forget how I let that elk get away with barely a wound. Luckily, that cop was a bad shot.

"Whose blood is this? Yours?"

Tears streamed down my face, I took off my glasses and wiped them away before I nodded again.

"Okay." Her hands were gentle on my shoulders and her voice was so calm I almost forgot what had happened. Almost.

"Get in the truck."

METAL BARS MADE up one wall of the tiny holding cell. With only a thin cot to sit on, I pulled my feet up under me and tried to get comfortable. My entire body ached not only from being shot, but also from holding all my emotions inside.

Hiding always kept me safe. Nervous reactions to every little sound or movement forced me to stay tense for hours on end.

The previous week had been a blur. Nurses in the emergency room cooed and kept their voices soft. As they cleaned my wounds and pulled the bullet from my shoulder, I got the feeling they felt sorry for me. *They couldn't have known that it was a cop that shot me, could they? Did they know my story?*

Stitches closed the hole where the 9mm slug called home for a few hours. If I wanted to put a positive spin on the entire situation, I could say I had street cred; I had been shot. Not everyone could tell that kind of story. Then again, not everyone could tell the story of killing their own dad, either. Not even after a million questions did I admit the entire story, certainly not to the nice nurses. I liked how they felt bad for me; if I admitted to them who I really was, I imagine their view would change. Then they would look at me with disgust, like my dad had.

The time spent between the police department and juvenile detention had been a blur of cold handcuffs, interviews, court, and small holding cells. At first, the police officers had treated me like a victim. In the end, I broke down and admitted what I had done and why. As I knew it would, my entire world turned upside down. I gave a short explanation, but the officers understood how I had been abused for longer than I cared to admit, my entire life, really. I had thought long and hard—the entire summer—about how to make up for my actions, but nothing could even the score for killing my dad.

I had known that eventually someone would have discovered that my parents had gone missing. That I had also gone missing. I knew when that day came, my story would need to be solid. No holes. Even details of the truth were hard to keep straight. I had spent hours upon hours and day after day trying to figure out the best way to phrase the explanation for why I did what I did.

The more time I spent thinking about it, the more I convinced myself that I wasn't the same pitiful kid I had been the day he killed my mom. The day I killed him.

I had to face it; I would officially be labeled a murderer. During the bouts of quiet time, I tried to remember who I had told the most details and who I had lied to. Well, not really lied, more like omitted specific details. Details that may make me look like I deserved to be abused.

I mean, I didn't tell them how much I had talked back or that I broke things on the farm. When Dad hit me, I learned not to do it again. I totally deserved the punishment he had doled out.

Most of the officers treated me like the scared kid I

was, but a couple looked at me like I had murdered my parents or something. They were rough when transporting me from the interrogation room to the cell—my cell—and back.

Turns out that my school called the police concerned because I hadn't been registered for fall classes. My mom was friendly with the social worker and although they weren't close, she knew my education was important to Mom. The counselor knew that Mom would have told her if we had moved away; she was very organized that way.

My mom had hidden the worst of our home life from me. It was only after being detained that I learned how my dad chose the ranch in Moose Pass for his hidden drug lair. One of the special agents pulled me into a private room and asked what I knew about the illegal activities.

Obvious to him, the questions confused me. He understood I had no knowledge of what my dad really did for money. I always thought he worked as an architect, at least that's what Mom told me.

The parties my dad held for his so-called friends turned out to be a way for him to distribute drugs through his dealers to the entire Kenai peninsula. He spent most of his time in Seward convincing dealers to do his dirty work. They never figured out where he stayed, so he must have had some girlfriend in town.

When Dad got greedy and tried to take over Anchorage, the undercover cops infiltrated the group and convinced my mom to talk.

When one of the undercover officers, Tom Johnson, took her into the barn for a "tour," my dad thought he was using her as a bonus for dealing with my dad, like others had done in the past.

Sick as it had been, it was Dad's way of showing his appreciation for the secrecy. Instead, he had convinced Mom to confide in him. Tom had planned on saving us, but he was too late.

If I hadn't taken my dad out last spring, the police would have had enough to put him away for life. We were all better off, so they say.

This news hit me like a ton of bricks; I felt like I had been hit by a Mack truck. My entire body ached, and my head spun. I attempted to make all the puzzle pieces fit but thought my head would explode.

Tom. The one person I had a positive feeling about was actually a good guy. Chills ran up my spine knowing my assumption had been right.

Even though I had eliminated the biggest drug dealer in southern Alaska, the fact was that I had committed murder and the state made me pay for my crime.

Unfortunately, I was forced to endure a trial and my lawyer convinced me that by pleading guilty, which I was, I would be charged as a juvenile instead of an adult. He was right; I was sentenced to juvenile detention, which meant I would be released when I turned twenty-one.

MCLAUGHLIN Juvenile Detention Center's secure treatment unit would be my home for the next five and a half years. Fifteen-year-olds aren't supposed to cry, but I couldn't help myself. Change is hard in general, but going from a four-hundred-acre farm to sharing a ten-by-ten cell with another boy was a bit extreme.

I wasn't sure how to live without being outside, without soaking up the sunshine, without drinking a glass of iced tea with my mom at the end of a hard day's work.

When I finally got comfortable—or exhausted—I dreamt. Mom floated beside me over our property. She held my hand and told me everything was going to be okay. I wanted to believe her.

My face throbbed with pressure; I woke to find a fist slamming into my cheek. I backed away before the second hit connected. My roommate had dropped from the top bunk, grabbed me by the hair, and with his nose almost touching mine, whispered, "Shut the fuck up."

"Sorry." I sniffled.

"If you keep making so much noise, they're gonna

come in here and search our room. If they search our room, you're the one who will be in solitary, not me. I'm not getting put in that hell hole again. Got it dickweed?"

"Got it."

"Now. Shut the fuck up." He climbed back to his bunk.

Mom? Can you hear me? I'm so scared. What's going to happen to me? What's going to happen to the farm? Am I ever going to be able to go back there? Shit. I didn't grab any of our pictures.

Chapter 10

Kennedy, age eighteen-March 2006

SPRING BREAKUP soaked through the UGGs I found in Megan's closet. My feet grew numb on the walk home; I knew better than to forget the plastic baggies. *Why did Cody have to ruin my boots?*

Not only did the ice and water slosh beneath my feet, but I heard it creak and crackle under tires behind me. I turned to see how much time I had before I needed to move to the side of the road, but there was only darkness as far as I could see. Strange. On alert, I continued to walk toward my trailer park.

Then, I heard it again. This time, though, I waited to turn around. Lights moved in the other direction; someone had come off the side road and headed toward town. I released my breath.

My nerves were on edge; every sound after that made me jump. For the third time this week, the same car seemed to appear in this same spot. I couldn't help but wonder if John had come for me.

Each time he bought a dance, his sessions grew more intense. He started off a little rough, sure, but over time he added new positions and demanded I do things that hurt. He was usually my last customer of the night; each time he left the bar, I hoped to never see him again. It had become harder for me to control his actions; he shared a shot and an Oxy with me when we spent time behind the curtain. He knew it made me less apprehensive.

When he put his hands around my neck tonight, though, I told him "No." He didn't listen. I tried to push him off me, but he reminded me how much I liked what he did to me and threatened to take his payment back. I gave in and allowed him to continue because I needed the money.

Even the pills wouldn't dull the anxiety of not being able to breathe, though. Scared that he would kill me right then and there, I bucked under him, but he held tight, getting off on my fear.

The more I struggled, the harder he squeezed. His eyes turned dark, and I tried to scream. Eventually, I turned over a table and it crashed to the floor. I guess I had made enough of a ruckus because Willy arrived and pulled him off me. Yelling obscenities, Willy forced John, pants down, through the bar and out the front door.

I tried to act like it was just any other day but when

the owner, Mr. Peterson, peered into the backroom, I had been re-applying my makeup. I'd only met him a couple times, but he seemed like a nice guy.

"I've turned a blind eye to what happens between you girls and the customers back here, but please believe me, I didn't know anyone was hurting you. I'm so sorry." The apology fell short. "Kennedy. Go home. Take the week off, I'll consider it vacation time. You'll get your full pay. Don't worry about Hannah and Yasmine; they'll be okay without your support for a little while. When you come back, things will be different, I promise."

Sweet, but he obviously didn't understand how much money Hannah and I pulled in from our activities in the back room. There's no way the owner would put up a couple thousand of his own dollars to cover my absence.

Slush splashed on my legs, bringing me back to reality. An engine revved as a vehicle sped past me; lost in thought, I hadn't heard the truck approach. My ears perked up again as a vehicle without headlights slowed to a stop behind me.

I picked up my pace and ran. The car crept closer but didn't pass. I turned to see what make or model it was but couldn't see without any moonlight. *Is it John? I hope to hell he's not back for revenge.*

Whoever it was, decided to stop and back into a

driveway, then turn around. I didn't slow my pace after they left; I ran the last half mile to my house. Sweat dampened my hairline and I became breathless.

I closed and locked the door behind me. *What if John had come after me? What would I do to protect myself? I need a car.*

I should have let Hannah drive me home. It wasn't that far, so I figured it would be okay, just like any other night.

One day, though, I wouldn't need to worry about who wanted to come after me. There would be no need to think about how much it would cost for my sibling's clothes for school or groceries when my mom refused to go out.

Cody and I planned to have a little house somewhere in the lower forty-eight—somewhere warm—with black shutters and surrounded by a white picket fence. *We'll be happier than anyone on this earth.*

IF I WANTED MY choice of cereal and lunch meat, mom forced me to go with her to Safeway. The local grocery store was the only place I could find Froot Loops. Emily liked it when I brought home treats for her. Nathan always asked for a toy car to add to his collection. Since I started working, I stopped asking Mom to buy things for me. Or for them.

Little did Cody know, I continued to work at the bar to make ends meet. If he knew, he'd probably kill me. The threat to leave me if he found out stuck with me and I prayed he would never know. It was a chance I had to take, though. As much as I loved him, Emily and Nathan being hungry wasn't an option.

At least now it was just the younger kids I needed to worry about. Zach was safe with his dad and Megan moved to Los Angeles last year hoping to make a positive change in her life. Jealous as I was, I told her I was happy for her when she found a guy and got married. Her husband was in a rock band, and they were on their way to the big time.

Mr. Ripple winked at me as we entered the store. Embarrassed, I tucked my head and pretended not to see him. After his time on the couch, he always tipped at least a twenty for drinks. As reserved as he was in real life, it still surprised me every time he laid a hundred on the table.

Mom had noticed how much money I spent and asked where I had found a decent job in this shitty little town. I had lied and told her I worked with Mr. Ripple most evenings. Well, it wasn't a total lie.

"Where's the dill pickles?" Plastic wheels squeaked from the shopping cart my mom pushed.

"How should I know?" Cranky and hungover, I forgot about the white lie.

Lettuce and tomatoes filled crates all around us. "Well, don't you work here?"

Shit. I grimaced. "They're not in the produce section, that's for sure."

"You should know where everything is. Or are you that slow it takes six months to figure out which aisle the pickles are in?"

As we turned the corner, a pudgy man in a white shirt stopped short. Mom gasped and put her hand over her heart. "Excuse me, Mr. Ripple." She moved her hand to her hip and tilted her head. "You startled me. I nearly ran you over. Please forgive me." Her fake apology annoyed me.

He looked her up and down. "No, Mrs. Smith. I'm the one who should be sorry." He licked his lips and glanced at me. "It's so nice to see you both."

"Likewise. I've been meaning to ask how you've enjoyed working with my Kennedy?"

"Oh." Surprised, he lifted his eyebrows and stared at me. "Let me tell you, you've raised a fine young lady."

"CODY!" *HE DID come back for me.* He promised he would, but I didn't know if he was serious or just trying to keep me from working. *Our love must be real if he came back.* I ran out the door of the diner into his open arms. Still shaken from the stalker incident, the warmth of my boyfriend's embrace comforted me.

"Hey, Kennedy. I missed you so much, my princess."

His kiss breathed a renewed energy into my lungs, and I held on for dear life. He leaned me against his truck and made it clear to everyone who could see us from inside the restaurant that I belonged to him.

"Baby, let's get out of here," he whispered in my ear, and I knew what he wanted. I didn't even bother to tell Brittany where I was going; she'd figure it out.

I hadn't paid attention to which direction he drove; I expected him to take me to his house so we could make up for lost time. Surprised when he pulled into my trailer park, I asked, "Why are we here? I thought ..."

"Well, you thought wrong." The truck jerked to a stop, and he jumped out, tapped on the hood as he rounded the front, then swung open my door. He had never been to my home before, so I wondered what he had up his sleeve.

A red Camaro sat in the driveway—Steve. Mom was entertaining in the middle of the day. "What are we doing here?" The key stuck in the door, and I had to wiggle it to make it come loose.

"Come on. Hurry up."

"We need to be quiet; my mom has company." I grabbed Cody's hand and led him to my room. I tossed my hair over my shoulder and started to unbutton my shirt. I didn't even care that he saw the disgusting kitchen and messy bedroom, I just wanted to be with him.

He furrowed his eyebrows and shook his head. "Where's your suitcase?"

Confused, I frowned. "I don't have a suitcase."

"Well, grab something to pack your stuff. You're coming back to Anchorage with me."

Stunned, my jaw dropped open and he chuckled.

"Hurry up."

We spent the next five minutes packing some of my favorite clothes as quietly as we could. I was excited to spend a week in Anchorage; it must have been meant to be that my boss gave me the time off to recharge my batteries. I was determined to make the best of my time with Cody.

Two garbage bags later, we jumped into Cody's truck and headed north. I couldn't wait to see where he lived and went to school. My mom didn't need to know I had left; I would call her later to tell her when I'd be back. It's not like she would miss me.

Fantasies of touring the city and going to places I'd only heard of, like Talkeetna and Denali, flooded my mind. "I'm so excited to go to Anchorage. I've only ever been once before. I can't wait to see the zoo.

"Sure, Seward has the Sealife Center, but I want to

see an elephant and a giraffe. I've heard Denali is even more beautiful than Homer Spit. Can we go there, too?" Without letting him answer, I chattered until we reached the Tern Lake Pullover.

Glass-like water reflected the mountains in the form of a "V." Clouds scattered in the bright blue sky and green spread across the panoramic vista. Each time I gazed into the snow-tipped mountains, I swore I would never tire of the calmness it brought.

He stood behind me, moved my hair over one shoulder, and put his arms around my waist. I loved it when he nuzzled my neck and tilted my head to allow him more access.

"Just you and me, K." Sharp nips on my skin made me squeal and gave me the goosies. "This is our world; isn't it gorgeous?"

I nodded and squirmed, rubbing my backside into his growing front. His reaction reminded me how much he couldn't resist my shenanigans.

His lips moved over my neck and his hands moved down my hips to the hem of my skirt, lifting it. "We're going to make it, you and me." He groaned when he discovered I wasn't wearing panties. "I love when you prove how much you love me."

I turned in his arms and unzipped his pants; he was ready for me. He held me to him with one arm around my waist and the other wrapped in my hair. With a tug, he silently asked me to give him my neck. He bit me harder than he had before, but I liked it and moaned.

He slid his hands down my thighs and lifted me off my feet and onto his erection. I cried out in a mix of surprise and pain.

Surprised at how much I enjoyed being suspended, I almost didn't hear another vehicle pull into the secluded parking lot. "Cody, stop." When he ignored me, I tried to put my legs down, but he trapped me against the truck. Panicked that someone would see us, I asked him to stop, again.

In response to my defiance, he growled, "I'll stop when I'm finished fucking you."

CITY LIGHTS SHINED brightly in the dark Alaskan sky; we'd made it to Anchorage. The college didn't offer dorms for juniors, they usually lived off campus. Cody's dad owned a house in the Tudor area, a subdivision just east of Midtown.

The four-bedroom bi-level home was shabby compared to the main house in Seward. Outdated and cluttered with hand-me-down furniture, it served its purpose. My mom's trailer couldn't come close to any stick-built home. Period.

It was late and I was hungry; Cody didn't stop for food during the three-hour drive, and I hadn't eaten since the diner. For such a large house, the kitchen was tiny. Smaller than even the one in the trailer. The refrigerator door stuck as I tried to open it and Cody chuckled. "Like you need more food."

I turned and frowned. "What's that supposed to mean?"

Without uttering a word, Cody grabbed my side and raised his eyebrows. My stomach had always been flat, so I didn't understand why he would suggest I needed to lose weight. *Whatever.*

We were both tired and I wasn't in the mood to argue. I opened cupboards trying to guess which one held glasses. All I could find were Solo cups, so I filled one with tap water.

"One of the guys on the crew, John, told me you're still working."

I hadn't realized Cody had snuck up behind me. His whisper in my ear startled me almost as much as his words. "John?" Did he know my most frequent regular?

Leaning against the counter with his arms crossed, he smirked. "I didn't believe him until I saw you walking home last night."

Heat creeped up my neck and I could feel my cheeks redden. I tried, unsuccessfully, to calm my nerves. My voice shook. "That was you?" Unsure of where this conversation was headed, I tried to diffuse it. "Jesus, I thought someone was stalking me, trying to figure out the best time to kidnap me."

Cody raised his eyebrows. "So, you admit that you didn't quit the bar?"

Ugh, this isn't going to be good. "I couldn't. My sister …"

Cody pursed his lips and opened a drawer beside the stove.

"When I tell you to do something, you do it. Do you understand?"

"But Cody."

"But nothin.' If you don't obey me, you'll be punished." A metal rod with a capital "M" on the end sat on the counter while Cody dug through another drawer.

"Punished? I'm sorry I didn't quit, but I will the minute we get back to Seward, I promise." I had no idea what this punishment would involve. Whatever it was, he was serious. His eyes turned black, and wrinkles creased his forehead.

"We're not going back. You're staying here with me so I can keep my eye on you."

"What? But …" So many thoughts ran through my head it was hard to put them in order. I said the first thing that came to mind. "My mom will miss me. I need to tell her where I am."

"Will she, Kennedy? Really? How stupid are you? She will be so much better off without you there to interrupt her partying. You're just a burden."

My mom had said those exact words just last week; how could he have known? I don't remember telling him about her trying to talk me into getting my own apartment.

With a small torch in one hand and the metal stick in the other, Cody held the flame to the "M" until it turned orange. "Give me your arm."

What could he possibly do with that "M"? "What? No." I pulled away from his grip.

Evil filled his dark eyes, and I knew not to resist. He held out his hand, so I offered my arm and closed my eyes. It seemed like hours before he touched the hot metal to my skin. Pain worse than anything I had ever experienced overtook me and I thought I would pass out. I had never smelled burning flesh before, and I never wanted to again. My stomach turned and I gagged.

"Now everyone will know you belong to me. Only me. No one else will ever have you again. Do I make myself clear?"

Tears streamed down my face, and I gagged again. Finally able to pull away, I ran down the hallway.

"You better not puke on my new carpet."

The first door led to a powder room and, luckily, I made it to the sink before the contents of my stomach rose to the surface.

I STUDIED THE swollen, red skin which surrounded the "M" on my forearm. It didn't hurt as much after a couple shots of whiskey, but it still pulsed. As painful as it was, it actually looked pretty cool. If this was how Cody announced to the world that we would be together forever, I'd decided it could be worse. A ring would have been better, but I took what I could get.

Chapter 11

Jake, age seventeen—June 2002

OVERCOME WITH anger, I made a fist and plowed it into Mark's face—no one called me a psycho. The severe word was reserved for my dad, and I was nothing like him. The new kid fell to the ground and covered his face.

I could have easily kicked him in the ribs and listened to them crack. I'd done it before. As much as I wanted to watch him bleed for what he called me, I wanted my freedom more.

Two guards rushed into the hallway just as Mark wiped blood from his nose. "What's going on here?"

I lifted my chin and waited for Mark to say it was my fault. He hadn't yet learned how to play by our rules. Until now. Like a good boy, he kept his mouth shut.

I was kind of a big deal in my small town. Even though my dad was a psychopathic drug lord ringleader, somehow, I had turned out to be the bad guy. Society labeled me a murderer, even though he killed my mom, among others who had betrayed him.

Over the past two years, I had made a name for myself among the nineteen other boys who lived in my unit at McLaughlin. When I first arrived, the older guys made me cower, then, when I realized I had nothing to lose, I fought back. The first time I knocked out the leader of the bullies, his crew backed down. After knocking him out two more times, everyone in the block looked at me as the one to fear.

My intent was to protect myself, not to gain the respect of all the guys, but I'm not sorry that happened. Not a fighter at heart, I never sought out trouble. For some reason, though, it always seemed to find me.

From what I understood, no one else had killed anyone, but I couldn't be sure. It was a rule that we weren't to explain how we got here; some of us followed that rule, others, not so much. I couldn't be sure if anyone knew my story; if they did, it didn't come from me.

Most of the other kids who had been sentenced to live here only stayed until they turned eighteen. I was different from them. Sure, they all had anger issues and a bad home life, but not one of these kids showed any form of empathy. They didn't seem to be sorry for what they had done, which made it that much more difficult to see them as equals.

All they cared about was getting into a less secure

area of McLaughlin so they could make their escape. I actually wanted to finish my education, maybe even graduate so I could live a normal life after I was released. During lock down, I studied while others talked shit or practiced rapping. I learned how to create earplugs from a piece of my bed sheet.

Gray had fast become my most disliked color. Everything in here was gray. The floors, walls, ceilings, bars, tables, beds, toilets. Even the fucking plates were gray. I think they did it to drive us nuts. It kind of worked. I longed to see any other color, ease my brain a little.

During our daily one-hour in the yard, I allowed nature to fill my soul. Within a week's time, I had already memorized the mountains and trees. I found it reset my sanity; I skipped over anything gray. Clouds formed specific shapes in the electric blue sky; I gave them all names. One day, I would be free, and I promised myself I'd never do anything to get put back behind bars again.

Others played basketball to pass the time. Most of the inmates became too competitive to continue for long periods and ended up fighting. Now that I had made a name for myself, my goal was to stay away from trouble. I had fought enough in this place; it had lost its allure.

While other kids made connections, which I guess could be called friends, I remained alone—by choice.

Time in my room was sacred. Being in seclusion allowed me to remember the better days with my mom in the Pass. Silence had been my companion for so long now that I had learned to love it.

One memory never went away, though, as much as I tried to forget. My counselor made me keep a journal and the most significant day in my life ended every entry. I had a feeling that my life would revolve around that single moment forever.

I pushed my glasses up my nose and studied the words I had just written:

> *I miss my mom. I miss petting my kittens and riding Soloman. I hope whoever took him away is treating him well. I regret not being able to help my mom escape; I was just too young.*
>
> *I hate my dad.*

With my eyes closed, I remembered my dad's parties. Over drunken conversations, he and his friends reminisced about their high school days. They had grown up together and began harassing women early on. My face grew hot each time they would tease Mom about her frizzy hair and small frame; they said she looked like a boy.

As much as they teased her, they sure enjoyed it when Dad encouraged her to give them tours of our little farm. When she spent time with them, they all smiled and laughed at her jokes.

They took turns following her into the night. Only after the cops told me she was their informant did I catch on to what the other men had done to her. *Why did she stay?*

ONE OF THE BOYS who was just a year older than me tried really hard to break through my walls. Pete—he wouldn't tell me his last name—was always including me in conversations and giving me little treats. Whenever he had an extra cookie or chips, he delivered it to my room. He was the only one I talked to, but I still wouldn't call him a friend. I didn't want to stay in touch with any of the guys there. Nothing good would come of it.

However, he did have a secret cell phone. So, there was that. The first time he asked if I wanted to call anybody on the outside, I denied him. The next time he walked by my door, he paused, held his hand to his ear and raised his eyebrows. I shook my head and he walked away.

I didn't have anyone to call—or did I? The only person I would even consider contacting would be Scott, but would he even want to talk to me? I hadn't seen him since before my parents died and if he knew what had happened, I'm sure he would steer clear. My life was a train wreck and no one else would want to be involved.

For a few days, I thought about how I would tell Scott what had happened and where I was. If I made contact with the outside, maybe I could remain sane. Maybe I would have a reason to look forward to getting out of juvy. It wouldn't be easy to transition from this place to real life and I would need a friend.

"Pete." I caught a glimpse of him as he passed my door. When he backed up and caught my eye, I put my hand to my ear and nodded. His smile lit up his face; he had broken through my barrier.

Hidden behind a brick in the third bathroom stall on the left, someone had wrapped the cell phone in a washcloth and stuffed it into a baggie. Pete had given strict instructions. Cell phones were one of the only ways to extend your time after juvy; that and fighting. No names. Period. Only talk for two minutes at a time.

It had taken me two days of hard concentration to remember Scott's phone number and to come up with a code name. As I typed his number into the phone, I held my breath and prayed he would answer. He didn't, so I left a voicemail.

> *"Hey buddy. I can't say my name and I can't say yours. It's me. Your best friend since fifth grade when you moved here. I can't tell you where I am,*

but I need to talk to you. Call me back at this number. Please. Leave a message and say you'd like to talk with Moose."

Anxious for a return call—what would I say if he actually figured out what was going on?—I sat on the toilet for thirty minutes. *Did I have the right number? Did he know it was me? Would he even want to talk to me if he knew what I had done?*

I gave up waiting after about forty-five minutes, disappointment brought my mood from high and excited about the what-ifs to low and discouraged about the you're-stupid-to-think-it-would-work. I shuffled back to my room and moped for the remainder of the night.

My notepad had been my only friend, the only one who really listened, anyway, so I took advantage of it. If I had a conversation with Scott—if he ever called back—I would first apologize, then explain my past to lead into what I had done.

The idea of talking with Scott inspired me to write. The words flowed freely and without pause. Before I knew it, four pages were full of explanations and stories from my younger years.

The next week, I asked my counselor for another notepad. In these fake conversations, I found myself admitting things to my friend that I never told anyone before.

In my mind, I heard how my dad deserved to die. *Was that true? Did he?* I couldn't help but think the things he had done to my mom were so bad that karma worked its magic through me. I also couldn't find a reason why I would be special enough to be my mom's angel.

As much as I thought about talking with Scott, my mind also trailed to thinking about Sally Mae. I often dreamt about her and about what it would be like to touch her. She used to smile at me and stare too long. My heart would jump, and I had a hard time putting two words together, but when I did, she laughed. Her deep voice raised three octaves and my blood pressure rose enough that I could feel my cheeks redden.

Her dark hair fell just past her shoulders; it looked soft enough to touch. I never did, but I fantasized about it all the time. In my imagination, it was softer than a kitten. When I wrapped it around my hand, my pants grew tight. What I wouldn't give to kiss her and experience the sort of ecstasy Scott bragged about.

Our rooms were void of doors, so each time the thoughts of Sally Mae entered my mind, I found myself rushing to the bathroom to complete the fantasy with my hand.

BREAKFAST WAS the same each morning; it consisted

of cereal—boring Corn Flakes—and a muffin. Everyone gathered for morning check-in at seven am and ate their food in silence. We weren't permitted to talk until seven thirty, then it was a free for all. Volumes of twenty voices trying to outtalk each other gave me a headache. Another reason for earplugs.

Pete sat beside me and smiled. "I just got word; I'm out next week. I'm so fucking happy I can't see straight."

"That's great, man. Congratulations." For the life of me I couldn't figure out why he thought I would care. But, whatever.

"Listen, you're the only real friend I have in here."

Saddened that poor Pete didn't have anyone else, I tried to be empathetic. He wasn't a bad guy, just a little annoying. Who wouldn't be in such a small space with all these guys?

"My family has a chunk of land in Talkeetna. I want to give you my number so you can call me when you get out. You can live there in one of the cabins and I can get you a job on the oil fields; my brother is a manager and helps guys like us."

As long as I had lived in Alaska, I'd never been to Talkeetna; always wanted to go, never really had the chance. Or a reason. "Thanks, man. That means a lot." I chose to keep to myself; I didn't think I needed friends. Maybe I had been wrong.

Chapter 12

Kennedy, age eighteen-October 2006

WHILE CODY attended classes, he instructed me to stay inside. No one could know that I was there with him. Cody knew I hated to be trapped, but insisted I not even open the curtains. It drove me nuts that I couldn't simply enjoy the scenery. His daddy was paying for everything and if anyone found out I was living in the house, he said we'd both be out on the streets.

Without an education, Cody wouldn't be able to take care of me. Without him, my life would be worthless. Even a high school diploma wouldn't have made my life better. Like Cody said, I didn't need to graduate and go to college; he was doing that for us both.

His degree in psychology would take us wherever we wanted to live. We could stay in Alaska or move anywhere in the lower forty-eight. He talked about moving to Dallas all the time, but I wasn't sure why. I would follow him anywhere; he was my future. Without graduating from high school, I wouldn't be able to make a career for myself, so I depended on him.

Even though the sun was out and the weatherman on channel two said temperatures would reach sixty-five, I knew better than to open the door. Or window. Cody had been so paranoid about his dad finding out about us that he made me a prisoner. Last time I sat on the balcony, I got another bloody lip. Getting slapped hurt worse in Anchorage than Seward; I wondered why.

As much as I hated to admit it, Brittany was right. She said Cody had to be in constant control of everything and that he wouldn't approve of my job. Even though she was the one who set it up, she suggested I quit. If I was allowed to call her, I'd tell her she was right and apologize for being so hard-headed.

I'd also call my mom. Cody said she didn't miss me, and he was probably right, but I would still like to talk to the kids. I didn't have a chance to say goodbye and they probably hated me for just up and leaving.

Maybe if I gave him what he wants and act like the loving girlfriend I know he needs me to be, he'll give a little in return. Maybe he'd let me call home.

Bored out of my mind, I begged Cody multiple times to get me out of the house. I wanted to see the countryside or at least the zoo. Maybe just a nice dinner somewhere that offered more than sandwiches. He refused. Each time a little more passionately.

It took me all day to work up the courage to ask, "how much longer do we have to live this way?" Whining wasn't my style, but I couldn't help the squeak in my voice. In my mind, it was better than crying.

Again, my timing was off. I should have waited to say something after we finished dinner. Plates with ham and cheese on hamburger buns sat on the kitchen counter.

"Don't you listen to anything I say?" A roll of his eyes emphasized his annoyance. "My dad can't find out about you. He has people watching me. I see his friends all the time. They follow me all over campus and the city. God, I can't believe you're so ungrateful."

He rounded the counter and towered over me. With my chin in his grip, his nose almost touched mine. "Don't you ever forget where you came from. Your whore of a mother made you follow in her footsteps. I saved you from her and from yourself. I think you liked "dancing" for those men. How do you think it made me feel to hear how everyone in town knew my girl was fucking any random yahoo who paid her enough?"

"I didn't like it, Cody. I hated …" The instant his fist connected with my eye; my head pounded as if it would explode. I fell to my knees and sobbed.

"Don't make me discipline you again. I hate making you regret your decisions. And don't ever talk back to me." He held a glass of honey-colored liquid in front of me and I took it. I also took the two pills from the palm of his hand. I wanted to stop the horrible feelings of regret and bring back the joy Cody and I once had.

"Now, let's remember why we're here. I'm getting my psychology degree so I can get us out of Alaska and start our life together. That's what you want, right?"

It was what I wanted. "More than anything." I nodded and smiled.

"That's my girl. You don't need anyone but me. Our love is enough to get us through. You're supposed to be pure and together we can make up for what's been lost. I can help you redirect your life so we can be the kind of people others respect and hold in high regard."

His warm hand on my face and the sparkle in his eyes made me believe he would make our life perfect. Soft kisses peppered the bruise forming on my eye, when he backed away and smiled, I knew we would be okay. A sense of belonging and hope ran through my soul.

"We only need each other, Kennedy. You and me, together. Forever."

The pills had allowed me to speak my mind; Oxy always had that effect on me. "I'm lonely, Cody. I miss my friends back in Seward."

With his fingertip, he wiped away a tear. "But, K, don't you see that they're all worthless sluts?" He handed me another shot. I wanted another pill but was afraid it would be too much. My head bobbed from one side to the other and I practically fell asleep during blinks.

I didn't understand how such hurtful words could be said with such sincerity. It almost sounded as if he was being nice. "I feel like I'm being smothered; I can't breathe. What am I doing so wrong that you need to know every step I take? I quit my job when you asked me to, so I could move here to Anchorage to be with you. You can trust me."

"I know your job was important to you. I wasn't around enough to make you feel wanted, so you found attention with those other guys." His strong arms wrapped around my shoulders, and I melted into his chest. When it was good with Cody, it was so good. He whispered the lyrics from my favorite song into my ear and I held on tight.

"Being with you is like heaven on earth. I don't know what I would do without you by my side. I need you. School is really hard right now, and I need you to understand just how important it is for you to stay out of sight. If my dad knew you were here, he'd cut me off."

"I'm sorry for being selfish, Cody. I love you. I understand."

"The best thing about you is that you're moldable. You don't know what it's like to have things and whenever I give you something, you appreciate it more than any other girl I've been with. You don't even care that this house is a dive. All the others tried to make me spend my dad's hard-earned money to update it."

I didn't know he had been with any other girls but was afraid to ask. If I did, it would prove I was a hypocrite. My previous job involved other men, so who was I to expect him to have kept his promise to only be with me? Still, it bothered me.

"When John told me he'd been you at the bar—again—I knew I had to get you away from that shit hole; that's why I brought you here. You promised yourself to me and I'm going to make sure you keep your word."

Shaking, I frowned. "Shit." I couldn't talk my way out of this one.

Like a flip of a switch, he instantly grew angry, and his jaw tensed. He pushed me to arm's length and smirked. My cheek stung the second his hand connected. "Dammit, K. Why do you make me do that? Why can't you just be a good girl and do as you're told? Now I have to prove my point."

"GET OUT, WHORE." Cody opened my door and pulled me out by the arm. He removed the blindfold and shoved me away from the truck. As he hit the gas, I turned away in time for the dirt that flew from his tires to pepper my back instead of my face.

The entire time in the truck, he ridiculed me for being easy with the guys at the bar. Even though he said he wasn't jealous, it had been obvious to me that he was. Very much so. I couldn't do anything but beg for forgiveness, which I had done every day since he found out.

A trailhead miles outside of Anchorage ran alongside the road, hooded by trees. The blindfold kept me from knowing exactly where I was. If not for the lights from the city, I would have been screwed. I walked as fast as I could down the uneven path until I reached the highway.

Temperatures had dropped and with minimal clothes, I shivered as I followed the signs to the city. Traffic was nonexistent after midnight, so no one knew I was out here all alone. It must have been two miles before the first exit to the city became visible. Exhausted, I pushed to pick up my pace and jogged down the ramp to the access road.

Shadows hid the beauty I was sure was all around me. Strange sounds came from the trees and on the ground. I was so pissed at Cody that I almost didn't hear the grunts behind me on the trail. I just wanted to go home.

By the time I made it back to civilization—aka a trailer park—I had gotten over being upset and just wanted to be warm. A rustling of sorts came from a nearby garbage can and I hoped it was someone I could go to for help.

I froze when the dark shape turned—it hadn't noticed me, yet. I was still drunk and the effects of the Oxy hadn't completely worn off. I stumbled, which made the bear turn and focus on me. My heart raced and I held my breath. *Is this it? Is this how my life is gonna end? Maybe if I don't move, he won't see me.*

The bear stood on his hind legs and sniffed the air. I knew right then he had caught my scent. *This must be my karma. This is God's way of punishing me for the life I've lived.*

My entire life in Alaska never brought me so close to a bear. My hazy brain made it hard to recall the training we had in elementary school.

Stay calm and identify yourself. That sounded ridiculous, but I was willing to give it a shot. "Hey mister bear. Or, God I hope not, missus. Please don't have cubs. My name is Kennedy. I'm a human. Please don't eat me."

Make yourself look as large as possible and don't scream. I raised my hands, palms out as if to inform the bear I wasn't armed and backed away slowly.

The monster took four steps toward me before I found enough strength to run. *Oh no. I forgot: don't run.* Focused on moving faster than the beast, I remembered not to scream. I was so scared, and it was so cold that my cries remained in my throat.

The first trailer I came upon had a shed positioned close enough to the house for me to fit between the buildings; the bear was too big. I forced myself into the small space at the same instant the bear slammed into the shed.

Somehow, I managed to squeeze myself further into the space just out of reach of the bear. Its claws tore the skin on my arm, and I forced a scream into the cold night air. A light turned on in the window beside the shed.

"I SUPPOSE YOU had to pay the nice gentleman back for the phone call. Did you go down on him? Did he choke you? You better not have let him fuck you; you know you're mine."

"What? Cody, no. You know you're the only one for me. I love you." The horrible argument from just hours before had been forgotten in the midst of the bear attack.

"How'd you get the scratches on your arm, then? That bullshit bear story is one of your worst lies ever. I swear I don't know how you got so stupid."

The ride back to downtown Anchorage made me uncomfortable. He seriously thought I had offered myself in exchange for a phone call. He didn't understand at all how scared I had been. The bear could have eaten me alive, and Cody didn't believe a word of my story.

Chapter 13

Jake, age twenty-one—July 2006

HEAT FROM THE high sun warmed my face differently than it had the previous five years. Six inches taller and muscled from working out—what else was there to do behind bars?—I could easily overcome any of the guards. Not that I needed to, but I learned to be prepared for anything. They were all fat, so it wouldn't have been hard to do. I pushed my glasses up my nose and smiled. A real smile, one I had hidden away for that very day.

Freedom felt good. A good in a way I didn't expect. The world was at my disposal, and I could do whatever I wanted. I wasn't forced to follow anyone's rules or to room with some asshole who cried himself to sleep every night.

The opportunity to start over was almost within reach. If I played my cards right, I could put the past behind me. At least, that's what my counselor drilled into my brain. I almost believed him.

One problem: I was a twenty-one-year-old convicted killer just released into the wild. Who would hire me? The only option I had was to call Pete and accept a position with his brother's crew. Or clean motel rooms, but who wanted to mop up someone's whiskey-laced puke?

There was nothing left for me in the Pass. I'm sure all the critters had been sold off to neighboring farms, and the house had a new family. In my fantasy, the new owners kept all the animals, so they didn't need to go through the stress of being rehomed. Especially Soloman. For the people's sake, I hoped my dad wasn't haunting the barn.

During my stint, I had plenty of time to think about what I would do when I got out. Without any family to speak of, my grandparents lived somewhere in the lower forty-eight—if they were even still alive—but I had never met them. I understood I had nowhere else to go and had to be methodical with my plan.

"Where to, friend?" An Inuit man opened the back door to his taxi.

"I'm not your friend." I tossed my duffle bag into the back seat and ducked so I wouldn't hit my head. Release from McLaughlin included five pairs of underwear, two pairs of jeans, two white t-shirts, a parka, my state ID, and five hundred dollars. Barely enough for a month in a shitty motel and some food.

Supposedly, it would be enough to last until I could secure a job, then an apartment.

"Cheapest motel around."

Lucky for him, the taxi driver understood how keeping his mouth shut during the short drive would be better than asking tons of questions. He pulled into the parking lot of a run-down building with three levels.

Two o'clock in the afternoon must be when the crazies came out. Four men stood outside the office door and shared a bottle of something wrapped in a paper bag. Used needles littered the ground and graffiti covered one wall. At the far end of the property, scantily clad women flirted with men walking past. The neon sign was rusted and had long been broken.

Sketchy. I like it.

After negotiating a weekly rate with the hotel attendant, I pushed two hundred dollars into his hand and pursed my lips. *Highway robbery.* I followed him up cement steps to a blue door with chipped paint. It wasn't unlike all the other doors.

Dirty carpet covered the floor of my second-story room; the sheets weren't much better. A faint odor of—what was it? Dirty underwear and spoiled milk?—lingered. The clock beside the bed flashed 12:00 as if it didn't matter what time it was inside this room. I lifted an eyebrow and chuckled. "Classic."

Not sure what to do next, I sat on the bed and

pondered. A bug escaped from under the TV stand, and I shuttered. At least juvy had been clean. I wondered what the bathroom looked like but decided not to look. When the time came, I would use it and get out. For now, I just wanted to enjoy being on the outside, but it wasn't easy to do here.

The freebie parka was too heavy and the t-shirt too thin; I needed to get some essentials. The crowd surrounding the bottom of the stairs had been surprisingly helpful when I asked for advice on where to get a jacket.

They pointed towards a secondhand store and, in slurred words, told me the only taxi they had seen in months was the one that dropped me off. I would need to walk if I didn't have a car.

The Attic was located a few blocks away, down on Gambell Street, so I took off on foot. It's not like I was in a hurry. Five dollars and sixty minutes later, I had a nice new-to-me spring jacket. It was a little too big and an ugly mix of red and yellow, but it was mine. I bought it with money I had earned by spending time locked in a juvenile detention center.

DRUNKS TURNED friends welcomed me into their circle when I couldn't fall asleep and ventured outside. Nightmares replayed the gun going off and my dad dropping to the ground almost every night. Still haunted by my actions, I joined in conversations to redirect my thoughts.

Various bottles of liquor exchanged hands as everyone in the circle took a swig. At first, I was intimidated by the sheer amount of alcohol they consumed, thinking they would pass out and die right there on the steps. Somehow, they all made it to wherever they called "home" after the bottles ran dry.

My next move needed to be strategic. I tapped my chin with one finger as I sat on the steps of the motel. All sorts of dirty, skinny men and women, most likely drug addicts, came and went throughout the night; somehow, I didn't feel threatened. It worried me that they thought I was one of them. *Oh well, at least they didn't mess with me.*

Before my release, my probation officer communicated the rules tied to my freedom. He told me counselor appointments for the upcoming year must be pre-scheduled, so I made it a point to ask for someone in Talkeetna, where Pete offered me a place to stay. I had decided long ago to take him up on his offer but had some business to take care of before leaving the city.

A small envelope, what I referred to as my exit package, included, among other things, bank information. When the release agent handed me the envelope, I had no idea what it contained, but never imagined a savings account statement.

I don't know how McLaughlin got ahold of it, but somehow it found its way to me. Leave it to my mom. She promised to always take care of me; this proved it.

Over the weekend, I explored the city. The bank sat in the middle of town, and I made a plan to arrive first thing Monday morning. The statement seemed to burn my fingers each time I studied it. Three pages listed dates of deposits and, most importantly, the account number.

Based on the history, my mom, the smart and slightly cunning planner she had been, opened the bank account in my name years ago. Every week, she deposited a few dollars behind my dad's back. Just in case. It paid off. By the time I was ready to dip into the savings, it had grown to nearly ten thousand dollars.

The teller who helped me had all kinds of options for what I could do with my money. I wanted to apply for a debit card but didn't have an address to receive it in the mail. Since I planned to leave, it didn't make sense to wait for it.

The teller assured me that the bank had branches all over the United States and all my needs could be covered from anywhere. I withdrew some cash and decided to finish my banking business in Talkeetna.

UNABLE TO DIAL long-distance from the motel, I shoved the paper holding Pete's number in my front pocket and left my room. Payphones didn't really exist anymore, from what I'd been told, so I needed to ask for help. Not one of my strengths.

"Hey, man. Can I use your phone?" I asked the first person who wandered past. He responded with a scowl and kept walking, so I asked the next person. Another scowl.

One of the regulars who hung out in the parking lot recognized me and lifted his chin. "Ten bucks."

Highway robbery. I pulled the money from my pocket, and he handed me the phone. Not knowing how these things worked, I stared at the device in my hand and raised my eyebrows. With a chuckle, the guy asked for it back and I gave him the number. He dialed and put the phone back in my hand.

A deep voice answered on the third ring. "Moore Industries, Pete speaking."

"Wow, you sound so damn professional."

Silence.

"Oh, sorry. Dude, it's Jake. Moose from McLaughlin."

"Jake! Oh my God. You're out—so cool." Rustling papers filled the background noise. "Let me give you my address. How soon can you get here?"

"Uh, I don't have a ride. I just got out on Friday."

I practically witnessed the smoke rising from his ears, even though he had been over a hundred miles away.

"Okay. Let me think. How can I get in touch with you?"

"I borrowed a phone. I'm staying at a motel in Anchorage. I don't have the number to either."

"Well, then. If you can hang tight until the weekend, I'll come get you Saturday. Where are you staying?"

AS PROMISED, Pete pulled into the motel parking lot on Saturday and honked his horn. I tossed my duffle in the back of his truck, and we headed north. Mountains in the distance grew larger as we got closer to Talkeetna.

Awkward silence filled the cab of the truck. *Should I be asking about his life even if it doesn't make a difference to me? I guess I should get to know him if I'm going to live on his property.*

"So. Pete. How've you been?"

One simple question led to an hour of mundane chatter. My old friend rambled on about how happy I'd be in his hometown. "Even though the Iditarod doesn't come directly through Talkeetna, the entire town still has a huge party the entire time the dogs are running. Will you be here in March?" At least the tension subsided.

“I’m not sure, man. I hope so.” Since he promised me a job at his brothers company, I thought it was odd for him to ask how long I would be around.

“Oliver just filled an opening for a floorhand, but I’m sure we’ll be able to find an open position for you.” As we got closer to the city, Pete pulled off the road to an overlook. “You ever seen Denali?” Assuming my answer would be “no,” he parked. “Check this out.”

Being trapped for years surrounded by a dull gray, the captivating blues and greens took my breath away. Snow covered the peak and I thought of home. I missed home. I missed my mom. I almost cried. “Amazing.”

“Feels good to be out, huh?”

I chuckled. “You would know.”

He grasped my shoulder. “Damn good to see you, bro. Let’s get you back to normal life.”

Off the beaten path, situated within a forest of tall trees, the Moore property stretched for hundreds of acres. Pete dropped me at one of the cabins and said he’d be back later to take me into town for supplies.

Enclosed within the small four walls were a bed, couch, wood stove, a small TV, and a smaller kitchen. No bathroom. *Shit*. I chuckled. *Literally*.

It didn’t take me long to unpack, I didn’t own much these days. *It will be so good to make something of myself, to prove I’m a decent human being despite my past. If not to anyone else, to myself. To Mom.*

"Next page, Mom." I stepped outside and found a chair on the back side of the building. A small firepit offered a place to burn a natural fire. Mountains filled the distance beyond the lake. Any anxiety about my future disappeared as I took in the sounds of nature. Songs of various birds, a growl, and a grunt came from the forest.

Hesitant to close my eyes, afraid I had been in some weirdly wonderful dream and would wake up back in McLaughlin, I took extended blinks. "I have a good feeling about this place. Mom. Pete tells me that jobs in the oil field are hard work, but they pay really well. I'm excited to be able to work off some of my energy."

A whisper tickled my ear, and I turned, expecting to find Pete playing tricks. Tears stung my eyes, and I knew. "Mom. I'm so sorry I couldn't save you. I know I've said it a million times, but I mean it more every day. I hope you can find it in your heart to forgive me."

As hard as I tried, I couldn't keep my eyes open. I didn't want to miss the view, but exhaustion took over.

I was startled awake when Pete closed his truck door. "Let's go get you some things."

FLAMES LICKED the sky from within their contained area. As much as I would love for them to roam free, the rest of the mountainside would not be happy. Especially

Pete and Oliver.

With a stocked refrigerator, I invited Pete to stay for dinner. “My treat.” Hotdogs cooked over the fire are my specialty; my mom always loved it when I made my signature entrée.

“Listen. Moose.” Pete sighed and folded his hands.

The tone of his voice gave me pause. I could tell he didn’t want to deliver the bad news. Since he first told me about Oliver hiring a floorhand, I had a feeling there wouldn’t be room for me. To ease his mind, I let on that it was okay. It wasn’t, but he shouldn’t have had to pay for it.

“How long can I stay?”

“I’m so sorry. I did everything I could. I’ve been talking about you for months. My brother does whatever he wants, like he owns the company or something.”

“Doesn’t he?”

“Yeah, but still.” He stood and shoved his hands in his front pockets. “My brother rents these cabins on a week-to-week basis, so as long as this one stays empty, you’re good. It might be nice, though, to offer him a couple hundred a month. Maybe you can get a job in town. At the bar or something.”

Chapter 14

Kennedy, age nineteen-December 2007

CHRISTMAS LIGHTS twinkled along Anchorage's Main street like multi-colored beads of joy. Spectacular holiday celebrations were commonplace during the holidays. Snow fell in small flakes, adding to the festive live scenes of Santa, elves, and reindeer.

Horse-drawn carriages lined the streets where tourists readily paid for an excursion, even a week after Christmas. Residents dressed in parkas shivered as they rushed from building to building, bags of goodies in hand.

Tonight would surely be a night to remember. I had thought of everything for the most special occasion—our first wedding anniversary. The second Cody gave me the green light to plan a night out, I created a list of ideas. I spent the last month arranging everything down to the smallest detail. I said a silent prayer that all the specifics lined up well enough to please my husband.

Dinner reservations at the fanciest restaurant in Anchorage had been the most important part of my plans. I wanted to prove to Cody that I was elegant enough for him, that I wasn't a trashy slut like he accused.

Upon entry, the hostess took our coats in exchange for a call tag. Cody's eyes lit up, then darkened at the sight of my slightly seductive little black dress, which hugged my curves in all the right places. It had been short, but long-sleeved to cover the scars and recent bruises. I wasn't sure if he was happy or pissed, but I had to hope for the best.

It was completely possible he wondered where the dress had come from; he knew every bit of clothing I owned and hadn't seen this piece before. Cody hadn't known I had left the apartment. It was against the rules, after all. An ad on TV showed the dress during a commercial and I knew I had to have it.

The Maître D' led us to a table beside the window, just as I had requested. I could feel Cody's eyes on my backside; new three-inch heels made my legs and ass look fantastic. My old one-foot-in-front-of-the-other dancer walk had faded since leaving Seward, but when I put the shoes on, it came back as naturally as riding a bike.

Dark wood mixed with dark paint and splashes of burgundy throughout the intimate space exuded sophistication. I felt important and sexy, like I had a reason to be in the fine dining establishment. People looked at us as we walked past; I liked it.

Cody's eyebrows raised when he read the costs on the menu. He cleared his throat as he placed the wine list beside his silverware—which was actually gold. "Get whatever you want, babe. This is a day for you; live it up."

"Are you sure?" I held my breath, hoping he wasn't just patronizing me. It annoyed me when he made me believe he was genuine, just to punish me when I did something wrong. "Because I would really love to try the filet mignon. I've always heard that's the best piece of meat."

A smirk on his face didn't always mean the same thing. Some days, it meant he was playful and spunky, other days he was planning his next diabolical move. Not sure which day this was, I treaded lightly.

Nervous, my fingers danced over the heavy diamond necklace which laid cold and flat against my collarbone. The outlandish wedding gift weighed more than anything I'd ever worn around my neck. Cody had expressed how it had cost more than my mom's trailer and contained almost five carats. Whatever that meant.

"Of course, my queen. Whatever your little heart desires." His sweet smile calmed my nerves.

My confidence restored, I tucked one of my soft

waves behind my ear, only to be met with a frown. Cody demanded that my hair be perfect at all times, even though we never went anywhere. I refused to let my frizzy mop of straw ruin his mood. Every curl was in place and frizz-free; I made sure of it. So why did he frown?

While we waited for our drinks, Cody stroked the back of my hand with his index finger, then pulled my hand into his. The intimate gesture reassured me that this night would be glorious. He gazed into my eyes and slow-blinked.

My heart fluttered. *This is what it's all about.*

"You know that you're the most beautiful girl in this restaurant, right?"

Heat stained my cheeks red, and I tucked my chin.

"I mean it. Hell, K, you're probably the prettiest girl in the entire state."

"Come on, Cody. That's not true." Cloud nine was so squishy and light. I could swear I floated on fluffy bits of happiness.

"Of course it is. Most of the girls in this state are practically men, they have to work out in the cold beside their husbands. If they can even get husbands. There must only be six semi-attractive women in all of Alaska." He released my hand and sat back as the waiter poured crimson liquid from a bottle of wine.

I think he just insulted me, but I'm not sure. With a

chuckle, I squinted and wondered what he meant. I didn't dare ask; it would feel shitty to know that my husband compared me to semi-attractive women. I pushed it aside.

"After I graduate in a few weeks, I was thinking we could move somewhere warm. Like this spring. We should start looking for houses. What do you think?"

"But my mom ..."

"Jesus, do we need to do this before we even enjoy our food? You know how to ruin the best days." His first glass of wine disappeared in seconds. I managed to sip mine even though I thought my tongue would stick to the roof of my mouth, it was so dry.

"Sorry. I just ..." Determined to recover the mood, I forced enthusiasm into my voice. "Warm sounds fantastic. I would give anything to get away from this miserable cold. Where were you thinking?"

"Well, my counselor mentioned how Dallas is in a hiring boom and the hospitals pay really well, especially after the internship." Cody went on and on about our future in Dallas and how wonderful it would be to explore new areas. I still hadn't been any further than Anchorage and hoped we could see more of Alaska before we left. But I internalized the thought just in case Cody wasn't in the mood for my selfishness.

Dinner was a fantastic ensemble of flavors; the steak was superb, and the wine and dessert complimented each other. Wine had a different effect on me than whiskey; everything was funny, and I found myself giggling at the simplest things. After just one bottle, I giggled too loud, and my husband frowned.

TWO HORSES whinnied as we approached the final segment of my special night: a carriage ride through the snowy streets of Anchorage. The treat had been icing on the cake. Cody held my hand as I climbed into the tiny cart. His smile melted my heart.

"Wow, Kennedy, you went all out, didn't you?" Compliments in any form confirmed his love for me. Quoting my favorite song lyrics was my favorite; sometimes, he would do it in the middle of a sentence.

Cold air leaked into my parka. I shivered and Cody pulled the blanket over our lap and put his arm around me so he could pull me closer. "I never imagined I could love someone so much. You're my world, Kennedy. What would I do without you by my side?" He kissed the top of my head. "You complete me."

When it was good with Cody, it was so good; better than any life I could have imagined. *This must be what heaven feels like.* I closed my eyes and pictured our new home in Dallas.

A two-story brick with white pillars on the front porch and white doors and trim. A two-car garage with two new shiny cars parked inside. My dreams had grown with the amount of money Cody told me he would be able to make as a psychologist.

As I snuggled into his embrace, I pictured our future together. Cody said he wanted two-point-five kids and maybe even a cat named Snickers. We don't need a lot of land, just enough for the kids to play and be happy in the fenced backyard. Our life was going to be perfect. This was just the beginning.

MY HEAD SNAPPED back, and something cracked. If I had been cooking, I would have thought Cody cracked a carrot in half behind my head. *That's what breaking bones must sound like. Why would I think that?*

Everything moved in slow motion. My body twisted and brown curls spun out around my face like a fan. My arms went limp, and my knees buckled.

The edge of the Formica countertop connected with my chin on the way to the floor, a sound like thunder after a bright burst of lightning filled my ears.

Bright red streaks of blood spattered across the countertop and on the window above the sink.

Considering the position of my body on the floor, it must have looked like a scene in a murder mystery.

When I regained consciousness, I asked myself what had just happened, but the answer escaped me; my right cheek pulsed. It took me a minute to realize that he had hit me. I didn't remember him making contact, but he stood over me with his fist still clenched, huffing.

Not sure if I should laugh or cry, I did a little of both. Relieved, now that the aggression had left his soul, I was a little scared of what would happen next.

Tight and hot, my face hurt; the beginning of a bruise raised on my cheek. My head ached, more like pounded, and my heartbeat pulsed in my chin. Blood crusted at the corner of my eye. I assumed it had to be blood—how could drool reach my eye?

God, if you're real, please let this be a bad dream. I will settle for a nightmare. Please. This can't be happening again.

A voice reached my ears and for a moment, I thought God had answered me. Then I was able to make out the words.

"You plan a date at the most prestigious, most expensive restaurant in all of Alaska only to show up looking like a whore. What the fuck were you thinking wearing a dress so short? Your ass cheeks hung out. And so tight, you left nothing to the imagination. I could see your nipples. Dammit, Kennedy, you're my wife. You must have left the house to buy it—without my permission. Who the fuck do you think you are? You put our free ride in jeopardy. If my dad finds out …"

Speechless, I could hardly believe what had just

happened. From the floor, Cody seemed to double in size. His breathing scared me, his fists hadn't unclenched, and I wondered how many more punches were in my future.

No more punches, just a kick. My stomach absorbed his boot and I gasped from the impact; the breath kicked clear out of me.

"Did you see who sat at the table beside us? The fucking mayor. One look at you and he about lost his mind. His mouth dropped and drool practically dripped from his lips. His wife covered her mouth; I bet she was so disgusted by the sight of you that she threw up."

Calm came over Cody like a wave. His shoulders sank and his fists released. It seemed as if speaking his thoughts brought him out of his rage. He twisted the top off a bottle of whiskey and drank straight from it. Gulped.

Cody reached out his hand as if he wanted to help me to my feet. When his fingers wrapped around mine, he squinted. "And your fucking hair. How many times do I need to tell you? You know I don't want to see you without straight hair. You look like one of my prissy classmates. Like you don't appreciate what you have."

Halfway to my feet, he let me go; I landed sideways on my ankle and cried out in pain.

"Oh, did that hurt? Are you gonna cry now like a little baby?" Cody didn't like it when I complained. "So pathetic. How 'bout I give you something to cry about?" He squinted as he thought. "Maybe another 'M'? This time on the inside of your thigh. I bet you'd enjoy the pain."

"No, please." Like he would listen to me. Once he got an idea in his head, he rolled with it.

He tapped his chin with his finger and tilted his head. The smirk mixed with his black eyes made me think of a horror movie I had seen years ago. Just like in *American Psycho,* Cody's sick ideas made me cringe.

We kept the scissors in a junk drawer; chills ran up my spine at the sight of him holding them. He grabbed me by the hair and pulled me to my feet.

"Wait! Cody, no. Please don't. Don't do this. I'm sorry, I'll never do it again. I promise. Please don't cut my hair." Tears streamed down my cheeks and mixed with the already dried blood.

"Oh, now you're sorry. What, precisely, my dear, are you sorry about?"

"Whatever it is you're mad about. I'm sorry."

"That's your problem, Kennedy," he practically spit my name. "You don't even know what you did wrong. You're so fucking stupid that you have no idea what to apologize for. How can I be sure you'll never do it again if you don't even know what you did?"

He wasn't wrong. I didn't know what I had done to upset him so much. I just knew he was pissed. When I didn't answer him, he made the first cut. I cried out, again, this time in shame.

Silenced by humiliation, I closed my eyes as he made the second cut. My long hair had always been my best attribute; my pride and joy. He took it upon himself to wreck the one thing that made me confident.

How could I be so stupid to think he would like the curls? He bought me a straight iron last year for Christmas and demanded I use it daily. I knew he didn't prefer curls, but I didn't think it was a big deal.

WARM SHEETS comforted my sore body. Cody laid behind me in a spoon position. His arm rested on my hip. "I'm sorry if I hurt you; you just get me so worked up. You know how to push every one of my buttons." His words slurred and his breathing slowed. That was my cue that he was falling asleep.

Thank God. Tomorrow is a new day. He'll be sorry and shower me with love.

"I promise, we will have the best life. It's you and me against the world." Snores rang in my ear in a whiskey lullaby.

After I was sure Cody was in a steady drunken sleep, I slid out from under his arm. The mirror in the bathroom reflected a familiar, yet strange image. A sad, broken young woman stared back at me.

Purple and red surrounded my left eye and encompassed my chin, my nose looked crooked, and dried blood covered the corner of my mouth. The worst of it, though, was the short uneven tufts of hair which framed my face.

"What the hell?" I snorted at the vision of fire and brimstone surrounding me, my husband stood in the center.

Pain in my stomach forced me to double in half. Before I had time to think about the repercussions, a squeal escaped my throat. When I woke Cody from a deep sleep, he usually had words to make me regret it.

Blood dripped to the floor from between my legs and I gasped at another sharp pain. Instincts told me what had happened, and I sobbed. "Oh, no. No, no, no."

I had wanted to tell Cody about the baby after we got home, but he obviously had other plans.

Chapter 15

Jake, age twenty-two—August 2007

SUMMER IN ALASKA had always been my favorite time of year. Every animal that called this area home had come alive and roamed freely. From behind my cabin, sounds of the wild kept me company. I named each one of the chirps, grunts, howls, and growls as they happened and greeted them with positive energy.

I had become one of those animals. Although my things were stored in the cabin, I camped in the wild more often than I slept in a man-made bed. All I needed was a pack, which contained a small tent and supplies to keep me alive. I wasn't allowed to own a gun due to my history, but because someone left a loaded nine-millimeter under my bed, I took it into the wild for safety.

Most of the terrain had not been explored by humans until me. The only trails had been created by animals; I felt honored to use their roads. Oftentimes I felt as if something watched me—probably bears, moose, or mountain lions—but none of them ever bothered me. Our mutual respect allowed us to live in harmony. Mountain goats dotted the ledges of the horizon, and I longed to see a reindeer.

I had prepaid Oliver for two seasons because I had the money; Mom had left me enough money to live for a while. He assured me if I wanted to leave before the two years ran out, he would refund the months I didn't stay. I didn't have any reason to doubt him. From the way I figured, I could find work, either with Pete or maybe at one of the restaurants in the area.

The only reason I needed to go into town was to see my probation officer. I bought a bicycle, so I had a way to get around, but spent so much time in the woods being free, that I didn't focus on finding work.

While in the wild, I hunted and dressed animals. Cooking the meat from the kill gave me a feeling of being one with the land; I grew vegetables behind the cabin, making the need for groceries minimal. Just like in the Pass.

Fish played a major role in my diet. I rode to the river once a week to catch salmon. Bears usually showed up, forcing me to move downriver. No sense taking a chance that they had cubs.

From what Pete said, fire-roasted salmon tasted way better fresh-caught than in any restaurant. I had to believe him; I hadn't ever had salmon any other way. One fish would last me two days unless he came to dinner.

At first, I asked Pete every week if any positions had opened up where he worked. Then, when I realized I wouldn't get a job at his brother's company, I only asked every couple of months. As long as they didn't mind me living in the cabin—and why would they? I paid rent—I figured I might as well stay.

I was in no hurry to be a productive member of society. I had no skills and wasn't able to help anyone, so there wasn't any use wasting time looking for work.

When my money came close to running out, I'd decided to ask Oliver if he knew anyone in the lower forty-eight who could give me a job. It would be nice to live somewhere warm; the more I thought about it, the more appealing it became.

Pete was nice enough to drive me to my last probation meeting. My time in Alaska was coming to an end and I didn't know if I was happy or sad about it. More sad, I think. But there was a future for me in another area, I felt it. I asked if he would invite Oliver to Brian's Burgers so I could treat them to dinner.

"Listen, Oliver. Pete. I want to thank you for letting me stay in the cabin for so long." I paused and pursed my lips. As many times as I had gone over the speech in my head, I didn't anticipate getting emotional. "I feel that I've overstayed my welcome."

"What? No. Jake, please don't think that."

Pete didn't want me to go, I could see it in his eyes, but I needed something to give me a sense of accomplishment.

"I didn't think so when I first arrived, but I'm just wasting my life. I need to make something of myself." I focused on the older brother. "Oliver, do you have any connections in the lower forty-eight? I would really like to try somewhere warm."

"I do." He nodded. "When we get back to the house, I'll give you the name of a contractor friend in Dallas. I'll even put in a good word for you."

On my last night at the cabin, a large, majestic male moose came into view. Over the past two seasons, I had only seen three and they were not close to the cabins. An overwhelming feeling of peace relaxed my body.

My mom taught me that the Moose represents the wise elder. It describes someone capable of communicating the joy of life and sharing wisdom and compassion. I wanted to be that moose.

ANCHORAGE TO DALLAS didn't sound that far away. In reality, the trudge through four-thousand miles wouldn't be as simple as I imagined. The ticket agent delivered the bad news that trains didn't cut through

Canada, and suddenly Dallas seemed a million miles away. Then she offered the second blow: buses didn't drive the route, either.

I thought twice about leaving. I had enough money for a flight, obviously, but had never flown before. I didn't know what to do or if it was safe. It was my only choice, so I called for a taxi to the airport, paid for a ticket, and waited to board.

"Mom, can you hear me?" Nothing else to do, I gazed out the window toward the mountains, certain that I would never be back. "I'm sorry, Mom. For letting you down. If I had been big enough to defend you, you would still be here, and I wouldn't have to leave." I sighed and leaned my head against the window. "I don't mean to keep disappointing you. I just can't help it.

"I'm gonna do it, though. It's about time for me to turn my life around and make you proud. I haven't lived a life you'd approve of, and I've made some bad choices, but I can make it right. One day I'll have a career and a house and maybe someday a wife and kids."

A sardine can. The airplane was packed full of people like sardines. I only prayed the top couldn't roll back as easily. My stomach lurched at the first movement; backing away from the gate had been traumatic enough, how would I survive an entire flight?

On top of leaving everything I had ever known in the past, I was headed toward the absolute unknown. A new start, I told myself, as if it would help make the thought of moving to Dallas better. I get it: change is scary. I had good reason to be riddled with anxiety. *Will this new company hire me if they know about my past? Can I lie about it on a job application?*

The counselor at McLaughlin said no. If I did and my employer found out about it, they could not only fire me, but report to the state that I had hidden my past. Especially for murder.

The closer I got to Dallas, though, the more I thought about how leaving the old me in Alaska could be a good thing, the more excited I got. This new start of mine could be whatever I wanted it to be. And so could my past. I had the time to think, and I came up with a plan.

The story I would tell people could be a new me. When people ask where I'm from, I'd just say Montana. I would tell people that I just left the cold after my parents died in a car accident. I smiled as more of my fake-Jake childhood formed in my mind.

I made up an entire past, which was exactly the opposite from reality. My father was a very loving, caring man who gave my mom everything she could ever want. It was almost sickening the way he loved us both so much.

Our ranch style home sat on seventy acres outside of Helena. I had been an only child because my parents were satisfied with just one son. While my parents chatted and laughed on the back porch, a cold iced tea in their hand, I cared for all our animals. We had the perfect life; the only thing I ever longed for was to live somewhere warm.

Chapter 16

Kennedy, age twenty–April 2008

THE VETERANS Administration usually hires from within or hires veterans before opening positions to outside applicants, but Cody was such a fantastic student that his counselor sent a letter of recommendation to the head of Human Resources. Or at least that's what he bragged about during every conversation we had about moving.

Cody received the call along with a job offer and was so excited to tell me his good news that my good news would just have to wait.

"Before we decide on the best place to live, we need to get acquainted with the area and the people. For the first few months, we'll live in an apartment near the VA. I've already made arrangements. It will be ready for us next week. Until then, we'll sort of be on vacation. Our hotel room has a kitchenette, so we can think of it as a starter apartment. This is the beginning of our perfect life. Just like I promised." His hands cupped my face as he lowered his lips to mine. Soft kisses covered my mouth, cheeks, and neck. I held my breath and reveled in the way he loved me. He was right; this would be perfect.

Cody was so happy he lifted me off my feet and spun in a circle. "I love you, K. Forever, I promise." We laughed and kissed as we stumbled down the hallway to our bedroom.

For the first time in a while, he took his time with me. Gentle yet passionate, he undressed me, kissing every inch of my skin as each piece of clothing fell to the floor.

Naked and aroused, I positioned myself in the middle of the bed and reached for my husband. My love. My life. Darkness filled his eyes, and a smirk pulled his lips to one side as he tilted his chin.

Between my knees, he knelt and rubbed himself on me, asking politely if he could enter. I opened myself to him and we made mad passionate love. He made sure I was satisfied—twice—before he fell asleep wrapped in a tangle of legs and arms.

Satisfied, I was indeed. Cody's love filled me with every kiss, every touch, every gentle thrust. His compassion for me and desire to please me was not lost.

This precious time consumed me. I never wanted it to end, so I allowed my mind to wander about how our life would be in Texas. We would explore the city and get to know our neighbors. I wouldn't need to hide inside anymore; we could have friends. Our growing little family would consume our every waking moment and bring us even closer together. I just needed to tell him.

I had been studying maps of the Dallas area and hoped we would be near one of the large parks so I could spend some time outdoors near a lake. My entire life had been spent near water and I longed to maintain at least a portion of what I had become accustomed to.

Maybe when we settled, he would let me invite Brittany for a visit. I would love to show her around the city; have our own little adventure. We could explore different foods—find the best pizza—and make up for lost time.

I was sure she would understand why I hadn't called. My mom would be a different story, though. She'd never come to see me. Not even if I begged her to bring Emily and Nathan.

DALLAS WAS WAY bigger than I imagined. Sure, maps showed how expansive the city had become over the past decade, but I didn't think there would be a need to use the Metro to visit some historic sites and touristy locations. Unique landmarks dotted our new hometown. I couldn't wait to get out and explore.

Our first night in the hotel had been uneventful; Cody picked me up and carried me over the threshold, making me giggle. We both crashed early from the long flight and stressful taxi ride from the airport.

Cody had taken care of the moving details. All our belongings, except some clothes and essentials, would be shipped once we got settled. All I had to do was walk beside my man, and viola, like magic, we re-appeared four-thousand miles away in the lowest of the lower forty-eight.

He admitted to rushing as he got ready for work the next morning. It was unusual for an intern to start on a Friday, but his bosses wanted to get started with him right away. There was no time left to recoup from the travel day, but he got up early, put on his white lab coat, kissed me goodbye, and walked out the door. He looked like a real doctor; I couldn't have been prouder.

Thrilled that I would have time to sightsee, I dressed for a warm spring day in a skirt and a white V-neck spaghetti-strap tank top. The scars on my arms didn't bother me, not here. No one knew who I was or what I had been through. The brand looked like something that a tattoo parlor would do on purpose, not an angry husband. I could be anyone I wanted and make up crazy stories about the three parallel scars on my arm. Although, I'm not sure what could possibly beat "a bear attacked me."

Texas heat was a lot different than Alaska heat—because the latter didn't exist. At least with the short hair, there was no need to pull it up into a ponytail to keep it off my neck. Prepared with a map and some cash in my purse, I set off on foot.

The metro had been a little sketchy, along with some areas I had to walk through, but I held my head high and acted like I belonged right where I was.

Homeless men stared at me as I walked past. Surely, they had never seen a girl from Alaska walking their streets. I chuckled to myself; they probably hadn't.

I spent the day touring the free areas of downtown. More than anything, I had wanted to see where JFK had been assassinated. Without much money, I could only wander around the grassy knoll area; tourists took their picture on the "X" in the middle of the street. A little morbid, but I could see the allure.

Life-sized bronze statues of a cattle drive at the edge of town intrigued me. I spent all of an hour walking around Pioneer Park, which featured forty longhorns and three cowboys, as well as the neighboring cemetery.

My feet were sore before lunch, so I found a food truck and ordered a taco. The Texas sun licked my shoulders; my skin tightened with the burn.

Exhausted by the time I returned to the hotel, I locked the door and collapsed in the chair. Two hours later, I woke up with a stiff neck and made myself a stiff drink. In the shower, the heat of the water mixed with the heat of the whiskey made everything better.

PRESCRIPTION pads sat in a stack on the kitchen counter beside two bottles of pills, folded twenty-dollar bills, and the room key. Because Cody would be prescribing these pills to patients, he wanted to test them. On us. This was his version of "research."

Psychiatrists take the training required to prescribe medications, which is why Cody chose this field of mental health. They're qualified to perform a full range of tests; however, I don't think the study was meant to be done on himself.

Not only did he give me a glass of water and two green and white capsules, but he also took one. Only one. It had been the first time we both indulged together.

From what he had heard from co-workers, this particular prescription would make him last longer in bed. Like he needed to; he already lasted just a little too long for my liking. Not that I would ever admit it to him.

I followed him to the bedroom and kept my eyes closed as I let him undress me. Whatever effect the pill had on him didn't matter to me. It relaxed me enough to push away the anxiety of all the "what if" questions racing through my mind.

What if he didn't like my hair?

What if I hadn't showered recently enough?

What if I'd gained too much weight?

What if the sun burned me too much for his liking?

For once, I had been relaxed enough that his every touch made me want more.

"You left the apartment today, didn't you?" Hazy words in a voice which resembled my husband floated around my head.

I straddled him and lowered myself slowly, moaning with pleasure as I let him fill me. "I sure did; had the best day." His hands roamed my body, squeezing my breasts too hard. He leaned forward and nipped my skin, bringing blood to the surface. I groaned; the slight pain turned me on, but I don't think he meant for it to.

The pills disguised the slap across my face as a playful nudge; I didn't care that my cheek was on fire. All I wanted was for him to make love to me. It was as if I was back in Alaska, dancing. I missed the familiar sounds and smells; I missed my friends. Oddly, I missed my regulars. Only another shot of whiskey could make the experience better.

"What the fuck is wrong with you?" He wrapped one hand in my short hair and yanked my head back. He didn't expect me to moan and grind myself into him, hard. Either it pissed him off or turned him on, both resulted in the same reaction.

I held on for the ride. No matter how hard he pulled me down and pushed into me, I took all of him and made sure he knew how much I liked it.

The next morning, my body reminded me of what kind of night we had had. Along with my insides hurting, fingerprint bruises covered my hips, ass, and breasts. The playful nip ended up being a full-on bite; I could see his individual teeth marks on my skin.

Confused when I studied my face in the mirror and touched the purple around my eye, I wondered out loud, "Did he hit me?" As it turned out, the slap had been more than playful. No matter how many layers of makeup I applied, the unnatural coloring around my eye still peeked through.

BREAKFAST usually consisted of cereal, so when I woke the following morning to the scent of bacon frying, my heart raced. Excited, I strode into the kitchen with a renewed outlook on life. I vaguely remembered Cody being upset because I had explored the city on my own.

Our old life must be playing into the new. Pancakes, bacon, scrambled eggs, and English muffins covered two plates. We had always spent weekend mornings in bed in Alaska. *This is a nice change.* "Cody? Is everything okay?"

"Of course, babe." He licked bacon grease off his

fingers. "What? Am I not allowed to make my best girl a nice breakfast? I figured we could spend the day strolling around the local area. Maybe get to know some of the business owners."

"That sounds great. And this smells fantastic." I wrapped my arms around his chest from behind and inhaled. "Almost as good as you."

Family stores within a five-block radius sold everything from groceries to liquor to clothes and shoes. I had stopped at a couple of them on my first day out, but I didn't want Cody to know I had experienced something without him. We entered every open door and introduced ourselves to whoever would listen, which I thought was a bit odd if our plan was to move by the end of the week.

Elaine's Kitchen sat at the corner of Martin Luther King Jr. Blvd. and S. Malcolm X Blvd; Cody suggested we stop for a snack. Six tables lined the front of the restaurant, three on each side of the door. Ten stools sat in front of the bar, nineteen-sixties style.

We sat at the only empty table and ordered jerk chicken. "Listen, Kennedy. I'm not going to make enough to cover the full expenses; you need to find a job."

I couldn't believe my ears. *That's it? No apology, no explanation?* "Um. Okay." Unsure of how he expected me to respond, I paused.

"Your little day out cost us too much money. Not to mention, you spent too much on food. I don't know who taught you how to shop, but now that we're paying our own way, everything you put in the cart needs to be on sale. Period. Besides, the hotel will drain my pocket faster than I thought, too. If you weren't so needy, I'd have stayed in a shithole."

He was wrong; I barely spent any money on the day I explored. He didn't even look at the grocery receipt, so how would he know what anything costs? Prices were different than in Alaska. And I thought I understood his hotel rating, but I had obviously misjudged; we were already staying in a shithole.

"Why don't you ask if this place needs help? It's close to the hotel and looks pretty clean. Besides, it will do you good to learn how to do something besides dancing for money."

Ouch. I raised my eyebrows and waited for him to give a better reason for the sudden request. *Couldn't he sell something? Like his watch or my necklace?* I didn't dare ask; he'd probably punish me for talking back.

Taking both of my hands in his, he gazed into my eyes and confessed. "The application for the apartment is on hold until I can prove we'll be able to pay the entire amount each month. I thought I'd be making more, but the number they quoted me is what I'll make after my internship. I'm a little pissed about their error, but we can make it work if you get a job, too."

"But you said you didn't want me to work. You hated my job in Alaska."

He leaned closer and hissed, "Did I say I wanted you to fuck the entire town of Dallas? Jesus Kennedy, when did you become so brainless?"

"Well," not wanting to draw attention to our conversation, I ignored his comment. "I don't have anything to keep me busy until we get our own place, so it doesn't sound like a horrible idea. I've never worked in a diner before, but I guess I can ask if they have a position open."

Our hotel sat just four blocks away, and the bus stopped in front of both buildings, which made it a perfect location for me to work. The more I thought about it, the better the idea of having a job sounded. "Hey, maybe I could put an application in at the water park or even the zoo." My eyes lit up as excitement made my heart swell. "I saw on the news that the state fair is coming in August; people swarm the fairgrounds for an entire month. I bet I could get a job there."

Cody sighed, bored with my ideas. "And just how do you plan on getting that far? You certainly can't walk, and my hours will definitely be different than yours, so I can't drop you off."

"I'll take the bus."

"The hell you will." Releasing my hands, he leaned

back. "You're trying to make us broke before we even get started. Come on, Kennedy. Use your head, for once, would you? Think."

MY PATH TO work took me under one of the major highways; I-45. Homeless men had constructed makeshift homes from tents, tarps, and cardboard. I couldn't help but think about how these men who involved themselves in a tawdry scene had arrived at such a sad segment of their lives.

Crack pipes and heroin needles scattered the ground around them. Chills ran through me as I tried to tell myself I was safe. It was early, so most of the men were still sleeping; those who weren't kept their eyes glued to me as I passed.

Finding a job had been unexpected and having to walk in an area which wasn't the safest made me nervous, but I figured if I could make friends with some of the people in the area, I would be better off.

I waved or nodded at the residents under the bridge, hoping one day, they might have my back. Memories of walking home in the dark after working at the bar brought a familiar feeling of unease. At least in Dallas, bears wouldn't be a threat.

Elaine greeted me with a smile as I entered her restaurant; I reciprocated. My experience as a server had gotten me the job. Waitressing wasn't rocket science, but it took a certain kind of person to treat all the customers in the same manner.

"Learn the menu, taste the food, write orders clearly, give correct change, be kind. It's that easy." Elaine introduced me to the cook, her husband, Dane. "Kennedy is going to be asking for taste tests, D."

"Zeen."

I tilted my head and raised my eyebrows at Elaine. My straight locks swayed into my eyes.

She chuckled. "You'll learn his little comments, soon enough. He's from Jamaica and desires to keep his authenticity not only in his cooking, but also in his every way of life. Zeen basically means, 'got it', it's slang for 'seen.'"

Aprons hung on a hook behind the door between the kitchen and dining room. Most of them were covered in grease stains or hadn't been washed in days. I pulled the cleanest one off the hook and tied it around my waist.

Complete with a notepad in one pocket and a pen in the other, my waitress outfit made me feel like I had a new purpose. My husband needed me to help save money for our future home and I was more than happy to help.

"Now, darlin', I have a specific preference about how I wish you to wait tables; customer service is the most important aspect of this job. You must remain peppy and smile. If you desire great tips, never forget an order, always read your customer. Know what they want before they do."

"Noted. When I served in Alaska, I took pride in getting to know my customers well. After only a short time, I could anticipate their needs." It wasn't a lie, but I obviously didn't share the context.

"I chose Monday for your first day because it's the slowest. Figured we could get to know each other a little bit. Be ready for tomorrow, though. Our lunch specials draw a good crowd."

"Okay."

"Dane! We need to test a Tuesday lunch special." Elaine raised an eyebrow. "You hungry?"

I was. The food was different than anything I had ever tasted. I liked it. A lot. I wouldn't have a problem authentically raving about Dane's cooking.

The entire day, four sets of customers came into the store; because I didn't have much experience with food, I shadowed my boss to learn the ropes.

By the end of the day, I didn't have much more experience than when I started. Elaine was a great teacher, though. I feel like if anyone did want to place an order with me, I could have done a great job.

Chapter 17

Jake, age twenty-three—April 2008

NEIGHBORHOODS surrounding south Dallas used to be filled with middle-class families living life to the fullest. In the past decade, things had changed. Before I moved to this strange city, I did a little research. On one of my last days in Talkeetna, I used the computer in the library—and the help of the librarian—to learn about my new home.

At one time, property around Fair Park, the site of the Texas State Fair, was highly sought after. When the real estate market crashed, values lowered and people who didn't have much money moved in. Now, the area is home to those without jobs, without homes, without purpose. Sounded like I'd fit right in.

I found a cheap motel on the south side of town which reminded me of the place in Anchorage, drunk men and all. Five men stood in a circle at the other end of the building; their voices carried as they passed a bottle in a paper bag.

Sun beat down on the pavement, warming the space to an uncomfortable temperature. If I were in the crowd, I would have suggested going somewhere cooler. But I wasn't.

I needed a place for the contractor to return a call and I hadn't bought a cell phone because it was too expensive. The screen door slammed behind me, closing me into a small reception area of the motel.

"Hey, friend. What can I do for ya? You need a room? It's fifty a night."

The name tag on the man's shirt read Quinn. "Do you rent out by the week or month?" Exhaustion took over and I felt light-headed. My eyes grew heavy, and a faint throbbing formed behind my eyes.

Quinn held my gaze; he must have been trying to determine if I would be a good tenant. "I'll take four-fifty for the month. You pay up front. If you leave early, I'll give you half back. I force you to leave, no refund."

"I'll take it." Not knowing if that rate was more or less expensive than other places around, I jumped at the chance to have a warm bed. I would have preferred to compare prices but wasn't in the best position to do so. Wandering from hotel to hotel didn't sound like the best idea.

Quinn seemed glad for the opportunity to fill a room. "We don't get many tourists or out-of-towners." He grabbed a key off the wall and wrote the number in his book. With his hand held out he continued, "It's a pretty quiet place, most of the time."

After I paid in advance for the room, I put on my nicest voice. "Do you have a phone I could use? I'm new in town."

"Sure thing." Quinn placed the receiver on the counter, nodded, and left the room.

A slip of paper with the contractor's cell phone number had practically burned a hole in my pocket. I couldn't wait to have a real job and a real promise for a better life. I dialed the number; it rang four times before voicemail took over.

"Hello. My name is Jake Knight. I was given your name by Oliver Moore in Talkeetna, Alaska. He said you had open positions, and I was hoping I could meet with you to discuss working for you. I'm staying in South Dallas for at least the next week. You can reach me at my motel." I picked up a business card and rattled off the number. "Thanks. Hope to hear from you soon."

As if he had listened to my one-sided conversation, Quinn returned as soon as I disconnected. He didn't need me to ask if he would mind receiving a return call. "I regularly take messages for the people who stay here. I understand the situation of my customers and do what I can to help y'all out while you're in the in-between."

"Thanks, Quinn. I appreciate your help."

DUSTY SCREENS covered the open windows of the second-floor room. A mild breeze had been refreshing considering it was close to ninety degrees. It would have been nice to have air conditioning; if I had known it was going to be this hot, I might have decided against Dallas. But now that I'm here I need to figure out how to make it work. Mom always taught me to make the best of what I had.

Stains spotted the green carpet and the cream-colored walls. One lamp offered light from an end table between the two small beds. A TV took up little room on top of the dresser and the closet door sat crooked on the hinges. The room also reminded me of the motel in Alaska. I put my clothes in the dresser and lowered myself to the bed.

I made a promise to myself: if I get this job, I'll do whatever I need to keep it. If there was a God, I might pray and ask for him to put in a good word with the contractor. I needed a job and I needed to make up for what I had lost.

With nothing else to do, and suddenly wide awake, I decided to explore the area and pick up some necessities. More men had gathered in the parking lot, and along with the bottle, they passed a joint, each taking a small hit and holding their breath. Drugs and alcohol never appealed to me, so I made it a point to steer clear.

The group chatted and laughed. They seemed like a fun crowd. An additional three men formed their own group and two women stood at the far corner, waving at passing cars. I didn't feel threatened, but I did feel a little out of place.

Heavy plastic bags hung from my hands as I returned to my new home; I nodded to the men as I climbed the stairs. The few necessities I brought from Alaska weren't enough to last long.

With nothing to do but sit on my bed in the stuffy space, I decided to make a presence outside, who knew how long I would be in the motel. It was always better to make friends with those who knew the area; in a new town—a big city—there might be a reason for someone to have my back.

"Vato!" A short, skinny Mexican guy lifted his chin. Seven other men stood with him in a circle. "What's your name, amigo?"

Spanish had been the only language of which I had picked up a few words. I understood "vato" and "amigo" were friendly terms. If I wanted to have any type of relationships in Texas, it probably wasn't smart for me to retort. "Name's Jake but my friends call me Moose. You?"

"Felix." He lifted the bottle to his lips, took a hard

swig, and held it out toward me.

An offering from a stranger; I had no idea where his mouth had been, but figured the alcohol would kill any germs. Even though I wasn't much of a drinker, I understood it would be best for me to accept the drink. I nodded once and took the bottle.

"Dallas has always been home," he rambled as I drank. "But I left for a few years. Just got back about a week ago. Where you from?"

"Just got here from Alaska. I'm waiting for an oil contractor to return my call so I can get to work."

"Alaska, eh?"

Shit, I already forgot to spin my lie.

HEAT PUNCHED me in the face as if I had walked into a convection oven. The office screen door slammed behind me as I stormed outside. *Dammit Texas is hot.* Frustration encompassed my entire being. *Why would Pete's brother lie to me?*

"Moose." Felix approached and stopped short. He tilted his head; he'd never seen me upset. "Vato, what's up? You look like someone just killed your dog."

"I'm empty." Not a lie, but not the reason I was so pissed. "Need to refill."

On my heels, Felix bounced behind me like a Chihuahua. Both of us grabbed a bottle of liquor and sat it on the counter beside a register. I paid the clerk for both, and Felix slapped me on the shoulder in thanks.

"Okay, Amigo." After a couple shots, we strolled back toward the motel. "Now, tell me what's really bothering you."

Felix had become a sounding board to bounce ideas off of and an empathetic ear. We had discussions about life, but neither of us had revealed deep truths.

"I can hardly believe I'm saying this. A buddy promised me a job with an oil contractor down here. Gave me his number and everything."

"That's great."

I stopped and stared at my new friend.

"Sorry, continue." He took a drink.

"I left three voicemails, and the dude never called me back. Finally answered today—my fourth call. He told me he had never heard of my buddy; no one ever contacted him about a possible hire from Alaska, and he doesn't have any openings. Doesn't expect to in the near future."

"Awe, Moose. That's rotten."

"I gave up my entire life for this job. I had almost nothing, but I placed all my cards in one basket."

"I don't think that's the right saying."

"Who the fuck cares?" Annoyed, I sighed and shook my head. I was done talking. The whiskey had already started to soothe my anger. In the last two weeks of waiting for the guy to call me back, I had become accustomed to having a drink with my new friends.

"I have something for you in my room. Got it from Dennis. Follow me."

Some of the guys were sharing rooms to split costs. Felix and another Hispanic guy kept their minimal belongings in a room on the first floor. Four men sat around the coffee table and didn't bother to stop their activity when we entered. I had never done coke, never had the desire.

Felix went into the bedroom and came back with something in his closed fist. "It's hot and crowded in here, let's go sit on the stairs."

"What's in your hand?"

Two pills sat in his palm, he took one and nodded for me to take the other. Without any idea what it was, I popped it into my mouth and chased it down my throat with a gulp of whiskey.

TIME SPENT WITH my new friend helped the days pass. After we got to know each other, we agreed to share a room to save money. Felix's roommate had decided he was too pushy and chose to room alone. They'd been friends forever, so Felix took the rejection in stride.

"Maybe when we save enough money, we can rent

a house. Wouldn't that be cool? A place we could call ours. Maybe in Cedars, a nicer area than this. I can already see it. A little white house with a little fenced-in yard. Maybe we can get a dog. You like dogs?"

"I do. I like all kinds of animals." The dream was a way to fantasize about a different life—a better life—and I liked it.

"We need to have enough for first and last month's rent, electricity, and water, but that shouldn't take very long to save."

Felix knew way more than I did about what bills we needed to think about. I had no idea paying for water was a thing. We had a well at the farm and I assumed everyone else did, too. Paying two months' rent before even moving into a place didn't make sense to me. Like, why would I give someone money for something I hadn't done yet?

The whiskey bottle grew heavy in my hand; I felt the need to lighten the weight of it. Three gulps later, I wiped my mouth with the back of my hand before passing it to Felix. Cable was not an option and the TV only offered three channels. Two showed the news, relaying information in Spanish.

Exhausted and a little drunk—okay, a lot drunk—I just wanted to get some sleep. The sound of Felix's voice mixed with the words I couldn't understand irritated me. I ignored him and closed my eyes.

"We should go to the Stop and Shop and also Irene's restaurant in the morning to see if they have any openings. I bet they'd give us dishwasher jobs or stockers, or something."

"Mmm hmm." I closed my eyes and allowed the room to spin around me, kind of like my life in general.

"BEFORE MY COUSIN went to prison, he knew everyone. I haven't been around for a while, but he assured me that all I need to do is mention his name and people will do whatever we want," Felix said. "For sure, someone who owns a gas station or restaurant will let us work for them. Maybe even a handyman. I know how to fix most anything. Except cars."

Vehicles rolled past as we trudged to the next gas station. The manager wasn't available at the first place we stopped. Felix entered the door to the next location with confidence to spare.

"Vato!" Felix greeted the attendant like he was a long-lost friend.

The man tilted his head. "Do I know you?"

"Amigo, it's me. Felix."

An empty stare was his only response.

"Felix, you know. Armando's cousin. Armando from Mexico."

The man lifted his eyebrows, shook his head, then

turned away. Another rejection.

Every day for a week, Felix and I walked down the street and asked every gas station we passed if there were any open positions. Either the manager wasn't in that day, or they flat-out denied us an opportunity. I didn't let it bother me, though. I figured eventually we'd find something. Every evening, we drank and played cards while the TV rambled on in Spanish.

We quickly fell into a comfortable routine. By week two, we had exhausted our gas station possibilities and decided to start visiting restaurants. There had to be someone willing to give us a chance. We popped some aspirin, took a shower, put on semi-clean clothes, and headed out the door around one o'clock.

The way we figured it, after the busy lunch hour, the owners would realize how much they needed another employee or two and would give us a job.

"Y'all find anything, yet?" Dennis spent most of his time either in the parking lot with some friends or walking to and from the nearby homeless camp under the freeway. He had been watching our job hunt and encouraged us to keep looking.

"Not yet. Today we're going to some restaurants and bars. Someone has to need extra hands." I shrugged.

Felix took the brown bag which Dennis held at arm's length and took a big gulp. He handed it to me, and I followed suit.

"Good luck." Dennis nodded and turned back to his group. I heard him laugh as we walked away.

The first three restaurants we entered said the manager wasn't there; seemed like a common theme. The next two said they weren't looking for help.

On our walk back to the motel, Felix dreamed about what life would be like after we started making money. My spirits were lower than at the beginning of the day but not quite broken. Yet.

He kept chattering. "We'll rent a little place in Cedars; it's a nicer area than South Dallas. We'll have a car, so we can live a little ways from work. Maybe we'll get a job in one of the warehouses, I hear they pay more than minimum and offer insurance. Vacation time, even. We'll name our dog Oliver." As if we had finished our conversation, Felix changed subjects. "Hungry?"

"The usual?"

Street tacos were a common lunch offered by vendors on the corner of most intersections. For a dollar apiece, we could fill our stomach on the cheap. I didn't know for sure, but I had the feeling Felix didn't have much money left. I needed to conserve what I had, too, so we made it a point to not spend what wasn't necessary. We didn't have a refrigerator, so we needed to eat out.

"Hey, why don't we try that place Dennis mentioned. It's on our way home. I wonder what time the lunch special ends? It's probably time for dinner by now. I could really go for a good meal." His steps quickened and I picked up the pace to keep up.

"Yeah, me, too."

Elaine's Kitchen was the best place in Dallas for Caribbean food, as far as Dennis had told us. He said the dinner was a really good deal; for only five dollars, you could get a big piece of jerk chicken, greens, and a huge scoop of dirty rice. Even if it was left over from the night before, or two days before, it was still good.

The chime signaled the opening of the door into a small but full restaurant. A pretty, young brunette turned and greeted us with a smile that reached her big brown eyes. Her hair fell straight to the nape of her neck. After showing us to our table, she turned and brought us glasses of water and menus.

In a shy, unsure voice, she asked if we were ready to order. I hadn't been able to take my eyes off her long enough to look at the menu. She had a gleam in her eye, and I instantly understood that at one point in her life, she had been audacious. She hid her beauty like she was saving it for someone special.

I pushed my glasses up my nose. "I'd like the special, please."

"Make that two," Felix added.

Her chuckle made my heart skip a beat. "But I haven't told you what the special is. Would you like to hear it?"

Felix and I both nodded.

"Jerk chicken, dirty rice, and greens. Five dollars." She tilted her head.

"I'd like the special, please."

"Make that two," Felix added.

Our repeated request was met with a full-on laugh. For a moment, I heard angels singing. While we waited for our meals, she checked on us multiple times between delivering food to other customers.

"You worked here long?" Felix raised one eyebrow. I was unable to form any words. Her aura mixed with the whiskey left me dizzy.

"Just moved here about a month ago." She shifted her eyes down and played with her apron strings.

Before we had a chance to get to know the pretty waitress, the chef rang a bell. "Order up."

"That's for you." She turned and I couldn't help watching her backside as she walked away. I knew almost nothing about her, but I got the feeling that she was sweet and maybe a little down on her luck, like us.

WAITING FOR THE night to end, Felix and I sat on the bottom step and enjoyed the finally mild weather. We had only half finished our shared bottle when my friend got froggy. "So, you and the pretty waitress, huh?"

"What?"

"She looked at you like you're her long-lost love. Like she has a connection to you. Like the two of you belong together."

"Listen, Vato, women are the last thing on my mind." I took a hard swig and shook my head. Lowering my voice so no one could hear, I admitted, "I wouldn't know the first thing to do if I was alone in a room with her."

"What? A good-looking dude like you don't know what to do. How did that happen?"

The whiskey hit me hard, and I blabbed about everything. Everything. From my dad hitting my mom, to the night they both died, to my time in juvy. I half expected him to laugh; when he didn't, I expected him to run. I wiped my eyes and waited for his retort.

After a long pause, he pursed his lips. "Moose, man, I'm real sorry. I'll always be here for you. And if you ever need to talk again, we can. My story isn't that far off from yours."

"You can tell me about it if you want." If he swore to stand by me, then the least I could do was repay the favor.

"My mom died of a drug overdose about ten years ago. My dad left long before that. The state took my sister and me. Separated us when we entered foster care. I bounced around for about six years before I got sick of the bullshit and ran away.

“I decided living on the streets would be better than having to deal with my so-called dad crawling into bed with me every other night. If I stayed, I swear I would have killed him.” He glanced at me and squinted. “Sorry.”

I shrugged. The abuse he had been forced into was far worse than what had happened to me. He didn't give any real details, but from the tears in his eyes,

I understood that if I had been in the same situation and my foster daddy forced me to do things with him, I would have killed him too. Felix was a better man than me. He resisted the urge, ran away from it. I hadn’t.

Chapter 18

Kennedy, age twenty-May 2008

DAYS WITH specials were, in fact, busy at Elaine's. With every table full, there was little time to rest. However, I made it a point to make connections with everyone who placed an order. Impressed with my people skills,

Elaine praised my ability to upsell and bring in just a little more cash. When she talked to Dane, I overheard her say how I was a good hire; the best waitress they'd had in years.

My tips confirmed her words. I had been hired at minimum wage—six twenty-five an hour—however, my first check added up to seven dollars an hour. Because I enjoyed working with Elaine, I had to be sure it wasn't a mistake. If it was a test, I wanted to pass. "Um, are you sure your math is right?"

"Yes, dear." She raised one eyebrow.

"I didn't mean anything by that, I'm sorry. But," I

added the amount in my head again. "We agreed on six twenty-five."

"And you're worth so much more, *puttus*." Her warm hand touched my cheek.

Still getting used to the unique terms, I grinned.

"It means sweetheart, it's affection. I wish I could pay you more."

Floored at how she had given me a raise within my first week, I hugged her and waved to Dane on my way out the door. I skipped back to the apartment; not really, but if I were still a kid, I would have.

Proud didn't come close to how elated I was to please my employer. If I had been honest with myself, it made me happy to not have to sell my body to walk away with money in my pocket.

PINK FABRIC hugged my curves on top and floated loose on the bottom as I sashayed from the kitchen to the dining room. My new dress made me feel pretty, not gorgeous or sexy, but pretty.

For me, it was a special day; a time to celebrate two-fold. Dinner would be ready for Cody when he arrived home from work, and I was ready to reveal my special news.

Cranky when he walked through the door, he didn't even notice me. Or dinner. He went right past me—more like around me—I stood in his path to be sure he saw how pretty I had made myself for him. Pork and barbeque sauce scented the room so I didn't understand how he could have ignored the entire situation. Heat rose up my chest and I knew to hide my emotions, so I popped one of the green and white pills I had hidden.

Thirty minutes later, with cold food layered on our plates, Cody sauntered out of the bedroom. Two glasses of whiskey sat in the middle of the table: mine had been emptied more than twice. I poured more and looked at him straight in the eye as I took a shot. I was pissed and I knew the action would provoke him, but the pill removed all ability to give a shit. Hungry, I asked him to sit.

"Why? So, you can serve cold food?" He huffed and pulled his chair from under the table. After the first bite, he pretended to gag. "It probably tasted like ass before it got cold, too."

Finally able to consume the meal, I pushed aside the flavor for substance. I hadn't eaten since lunch at the restaurant, and I knew that if I had eaten dinner without him, I would be punished.

"Where'd you get the dress?" His words pushed past the food in his mouth.

Not "it looks nice on you," or "you look pretty." Annoyed, I told him the name of the store. It didn't mean anything to him, he had no idea about the shopping areas around us. He certainly didn't understand that it was a secondhand clothing store designed exclusively for women.

"Drop the attitude, Kennedy. You don't have enough money to buy stupid shit like that." He shot his whiskey.

No way was I going to tell him about my raise; he'd want to steal all my hard-earned money. I kept my mouth shut.

"How did you get to the store?" His ridiculous line of questioning got old.

Without taking my eyes off his, I pursed my lips and poured him another drink, then quickly regretted it.

"I asked you a question." The drink went down in one gulp, and he poured another. "Answer me." His voice was barely a whisper.

"I took the bus." An unfortunate influx of my tone soothed him.

"And what have I told you about taking the bus?"

Shit. "You said I couldn't take the bus *to work*."

Cody inhaled and held his breath as he tilted his head back. I had seen this action in Alaska; it wasn't good. Last time, I got slapped for being stupid and had to use makeup to cover the fingerprints on my cheek for three days.

I flinched when he moved; I knew better than to walk away when he was in a mood. A pill I didn't recognize appeared in the palm of his hand; he wasn't aware how I had already taken something to relax.

"This will help you keep your figure; I noticed you've put on some weight. I don't like it. My woman will stay thin and keep a flat stomach."

My face drooped. He was not going to like my news. "What are they?"

"You don't trust me now? How dare you ask me what I'm giving you to better yourself. To make yourself more appealing to me—your husband."

Beside my glass lay a round blue pill. I glanced between it and Cody.

"You'll lose the weight. Do I make myself clear? Honestly, I thought you understood this requirement, but obviously not. You must be eating away your tips at the restaurant. I refuse to be married to a fat cow. Blubber is a turnoff and when I look at you, I want to instantly get hard."

He stood, unzipped his pants. As they fell to the floor, he reached for me with one hand. The other stroked his erection. "Let's get that childish dress off you." His lips twisted into an evil grin.

Apprehensive, I allowed him to pull me to my feet. I had angered and disobeyed him; usually, that meant rough sex. But his smile told me the whiskey had calmed his nerves.

He wrapped one arm around my waist and held me

tight enough that if I tried, I wouldn't be able to wriggle out of his grip. Warmth from his other hand on the inside of my bare thigh aroused me. He stared into my eyes, not offering any sort of kiss. He made sure I felt the enormity of his emotion. The soft fabric of my dress gathered as he reached under it and caressed my sensitive skin.

When he stopped, I gulped. His eyes widened, then thinned. The moment he felt the fabric of my thong, his demeanor changed. I had broken the golden rule.

A low growl escaped his throat, and he picked up a steak knife off the table. Without taking his eyes off mine, Cody lifted my dress above my hip and slid the knife under the elastic of my thong, cutting it and my skin in one swift movement.

I cried out in pain. The action may have been sexy if the blade hadn't cut me. Another scar to add to my collection. In one hard pull, the panties were ripped off. He discarded the knife on the floor then picked me up and sat me on the table. One cheek landed on a plate, and it broke under me.

Angry, he stood between my legs and stuffed the thong into my mouth. "What did I tell you about wearing skirts? Easy access all the time. Dammit, why do you deceive me?"

Pressure from him pushing fully inside me with one thrust took my breath.

I opened for him and permitted myself to enjoy his passion, whether it be created from lust or anger, or a little of both. I learned long ago that if I wanted to enjoy sex with my husband, I might have to endure a little pain.

When he was finished using my body, he pulled out of me and pushed me off the table. I caught myself before my face hit the chair. "Clean yourself up, you dirty whore. I don't know why I bother with you."

As I stumbled down the hallway, I wondered if it was blood or the remnants of sex that ran down my leg.

Chapter 19

Jake, age twenty-three—May 2008

BETWEEN THE TWO of us, the entire bottle of whiskey disappeared that night. We woke up later than usual and I had the worst hangover ever. We decided to take a day off from looking for jobs. Yesterday had worn both of us out, anyway.

Dennis had noticed how much I suffered and suggested I take a little white pill. I reached toward him not knowing, or caring, what it was. If it made me feel better, I'd take it.

He closed his fingers and stared at me. "Five dollars."

"Fine." At that point, I'd have probably done just about anything to make the pounding in my head go away. I gave him a five-dollar bill, took the pill from the palm of his hand, and swallowed it.

It worked a little too well. I felt fantastic within five minutes. My shoulders sank; I was more relaxed than I had been in a year. Although I was wide awake, my blinking slowed. Whatever worries had plagued me ten minutes prior were forgotten.

A slight breeze blew the hair out of my eyes. Sun warmed my skin, but not like it had in the previous days. *Must be nearing the end of this godawful spring. Summer will be even worse.* Not knowing where we were headed—and not caring—Felix and I followed Dennis' group through parking lots and down sidewalks. Horns honked and engines revved on the highway above our heads. It wasn't until we stopped walking that I figured out where we were.

Tents, cardboard, tarps, and garbage littered the area under an overpass. A bottle ended up in my hands and I didn't remember gulping enough to make me dizzy. Only Dennis and Felix stood before me. The others had spread out amongst the camp.

While we searched for work, Felix and I had passed the area multiple times. We had never acknowledged it existed; afraid we would one day end up part of the community. The realization of how it could happen sooner rather than later hit me, but not as hard as I expected it might—most likely due to the extensive amount of alcohol and whatever that pill was that clouded my thoughts.

"Easy there, cowboy. Save some for the rest of us." Felix's voice resounded in my ears, but I didn't see him.

The heft of the bottle no longer weighed down my hand.

“There’s room if y’all don’t find jobs.” A green tarp covered a yellow tent; personal items surrounded it as a wind blocker. Or maybe it was for privacy. A bike with a flat tire leaned against a grocery cart with two broken wheels. “Three guys moved on a couple weeks ago. Decided this wasn’t the place for them.”

I couldn’t imagine myself living like this. However, I could totally understand how living like this would make you want to hoard the items that you have. With twenty-some most likely unsavory characters surrounding me, I would make sure everything of value stayed on my person, if possible.

The bare spot of ground beside Dennis’ belongings was not quite large enough for the four lawn chairs which had been jammed in the space. “If you want me to save the spot, I’d be happy to. It’s only ten dollars a week.”

“Nah,” Felix wrinkled his nose at the rank smell which blew in with the breeze. “We’re good. But thanks.”

SOMEONE mentioned food; the long, boring, wasted day had somehow been exhausting. Felix and I followed a group of four from the I-45 overpass to a little restaurant a few blocks away.

Curry from the day's special hit me in the face as we walked through the door. I paused, inhaled, and smiled. *Heavenly.* The chimes sounded familiar, but until I saw her, I hadn't realized where we were.

Wispy brown curls danced around her face as she turned in our direction. Her bright smile warmed my heart. She recognized us. I almost gasped; she was so beautiful. The different hairstyle brought out her lively personality. She had a different air about her; she seemed happier, somehow. More vibrant.

Dennis and the others sat at one table and flirted with the pretty waitress as they decided what to order. "What's your favorite plate, darlin'?"

"I haven't been in the lower forty-eight long enough to have a favorite."

From day one, something about the way she spoke sounded familiar. Like she was literally the girl next door. Then she delivered the Alaskan phrase and it hit me.

I tilted my head and smiled. "Excuse me."

She lifted her chin in recognition.

"Anchorage or Seward?" I asked, guessing correctly.

She stared at me; her smile reached her wide eyes. "Seward."

"Moose Pass." Relaxed, I could barely string together more than a few words.

"Shut up! We're both Texan cheechakoes?" She sat across the table, beside Felix, and gaped at me in wonder.

"Prove it." The pretty girl made me sassy.

She pointed to her left bicep. "Bear attack."

My mouth dropped. She was serious. "Yup, we're newcomers alright." I touched a scar on her forearm. "What's the "M" stand for? I've never seen a tattoo like that. Where'd you get it?"

"My last name is Miller." Her eyebrows raised as if asking if that was the right answer. Then she changed the subject. "How did two Alaskans meet up in Dallas? I'm floored." Her smile lit up the room.

During our short discussion, Felix tapped the table with his fork. "I know y'all are getting to know each other and everything …" When we didn't stop talking, he raised his voice. "I'm getting kind of hungry."

"Oh," she laughed. "I'm sorry. What's your name?"

"Felix. Felix Ferguson."

"Felix Ferguson, it's nice to meet you. I'm Kennedy. What can I get for you today?" She glanced at me like she couldn't believe we had figured out the connection. Her pen in one hand and pad of paper in the other, she focused on taking down our order.

I pushed my glasses up my nose. Kennedy. A little dizzy, the effects of the pill from Dennis gave me confidence. I almost asked Kennedy on a date. Which would be ridiculous; I was practically homeless. I had no job, very little money, and lived in a shithole motel with my best friend. What could I possibly have done to impress Kennedy? I loved the sound of her name, though.

"Kennedy."

"Yes, um … I'm sorry, what should I call you?" Our eyes connected for a second too long and she blushed.

I hadn't realized I spoke her name out loud and tried to recover. "Jake. I'm Jake Knight. I'd love some water."

"Comin' right up, Jake Knight."

I watched her backside swing and felt Felix looking at me. "What?"

He lifted one eyebrow and in a sing-song voice said, "You're in love." There was no talking him out of it once he got rolling.

Kennedy placed glasses of water in front of us and I used mine to hide my grin.

Felix ordered right away. "I'll have the special."

"But I haven't told you what the special is."

"Have we had this conversation before?" I asked.

"Stew Chicken Roti. I had no idea what to expect; the food here is so different from Alaska. I had a piece earlier, though. It's fantastic."

"I'll have that," Felix smiled.

I nodded. "Make that two."

Chimes above the door signaled another customer. I hadn't seen Kennedy frown before. I didn't like it. A clean-cut, freshly shaved man wearing a button-up dress shirt and slacks strolled over to Kennedy and stood directly behind her. He whispered in her ear, and she instantly bowed her head.

Without raising her eyes, she pursed her lips and waited for the man to move away. She didn't look at either of us. "I'll put your order right in."

The man followed her behind the counter and leaned in close. If his face hadn't been so crinkled and angry, I might have thought he was about to kiss her. Heat radiated around my chest, but that's where my temper stopped. The pill I took earlier kept my emotions under control.

Red lines streaked Kennedy's pretty brown eyes and her makeup had smeared. It was clear she had been crying and my shoulders sank with compassion. She returned with our food but before she set the plates in front of us, her eyes followed the man out the door. When she sighed and shook her head, my heart broke.

"Are you okay?" It wasn't my business, but I couldn't help but ask. She had been so happy and lively before the jerk upset her.

She offered a weak smile and blinked away tears. "I'm fine."

Chapter 20

Kennedy, age twenty–May 2008

CODY HAD LEFT for work the next morning, leaving me lying in bed. He snuck out without saying goodbye. At first, I found it enduring how he let me sleep in knowing I didn't have to work the early shift. Then, as time passed, I understood his point.

Dinner cooled on the table as I waited for him to come home. He had arrived back to the room late before, but this felt different. I didn't know if I should be upset or worried; the sense of something being wrong filled me with fear. Unable to focus on mundane tasks, I wrapped up the food and put it in the fridge, then bounced from dishes to laundry to watching TV.

I tried to ignore my feelings but by the end of the night, my mind had me convinced he had been on the wrong end of a gun or knife. Surely, he had been killed. There was no other reason for him to not come home. I had never gone to bed without him before and it had been impossible to sleep.

He demanded I never call him at work, so the following day when he hadn't been home or called by noon, I seriously considered filing a missing person's report with the police. But what would I tell them? I had no clue how to act or react, so I went to work, like usual, and stumbled through my day.

By day three, I was beside myself. Again, I got ready for work. Like usual. I followed the sidewalk under I-45 to the restaurant. Like usual. I waited on customers, made small talk, and smiled. Like usual. Elaine sensed something wrong but didn't ask. She made eyes at Dane, and he shrugged.

On the fourth day, when Cody still hadn't come home, I was a mix between furious and terrified. I had been through all the emotions multiple times. *What if he's dead on the street somewhere? Would serve the asshole right.* Thank goodness I had the day off so my anxiety could be trapped within the four walls of our hotel room.

On the fifth day, tears streamed down my face; I couldn't keep them inside. I feared my husband might never come back, but I was also worried sick. *Did he leave on purpose? Did he move away, or will he be back?* I didn't have any choice but to stay. However, I couldn't afford to pay the nightly rate for the room. Not wanting to believe the worst, I chose to think he left because he didn't love me anymore.

What am I going to do if he left for good? What the hell is so bad about me that made him choose to leave? I do everything I can to keep Cody happy and prove myself to him. No matter how many times he tells me I'm not worth it, I try to prove him wrong. I am worth it. At least Elaine thought I made a good waitress. And back in Alaska, Willy used to tell me I was appreciated.

My mom used to ignore me and tell me I wouldn't ever make anything of myself; I thought Cody would take me away from that life and those thoughts. But here I am. I set aside my dreams of being a mother to please Cody. Maybe he would accept me gaining weight if he knew it was due to a pregnancy. He promised to never leave me again. Now he's gone. Fuck my life.

WITHOUT ANY lights on, our hotel room seemed like a cave. As I opened the door and walked in, an odd feeling of dread filled me. Chills ran up the back of my arms. The air conditioning blew from beside the window with a subtle hum. I didn't remember turning it down so low. Behind closed blinds, the setting sun from the long day was invisible.

I closed the door behind me and waited for my eyes to adjust. I hadn't yet become familiar enough with the small space to be able to move around without bumping into furniture.

Cody stood and I yelped. "Jesus, you scared the shit out of me. You're home. Thank God." He didn't acknowledge me, so I didn't rush him. It could be possible he was out of his mind. Some of the pills we had shared were capable of causing odd side effects. He could be hallucinating. If I interrupted his delusion, it could be dangerous to us both.

Silence and a stream of marijuana-scented smoke followed Cody from the couch to the light switch in the kitchenette. Weed wasn't my thing; it just put me to sleep. When Cody had smoked it in Alaska, it made him paranoid, so I knew I needed to tread lightly.

I needed answers, though, and decided to ask gentle questions. "Cody? Are you okay? Why were you sitting in the dark?"

He opened the refrigerator and selected lunch meat and cheese, then pulled bread from the cupboard. After he made one sandwich and popped a top off a bottle of Dos Equis, he moved to the couch and turned on the TV. Not once did he look at me.

Confused, I followed in his wake and lowered myself to the couch. "Hey. Where have you been? What's happening?"

Silence.

I had a funny feeling he was ignoring me on purpose, and I lost the ability to care if I "woke" him.

"What are you doing? Didn't you think that maybe I would want a sandwich, too?" I spoke to the cold air. The stupid ignoring game aggravated me.

"Fine. I guess I'll make one myself." He didn't react to the comment I made, apparently to no one. Stunned to find all the food in the refrigerator had been eaten, I scrunched my face. Only one piece of yellow cheese sat on the top shelf. It wasn't even in the wrapper anymore; it had grown hard and crusty.

"Did you eat all the food?" *What the hell is he doing? This is so fucking weird.* The empty bread bag in the sink led me to believe he had eaten the rest of that, too. I pulled open every cupboard door only to find all the groceries I had brought home earlier in the week had disappeared.

"Cody?" *Did he seriously eat everything? Or could he have thrown it away?* "Did you put the food somewhere else?" *Am I just imagining things?*

A commercial made him chuckle. I sat beside him on the couch and tried to talk to him, again. "Will you please talk to me? I don't know what I'm doing wrong. I'm sorry for whatever I did. If you tell me, I'll change."

It was as if I was a ghost. Like he couldn't see me, and I was hovering in a parallel dimension. I hated being filled with anxiety. Not knowing what I needed to do differently made me sick to my stomach. I poured a glass of whiskey and took an Oxy. I needed to forget how unimportant I was.

THE NEXT MORNING, he snuggled up to me, kissed my ear and pushed his erection against my ass. I was thrilled his attitude changed from the weird night before. I rubbed against him and repositioned myself.

With one hand on my hip, holding me steady, he shoved himself into me, and I whined even though I was ready for him. He liked it when I made it seem like he hurt me a little, even if he didn't. I loved it when he woke up wanting me.

He finished in a hurry but rolled me over right away and started from scratch. Soft kisses started on my lips, and I held my breath as he kissed me with the entirety of his passion.

The way he moved above me, teasing with soft touches, drove me crazy. His lips traveled from my chin to my breasts and warmed my core. He kneeled between my legs, and I moved against him teasing, making it impossible to resist me.

Sheets wrapped around us as we changed positions after each of my orgasms. Pillows had been pushed off the bed and softened the landing when we tumbled onto the floor.

We continued our love making in the compact shower, I wrapped my legs around his waist, and he held me against the wall. I didn't even care anymore where he had been. My husband was back. He was home safe.

Early in our relationship, Cody had asked which position I enjoyed the most. The shower was it; the angle allowed him to hit my sweet spot and I couldn't hold back the intensity of my release. Sometimes he would cover my mouth with his hand so our neighbors wouldn't hear.

Hot water streamed over and between us when an odd realization hit me: usually Cody was always vocal when we made love, but I still hadn't heard his voice. Not even a moan.

He stood behind me and nuzzled my neck, then whispered my name. I loved the sound of his smooth cadence and was thrilled to hear his voice. Although when I comprehended his words, I second guessed myself.

"I need to know something."

My eyes lit up; I was so relieved he wanted to talk to me again. I turned to face him and smiled. "Anything, my king."

"How many of Elaine's customers have you fucked?"

Stunned, I backed away and tilted my head. "What?"

"I saw how the guy with the glasses looked at you. Like you were a bottle of whiskey he wanted to drink."

I laughed. "Jake? He's harmless."

"Oh, you're on a first name basis with him? I suppose he's the reason you didn't straighten your hair the day I came to see you. Maybe he's the reason you're smiling more often."

Dammit; the curls. I knew better than to leave the house without straightening my hair. I'm so stupid. I tried to blow off the ridiculousness of his accusation but knew better than to roll my eyes. I did push my limit, though. "So, I'm not allowed to smile now?"

Anger laced his words, his eyes darkened. He gripped my hips with both hands, his fingertips practically punctured my skin. I was sure they would leave bruises. "How many times have you taken him behind the building and let him fuck you when he doesn't have money to pay his bill?"

This line of questioning had grown absurd, and it upset me more than it should have. I knew by now if I let him know he got to me, he would keep pushing. So, I chuckled instead of screamed. "You have quite the imagination, my love." I squirmed out of his grip, turned the water off, and grabbed a towel.

"So, you just let him bend you over the counter. I see. The food there is worth more than a simple blow job? Did you let him and his friend tag team you?"

I sighed and did my best to ignore him like he had to me the night before. At least now I understood why he was so upset. He was wrong, but the treatment made sense. He stared at me, waiting.

"Do you expect me to give you an answer to a question that doesn't make sense?"

GROGGY FROM having been unconscious, I kept my eyes closed until I could decipher what happened to cause me to go black. My jaw hit the countertop on the way to the floor. It must have, the slice in my skin and blood dripping down my chin told the story.

Along with the throbbing on one side of my face, I had bitten my tongue and swallowed pools of blood.

It took me a minute to remember what I had done to upset Cody. Again. *Oh, yeah. I told him he was wrong.* Cody is never wrong. About anything. If I had admitted to doing what he fantasized I had done, the punishment wouldn't have been nearly as bad. Or would it?

A faint memory of the dream I had had while I had been out hit me hard. I was in Alaska, shivering from the cold, having sex with one of the regulars at the Next-door. It must have been John because he was big; I could feel him filling me again and again. For a moment, I thought I was back in Seward. Then I realized my shoulders had grown numb.

Without any sense of time, I didn't know how long I had been handcuffed to the headboard. I pulled one arm just to be met with resistance. Dazed, it took me a minute to realize why I was so cold and what scent surrounded me. I opened my eyes to find a shirtless Cody and a naked man I had never met standing over my fully exposed body. Pressure between my legs told me they had been in the middle of using a sex toy on me when I woke up.

Disgusted, my stomach churned, and I gagged. "Who?" I could barely force the word past the gag which had been shoved in my mouth. I tried again, anyway. "Stop." Squirming to get free, I panicked. "Cody!"

Cody took a hit of the joint he held in one hand, held his breath, then passed it to the strange man. Then he took a swig straight from a whiskey bottle before he held it and a pill in front of me. "Shut up. Now that you're the sole income provider, you have a job to do. I suggest you make it worth my friend's hard-earned money."

He removed the gag, and I gladly accepted the white and green pill he offered and gulped the whiskey to push it down my throat. From the expression on his face, I understood my commentary would not be welcomed, so I kept quiet. I had a frightening idea of what he meant when he told me I had a job to do. *Did he sell me to this man?*

Cody's eyes turned black; I could only imagine that the devil himself had taken over his soul. He enjoyed watching, I knew that, but I never thought he would introduce a stranger to our sex life without my approval.

Uncomfortable with the entire situation, I tried to protest. “Please let me go, Cody. I don’t want to do this.”

“You think I give a fuck what you want? You’ll be a good little whore and do your job. Don’t disappoint me.”

The naked man held a hit from the joint, blowing the smoke out a little at a time. Nodding, a smile spread across the stranger’s squinty-eyed face. He stroked himself and practically drooled as he gaped at my breasts. Then he joined me on the bed.

The pill kicked in and I closed my eyes. I fantasized about a celebrity while the man touched me. Gentler than Cody ever had been, I kind of liked it. I pretended like I was back at the bar and moaned with fake pleasure. The man climbed on top of me and positioned me in a way I’d never tried before. He slid into me, and I arched against his weight.

If I opened my eyes, my pleasure would have halted, which would prolong the experience. I moved and moaned when I knew it counted; I rocked the strangers’ world. Honestly, I enjoyed sex with him more than my own husband. I almost didn’t want it to end. But it did.

“Best two-fifty I’ve ever spent.”

Chapter 21

Jake, age twenty-three—May 2008

TIME PASSED slowly and in a hurry at the same time. Whatever pill Dennis had given me made it possible for me to stop thinking for a few moments. A lot of moments. I don't know how much time went by or what happened before the sun went behind the highway, but I didn't care.

The camp was not a place I wanted to live, but I had a feeling it wouldn't be long before Felix and I made the move. I hadn't counted my stash in a few days, but it had gone fast.

The regular crowd gathered at the motel. Because we lived there, Felix and I had become regulars, too. Of course, we had too much to drink—it was our MO. It hadn't been a conscious decision, but something that had organically happened.

Loud exhaust identified a familiar truck as it slowed beside the ladies on the corner. No one paid attention until Brenda screamed for help. Everyone in our circle turned to find the man struggling to drag her to his vehicle. With his arm around her waist, he pulled, and she kicked.

"Help! Someone, help me!"

I stayed put while Dennis and his friends approached the guy. There was no need to let my anger get the better of me. Unless they really needed help. They scuffled for a minute before Brenda broke away from the man's embrace.

She hid behind Felix and her friend. "That's the asshole who raped me last week."

"You can't rape a whor—"

Dennis' fist connected with the man's jaw before he was able to complete the sentence. "Didn't you learn anything from the last time you were here?" Last week Dennis had pulled this same man out of the passenger side of a different car because he harassed Brenda's friend.

The next five minutes contained a cluster of fists, loud voices, and blood. Thuds from punches thrown, then a scream before the loud snap of a breaking bone filled the air.

Felix attempted to pull Dennis out of the mix but was unsuccessful. I rushed in and was able to separate everyone. Before the police could arrive, the crowd had dispersed. With nothing to investigate and no one to admit to a crime, the cops took off with only the names of bystanders.

"All right, y'all. You need to leave. Now." The owner of the motel kicked everyone out of the parking lot.

Felix and I crossed the lot to chill on the steps, but Quinn wasn't having it.

"All of you. Out."

Confused, I frowned.

"Get your shit. You're out." He stood with his hands on his hips, not willing to negotiate.

"For good?"

He nodded one. Finality.

Dennis had watched from afar and followed us up the steps to our room.

"Let me help. Y'all can stay at my place."

FOUR HUNDRED dollars. I arrived in Dallas with close to three thousand; less than two months later, all I had to my name was four hundred. *Shit. How in the hell did I blow through that much money?* Whiskey, food, pills. Repeat. I did pay for a lot of Felix's food and drinks, but still, I should have at least a thousand. I stopped counting a few weeks back. *Double shit.*

Goodwill had a store a few blocks to the east, Dennis led the way. We found a two-person tent, some camping supplies, and a couple of tarps. They were ripped but they would work.

As Dennis suggested, I kept my cash on me in three different places: my front pocket, sock, underwear. I bought what I knew I would need to live outside, just like in Alaska but warmer. Sleeping bag, containers to keep things dry, and a backpack big enough to store and carry a whole lot of stuff.

As we passed the liquor store, I bought two fifths of whiskey; if others in the community shared, I wanted to be sure we could repay the kindness to our new neighbors.

On the first day in our new home, we set up the tent and made our space as non-homeless as possible. After only an hour, we were finished.

Dennis walked us around the neighborhood and introduced us to some of the other folks. The commentary while we walked from one person to the next explained if the person was good or not so good. "Not everyone has your back, out here." He warned us to be careful. "You'll need those eyes on the back of your head."

"I'm not sure if anyone uses their real names, because who would name their kid Griffin? Seriously. That, to me, sounds like something you would name your dog, but what do I know?" Dennis explained.

"I get that. That's why Felix calls me Moose. I'm from Moose Pass, Alaska."

"See! That's exactly what I mean." His eyes lit up. "Me, too. Well, not Moose, but Dennis because I'm a menace. Get it?"

I didn't.

"Ah, never mind. Follow me, I'll show you around."

Most everyone had the same items stored in their area. A few things were considered community property. Five bikes, stacks of firewood, extra tarps, a large pile of rope, and two dogs.

At one time, these things belonged to an individual who most likely had thrown them in the garbage. Now, they belonged to everyone. It's true what they say: one man's trash is another man's treasure.

WE HAD SET UP between Dennis and another of the longtime residents named Jed. He wasn't one of the regulars in the motel parking lot, so we didn't know of him, but he wanted to be helpful. "I saw y'all come in last night. You look like bad news." He chuckled and held out his hand. "Welcome home. Newbies build the fire on their first full night." We instantly connected.

I was well aware of how to start a fire, Felix, not so much. He was a quick study, though, and picked up the technique quickly.

Jed handed us firewood once we got it stoked. "You know, this doesn't have to be permanent. If you want to get out of this situation and change your life for the better, just put your mind to it. You'll be able to do it."

"If that's true, then why are you still here?" I genuinely wanted to know. For some reason, Jed felt familiar. I saw a piece of me in him.

Lawn chairs placed in a circle around the firepit allowed us to sit and enjoy the warmth. Jed sat in one and told us his story. He had lost his wife and son in a car accident. "I tried to live a normal life again but ended up in mental institutions. I couldn't get a grip, couldn't keep a job or friends. So, this is my life now and I'm just fine. I make money where I can and if I can't, I take what I need and only what I need. I've never hurt no one."

Most of the camp residents would congregate at the firepit after dark. While daylight remained, only a few of the community members gathered. "How did you end up here?" Jed truly wanted to know my story.

"My parents died when I was fourteen. I lived alone for the summer before the cops realized I didn't have any supervision. I never had a job because my entire adult life has been spent behind bars—or outside with a bottle of whiskey in my hand. Like you, Jed, I never hurt anyone; I made sure of that." Eliminating portions of the truth was still a lie, but more to myself than Jed.

Clearing emotion from his throat, Felix joined in the storytelling. "I never thought I would follow in my mom's footsteps. When I was twelve, she died of a drug overdose. The state split up my family and I bounced around different foster homes until I was old enough to get out. Been living here and there ever since."

"I'm from Minnesota, originally." Dennis' voice startled me. "A little town outside Minneapolis. My best friend talked me into smoking crack with him one night and I never went back. I lost everything. I couldn't save my marriage and my parents don't want anything to do with me." He sighed and pursed his lips. "So, here I am. Making the best of my shit life."

Trying to stay upbeat, Dennis switched gears. "Y'all'd be surprised how much a person can make standing at an intersection with a styrofoam cup. Lots of people give a dollar and if I can get ten, I can buy my food and drink. That's all that matters. Don't need money for rent or electricity. No car payment, no TV. It's the best of both worlds. If I wanted a job, I could probably get one, but then I couldn't do all the other things I want to do all day. Like drink." He held up his bottle and gulped. "Or chill."

One of his pills appeared in his hand and he popped it into his mouth. It didn't hit me until we were in forced proximity: Dennis babbles like Bubba Gump when he's high. I wondered who he got his supply from; he always had a stash of pills. He'd been here for a while, so I was sure he had his connections.

"Eighty percent of the people standing on the corner

with a sign drive away in Beamers. The rest of us do anything we can to make a buck."

KENNEDY RARELY left my mind. It had been difficult to watch the man who took her behind the counter dominate her. My dad had treated Mom that way, like she was less than him. She wasn't, by any means.

Felix had teased me about Kennedy being someone who would be perfect for me. The more I thought about it, the more I wanted someone to love. It hadn't been the right time or place for Kennedy to be the one.

During a particularly bad day spent feeling down on myself, I wondered what to do next with my life. We had been to Elaine's a couple times the previous week and when one of the guys mentioned food, I suggested the restaurant where Kennedy worked.

Looking forward to seeing her smile, I decided to splurge. I didn't really have the extra funds, but I wanted to see my pretty waitress. Maybe she could lift my spirits.

Disappointed that Kennedy wasn't working, I asked the owner about her. "Elaine, where has Kennedy been? The last few times we've been in, she hasn't been working."

The simple question was met with a shrug. "She

just up and left one day. Husband came in and pulled her out by the arm. Haven't seen her since; one day she was here, the next she was just gone. Didn't even pick up her last check. To tell you the truth," she leaned closer, "I'm a little worried about her. I went to the address on her application to see if maybe she was sick. The office manager at the motel said they had checked out two days earlier. I hope she's okay."

Chapter 22

Kennedy, age twenty–June 2008

SUITCASES LAID open on the bed, half full of clothes. Cody packed our things in a hurry; most of the task had been finished before I got out of the shower. My entire body hurt from the previous week of pleasuring customers from all walks of life.

Each night, someone different knocked on our door shortly after Cody fed me two green and white pills and four shots of whiskey. The dose made me sleepy and agreeable. With just the right amount, I almost enjoyed the pain.

"Let's go."

"What about the rest of my stuff …"

He pushed past me with a suitcase and pointed to two duffle bags. Most of my summer clothes hung in the closet and my makeup littered the sink in the bathroom. I grabbed a grocery bag and threw whatever I could into it as he screamed for me to hurry.

A taxi picked us up and delivered us to the airport. I knew better than to question where we were going and why. I had to trust Cody; he was my husband and he had already made plans.

Everything happened so fast, I didn't have a chance to even tell Elaine I was leaving. Not only was she my boss, but she had also become my friend. My only friend. Although my last check wouldn't amount to much, I had worked for it and was upset that Cody made me leave so quickly.

At the ticket counter, Cody demanded, "Two tickets to Anchorage."

"We're going home?" My face lit up at the idea. I was so happy to finally leave the place that turned Cody into a bad person. While we waited to board the plane, I asked why we were going back to Alaska. "Not that I mind, I love the mountains and cooler weather. But how did this decision come about?"

Cody stared out the window and watched the planes move to and from the gates. Once on the runway, they sped and lifted into the air. He smiled when they disappeared into the clouds.

A frown took over his expression. "I couldn't make enough at work and my boss refused to give me a raise. He said I needed to intern for a year before I would start making any real money. Apparently, it was detailed in the offer letter. Like I would have read that." His scoff almost made me laugh, then I thought better of it.

Stunned by how he had confessed, I held my breath. He hasn't spoken this many words to me in months. If I moved, he might stop talking.

"I told them you needed mental help and thought my internship allowed me access to drugs to help my wife. They offered to refer you to a fellow doctor, but I turned them down. When he found out I took the prescription pads, he fired me. We're broke."

I placed my hand over my mouth and held in my gasp. His honesty surprised me. "So, it's my fault we had to move."

His eyes met mine and he squinted. "Without paying rent, we couldn't stay in the motel, now, could we? While you were in the shower, the office manager said we had two hours to vacate. If we didn't, we'd be arrested." Focused on his shoes, Cody mumbled something I couldn't hear.

"What?"

A growl escaped his throat, and he yanked the duffel from between my feet. He rummaged through the bag and pulled out a bottle of pills. He popped one and offered one to me. I took it.

"I called my dad and told him I needed help. He said if I could get to Alaska, he'd give me the keys to a house."

Okay, we can start over. I sighed and sat back. The

pill took effect after a few short minutes, and I closed my eyes.

“I’m sorry our time in Dallas wasn’t like I planned.” His shaky voice caught my attention. It was unlike him to be remorseful. “I wasn’t able to provide for you. I promise we’ll have the best life once we get back home.”

I believed him and pushed my luck. “How did we pay for the flights? Did you sell my necklace?”

A smirk transformed his face; he chuckled. “That necklace is fake. I found it at a Halloween store.” He glanced at me and frowned. “You really thought it was real? Awe, that’s so cute.”

When he stopped laughing, he answered my original question. “With your past, I knew you’d be happy to help. You didn’t think twice about having sex for money in Seward, so I figured that was the fastest way to make some cash.” He kissed me on the cheek. “You did good. We’re going home thanks to you.” He licked his lips and closed his eyes. “You did real good.”

I HAD ONLY EVER been in one airplane before: the one we rode to get to Dallas. My second experience was totally different. In so many ways. On the first flight, we were planning our life. Cody would make good money at his job, and I would be a stay-at-home mom once we decided to start a family.

In my head, the plans had a bright aura as if purity and positivity surrounded us. On the flight back to Alaska, we left behind a few dark months.

Our plans had backfired; Cody never really began his career, and I only angered him with how I wanted our life to come together. As much as I hated the things he made me do for money, he seemed to get pleasure from watching. I hoped that life filled with darkness wouldn't follow us home.

We landed in Anchorage late at night and hopped on a shuttle to the nearest hotel. Cody told the driver we had arrived for our honeymoon. The thought of newness gave me hope.

I wondered if my mom even knew I had left Alaska and thought about calling her. Cody wouldn't approve, so I pushed the thought out of my mind. I didn't want to cause any unnecessary tension.

The name-brand hotel had been too expensive, so he pulled the suitcase behind him and I carried both duffels alongside Spenard Road to the nearest run-down cheap motel. After a quick check-in, we pulled our bags up the steps to our room at the end of the hall.

Exhausted and feeling dirty from our conversation while we waited to board, I immediately opted for a shower. I had spent a long thirteen hours and two layovers thinking about how our life would be different once we got away from the negativity in Dallas.

Cody made a phone call, and I didn't question who was on the other end of the line.

The next morning, we took our bags to the motel office. "Did someone drop off a key last night for me? Cody Miller?" The attendant nodded and handed Cody a key and an envelope.

I followed my husband to an old truck which had been waiting for us in the parking lot. He loaded our bags in the back. "Ready to see our new home?"

Not questioning his connections, I shrugged. "Yeah. Where we headed?" I prayed now that we were back in the last frontier his demeanor would change.

"Surprise." An old-Cody smile spread across his lips.

My heart lifted, *Thank you, God. He's back. This is the man I fell in love with so long ago. We can do this. It must have been the stress of moving so far away that made him act crazy. I promise I'll do everything I can to keep my man happy.*

SNOW-COVERED mountains surrounded us on three sides. Even though it was summer, the temperatures stayed cool. Cold compared to Texas. The heaviness in my body diminished as we drove alongside Knik Arm. Mt. Baldy to our right rose above the arm like a protective big brother. *I feel safe again.* The thought surprised me. Had I really not felt safe in Dallas?

Cody must have sensed my relief; he grinned and pulled into the trailhead of Thunderbird Falls. “Detour?”

“Yes, please.” Energized, I jumped out of the truck, grabbed my jacket, and followed him to the trail covered with a wood-plank walkway. Birds chirped and leaves rustled all around us, in the trees high above and along the ground.

Water flowed down a slope between tall walls of rock, a mountaintop in the background. If Texas had more views like this, it may have been harder to leave. Cody stood behind me and wrapped his arms around my waist.

I leaned back, closed my eyes, and inhaled the scents that surrounded us. Cologne mixed with the piney scent of the forest and the fresh cleanness of the rushing water. I felt a cleanse just from connecting with nature and a renewed connection with my husband. *Beautiful.*

Relief pushed away any anxiety I had about moving back. It was hard to believe our life in Dallas had actually happened. Confused how the events could have occurred, I decided to put it in my past and forget the days. Easier said than done.

“I’m so glad you stopped and took the time to enjoy our Alaska. This place is so amazing. Incredible. Beautiful. Refreshing. Hard to believe I feel so renewed. Let’s start our life over.”

Cody turned me in his arms and placed a gentle kiss on my lips, then gazed into my eyes. "You have such great ideas." He pushed a stray strand of hair out of my eyes; love flowed from his touch. "Let's go home." A kiss on the tip of my nose sealed the deal.

We crossed the Knik River and slowed. Surprised when he pulled over, again, I smiled.

"I thought because you've never been this way, you might enjoy some different scenes. I want to give you the full experience."

Clouds scattered in the blue sky above the mountain peaks. Both reflected off the water and created a picture-perfect view. I couldn't believe how much I had missed this.

Tears filled my eyes, and I wiped them away before Cody could see; I didn't want him to think I was upset in any way. Joy spread through my body, not sadness.

"Thank you, Cody. I didn't know how much I needed this connection. To Alaska and to you." I snuggled under his arm and reveled in his embrace.

TWO HOURS LATER, we crossed a set of railroad tracks and pulled into a driveway beside an old single-wide trailer. White walls and what used to be blue trim had molded and faded over the years.

The screen door hung from one hinge and dragged

on the small concrete stoop. Someone had built a porch around the steps which sagged in the far corner. Boards covered half of the windows, making the structure appear to be abandoned.

I believed Cody when he said the house was safe; I didn't have a choice. Although this place wasn't ideal, I was willing to remain optimistic. "Where are we?" I wasn't familiar with the area we had driven. The buildings of a small town stood a little further past our turnoff, and I was certain we hadn't reached Denali.

"Just outside Talkeetna."

"Okay, I've heard of Talkeetna." One of my customers at the Next-door owned a dogsled tour company here and vacationed in Seward. I wasn't about to tell Cody how I knew about the area. Luckily, he didn't ask.

"My dad bought this place before I was even born. No one has lived here in almost as long. From what he told me, he paid someone to keep it secure and made repairs when needed."

He took my hands in his and smiled. "We can start over, here." He pulled the envelope out of his pocket and showed me the contents. "This money will help."

DUST COVERED the countertops and mud smeared the inside of the windows. Ugly wallpaper separated from seams in the middle of the walls and a stagnant odor filled the room. Old furniture with torn cushions filled the living room, so at least there was somewhere to sit.

The place would take some time to clean, but it might not be so bad under the layer of filth.

Cody pulled the suitcase down the hallway to the bedroom. "Look around in the kitchen. Make a list of what we need to live on for now. We'll pick up supplies when we go into town."

Excited to have the chance to explore Talkeetna, my mood brightened. I pulled an old envelope and a pen from my purse and wrote what necessities we needed to get by. Cleaning supplies, paper plates, plastic forks, paper towels.

The bathroom was simple, and dirty. I added toilet paper and towels to my list. Two of the three bedrooms held old, stained mattresses on the floor. No frames, no sheets. My list grew with each room I entered.

My stomach growled at the same time Cody asked, "Dinner?"

In town we passed a couple diners, some fast food, and ended up parking at the local bar. *Thank God; I could use a drink.*

"Hey friends, welcome to Brian's Burgers. Sit anywhere you'd like." A man behind the bar lifted his chin in greeting.

We sat by the window so we could look out over

the river. "Gorgeous." Happy to be home, I sighed and offered the love of my life my most sincere smile.

"Not nearly as gorgeous as you."

I blushed. *Who is this guy?* I hadn't realized just how much I missed his compliments.

A nice-looking older man smiled and placed menus on the table. "Haven't seen y'all here before. New in town?" I almost flinched at what I had always thought was a southern term. Obviously, people all around the world shortened you all to y'all.

I had been so taken aback by Cody's niceties that I hadn't even bothered to look around until the waiter sidled up to our table. The bar had a cabin feel with wood-planked everything. A fireplace and natural stone highlighted with antler accents. "Yep. Just moved in today." Cody didn't bother to return the smile.

"Burgers are the best in the area. We serve everything from reindeer to moose to elk, bison, and beef. Create your own with all sorts of great toppings." He opened my menu and pointed to a list. "Here, on the right. We have a nice line up of home-brewed beers and cider. Do you know what you want to drink? Or do you need a minute to look over our choices?"

"Two light beers." Monotone, Cody ordered.

Seemed as if it didn't matter if I wanted to try something different. I pushed the thought out of my head. *Don't be cranky. It's been a long day. Maybe after the first one we could change it up.*

"Yes, sir. I'll be back in a minute with your beers."

"Thanks." Cody's voice lowered; he practically spat out the last word. "Friend." His gaze through squinted eyes followed the waiter.

Chills ran up my spine. I wasn't sure what had bothered him and probably didn't want to know. My breathing increased as I pushed memories of cheating accusations to the back of my mind. I tried to redirect his attention. "What kind of work will you be able to get here?"

Still focused on the bar employee, he pursed his lips. "Not sure. I haven't looked through the paper. I'll need to draft a new resume and send it to the right people. It may take a little while to find something that fits my talents perfectly. That's why I'm glad my dad gave me some cash. Should get us by for a while."

Not knowing what Cody planned for our life, I made what I thought was an appropriate suggestion. "I can spend my time setting up the house while you look for work. Maybe I could call my mom and Brittany and have them help us get set up."

His tone sharpened. "What, you're not going to contribute to our life? You think you're too good to work, now that we're back in Alaska? And no. You're not going to call those losers. You really think your momma wants to hear from you? You were a burden to her; she doesn't want you. Never has."

"Cody …" My heart raced as the Dallas version of my husband returned.

"You listen to me." He leaned in so only I could hear him. "I'll not have my wife be an ungrateful, assuming, spoiled brat. I may have ruined you in Anchorage, but things are different now. You'll work for your keep."

"Okay. Yeah, you're right. That's what I thought."

Chapter 23

Jake, age twenty-three—June 2008

THINKING ABOUT the past was just a waste of time; just about as much as thinking about the possibilities of the future. The mountain of horrible things I had done could not be undone. The reasons leading up to my actions still confused me; *why did my dad have to be such an asshole?* Things could have easily been so much different.

I missed my mom every day. Her words of how to be a good man never left my thoughts, but I couldn't imagine a way I would be able to improve someone else's life. It took all I had to keep my own life moving forward. All I could do was ask for forgiveness and pray that one day I'd have peace. Which didn't make sense when I thought about it because I didn't believe in God. Not anymore.

It dawned on me how I'd never done anything good; never helped anyone when they needed it. Everything in my life revolved around my needs. The more time I had to think about it, the more it bothered me. If I had found a job and made something of myself, I wouldn't be in this situation. I wouldn't be relying on drugs and liquor for a reprieve to life in general which I used as a reason to continue down the path of destruction.

I knew it was wrong, but this was an incredibly difficult time; I had literally nothing to look forward to. The pills took away the physical pain and the whiskey removed my ability to give a shit. It was my way of escaping.

Some of the guys in the camp did more than take pills and drink whiskey. Most of them abused meth because it was cheap and readily available. From what they told me, the high lasted for hours. They could forget about their worries and just be.

Sitting in a lawn chair all day, doing absolutely nothing, certainly not anything productive, had not been any better than walking around looking for work. Nothing ever came from either activity. Life passed by a little more with every semi which rumbled above us on I-45.

Dennis and Felix made a few dollars a day at street corners, but I didn't want to beg. I still had a very little amount of money left and I thought about looking for a place to work. Doing the right thing appealed to me, but motivation was hard to come by.

If I could just gather enough cash to get another

motel, I could take a shower every day. I'd rather be broke with water than have a couple dollars and be dirty. My hair had grown out of control, and I couldn't remember the last time I shaved. Probably in Alaska. Felix didn't seem to mind, but he stayed high all day, so whatever had plagued him in the past didn't bother him anymore.

Somehow, though, the minute I opened my eyes, I could feel something was going to be different today. Storm clouds kept the sun from reaching us, but the day held a promise of sorts.

The camp of homeless men didn't usually come alive until after noon; most of the time the statistic included me. I fought through my hangover because I felt like I deserved to feel the repercussions of my actions.

Random passers-by typically didn't slow down as they approached the camp; they sped up and ignored our bodies lying in an open grave. This lifestyle is, in general, the end for most people. Our tents acted as a makeshift coffin.

A clean-shaven man with dark hair and glasses looked out of place as he and a friend with a mustache slowed in front of our camp. If it had been raining, I would've understood the need for them to wait under the bridge until it passed. I didn't expect these guys to approach anyone.

When they greeted the one person most of us stayed away from, I held my breath. Known as Crazy, because that's what someone labeled him a long time ago, his off-color actions and out of place outbursts fit the nickname. I think his real name may have been Bob.

Mustache offered Crazy his hand in greeting. After he inspected it from afar, Crazy accepted it and squinted. I couldn't quite make out what Mustache said to him, but when Crazy bowed his head, I knew it must have been something impactful. Crazy hadn't been known as accepting.

Offering his new friends a dirty lawn chair, Crazy invited the men into his sacred space, then he waved to me and invited me to join them. Most likely because I had been watching the interaction.

Three other men had observed the strangers and joined us around the firepit. I woke Felix and pulled him with me; this person may be offering jobs. Or money.

We all brought our own chairs and formed a small circle. Crazy introduced Andrew and Chad to eight residents of the camp and sat beside me.

Anxiety filled my chest like I was late for something or had somewhere to go. I almost wanted to leave but talked myself into staying. What else did I have to do? The rest of the crowd leaned forward, ready to discover why these men had stopped.

A voice full of joy and kindness reached my ears

when the man with a mustache spoke. His love for life was evident in his expression and stance.

"Hi, guys. My name is Andrew. My friend here is Chad. We came out here today to pray with you." He held up a bible. "We're offering the love of Jesus."

Underwhelmed, I rolled my eyes and almost got up. Seriously, to ask God to help us, as if was going to help, sounded ridiculous. I had asked God to help me throughout my entire childhood and nothing ever happened. Would it even be worth sticking around to hear what these yahoos had to say? Probably not. There had been no reason for me to believe such a being even existed.

One of the other guys did stand up and Andrew said, "It's okay if you wanna leave. I understand not everybody wants to hear about Jesus and not everybody wants to accept that people like Chad and myself are out here praying for you. If you just give me five minutes, I just want to let you know we are here. And we're thinking of you and want to support you. I would like to take a moment to say some words on your behalf. Would you let me do that for you?"

I knew it was all bullshit, but they also brought food. It wouldn't be right to take the food without listening to their speech. I decided I probably had enough time left in my day to sit and listen about this Jesus character, even though it went against everything I had learned about the world over the past few years.

"What's your name, sir?" Andrew nodded in my direction. I turned to see if anyone was standing behind me.

"Jake." I wasn't about to let this stranger break through my walls; he didn't know my story and I didn't like his reason for intruding.

"Jake. It's nice to meet you." He recognized my resistance and relaxed his shoulders. "Would you mind if I told a story about finding Jesus?"

I shrugged. "Isn't that why you're here? Go ahead and waste your breath. I'm only here for the food."

"Help yourself, we brought enough for everyone."

It would have pissed me off if he smiled and acted like he was doing me a favor. Instead, he made me feel like I was doing him a favor by listening to what he had to say. Maybe that's how he got to be so chipper, by offering helpful words that others could learn from if they just listened.

Chad stepped forward with scissors in his hand. "We're also offering a haircut and shave to anyone who would like one. We can talk and work at the same time if that's okay."

Crazy raised his hand. "Can I be first?"

Armed with a spray bottle and comb, Chad wrapped a cape around Crazy's neck and sprayed his hair with water.

"I grew up in an angry household," Andrew said. "Even though I thought it was normal, I learned later how my childhood wasn't healthy." Andrew shared his life story with the group and through his openness, I understood we weren't all that different. He had been abused, too, and watched his parents' tumultuous relationship fail. Of course, the one major difference was he had not murdered his dad.

AN AFTERNOON full of food, cold water, and nice people had been a good change of pace. Twelve of us got haircuts and a shave; my spirit rose just from getting clean.

Andrew pulled Felix and me to the side for a personal conversation. "There's a place in Tennessee called Second Chances. It's a sort of rehab for homeless people who are really trying to get back on their feet."

He paused and waited for others to pass. "I only recommend it for those who I feel have a really good shot at renewing their life. The two of you seem like you're just in a rut and you want to get out of this lifestyle."

I nodded.

"I'm right, aren't I?"

"Yes. You are." I admitted. "As resistant as I started out, your words really resonated with me today. I want to thank you, again for spending time with us, for making it a point to reach some lost souls."

"If y'all want to make some serious changes, get to Tennessee. Take a bus, hop on a train, just get there. It's a tiny home community founded by a previously homeless drug addict, dedicated to helping those who want to help themselves."

Although Tennessee sounded like a great way to start over, I knew what I needed to do. Alaska had been calling for me from the minute I left. I've heard her whisper in the wind but chose to ignore the pull. Until today. Dallas was not my home and would not be able to move forward here.

Mom blew my now clean hair from my eyes, confirming my desire. Or was that just the wind?

Chapter 24

Kennedy, age twenty - June 2008

VIEWS OF THE Alaskan countryside never got old. Blue skies surrounded the majestic peaks of Denali in the distance and the crystal-clear blue of the Susitna River reflected puffy white clouds. As much as I enjoyed the outdoors, I would have also enjoyed a ride to work.

The truck just sat in the driveway all day while Cody looked in the paper for jobs and crafted his new and improved resume. If he went anywhere throughout the day, I couldn't tell.

During my daily walks, I had plenty of time to think. Brittany crossed my mind at least every other day. I missed how we used to joke and laugh about everything. I can't remember the last time I laughed until I couldn't breathe. It had definitely been with her.

Although it was kinda nice to be away from my mom, and I knew she didn't miss me, I thought about Emily and Nathan all the time. Emily was probably dating, and Nathan surely had grown like a weed.

It saddened me to be kept in the dark, but Cody's plans would even out, and I'd be able to go back to Seward soon enough. He wouldn't admit it, but I could dream.

Work also consumed my thoughts. Anything to not have to think about the most recent bruises on my forearm and what I had done wrong to deserve them. My boss encouraged me to come up with ideas on how to improve customer experience. Instead of stressing about my future, I had another purpose. I put the time to good use.

"Hey, Brian." As I dried glasses and put them away, I hesitated to share my idea. What if he thought it was stupid? "I've been thinking. You should offer tastes of beer in little glasses, so customers know which one they really like before they spend their money on a full glass. Like a sampler platter for beers, instead of appetizers."

Silence had never been a positive in my life, so I made it go away. "Lots of people aren't sure what flavor they'll like—or whatever you call it—and I've given more than a few free glasses because whatever they ordered wasn't what they expected. I hate to waste so much by taking away full glasses."

A smile formed at the corner of his mouth. I'd seen that look on Cody; most of the time, it wasn't good.

"It's just a thought." I bowed my head and turned.

"Kennedy. Wait. That's the best idea I've heard in a year." Brian leaned back against the cooler and tapped his chin with a pen. "I'm going to make it happen."

I could tell how much the suggestion resonated; he began mulling it over in his brain immediately. For the first time in—well, ever—my opinion mattered.

Two couples entered through the front door and took in the unique interior of the bar. As if the original structure had been a ski chalet, a fireplace encompassed the entire east wall.

Brian had positioned couches and loveseats close enough so warmth would reach customers in the winter. In the summer, when the fireplace sat dormant, the closeness proved to be a more intimate setting.

I followed them to the couches and delivered menus. "Welcome to Brian's Burgers. Have you dined with us before?"

"Nope. First time." A petite blonde with joyful eyes smiled. "What's good here?"

"Everything. Seriously, I'm not just saying that." I explained the menu first, then, on a whim, described the new beer sampler. "For five dollars you can choose five different beers to test, that way you can find your new favorite."

After I noted their orders, I turned in the slip to Brian. "All four of them would like to try our new beer sampler."

Stunned and exhilarated, Brian nodded. "Nice job, Kennedy. Nice job."

We worked together to put the sampler together for the first time, then again ten more times that evening. It was a hit. My idea worked and my boss loved it.

I felt so good about my time spent at work that I almost didn't care about having to walk home. After all, it was nothing new; I had done it in Seward and Dallas. Now that we were back in Alaska, I needed to remind myself to be watchful for large predators.

A STALE SCENT of old wet carpet hit my senses as I opened the door. It would lessen the longer I saturated in it; I poured a shot of whiskey to make it disappear. To make this entire house disappear. I couldn't wait until we could afford our own place. Or at least to fix some of the brokenness of this one. Winter wasn't far off, and some of the windows were still covered by plywood.

"I had the best day." The smile on my face couldn't be replaced.

"I bet you did." Impatience laced Cody's words. Bent over the newspaper spread out over the coffee table, he frowned.

I ignored the negativity. "I did. I came up with a new menu idea and Brian loved it."

"I bet that's not all he's lovin'."

With the TV blaring, I almost didn't understand his comment. *Ugh, here we go.* "So many customers don't know which beer to choose, so I suggested a sampler platter. It was a hit. Brian is going to put it on the new menu starting next week."

"How many times did he fuck you to thank you? I can smell your sex from here."

"Come on, Cody. I'm not sleeping with anyone else. I love you; you're my husband."

"Didn't take you long to find someone to fuck in Dallas. Why should Talkeetna be any different? I've seen how he looks at you."

"You don't recognize that look because it's called respect. Something you've never had for me." I couldn't help pushing my luck. The far-fetched accusation pissed me off.

He stood and touched his nose to mine. "You can't deny it; I know how you feel when I fuck you and it changed in Dallas."

I didn't care if I pushed every one of his buttons; he ruined my night, and I was about to ruin his. "How am I supposed to stay tight with the things you and your Johns do to me? You're being ridicu—"

A FLASHBACK of a fist coming towards my face—fast—raced through my mind like a bad movie. My heart swam with the memory of five or six strikes, I had lost count after three. I reached up to the spot on the side of my head that hurt the most. Hair that was normally soft and clean had become stiff and gooey with a thick gel-like substance.

Fuck. Pain shot through my forearm as I reached for my throbbing chin and attempted to figure out what other body parts had been damaged. *Ow. Oh my God. It's everywhere.* Pain swallowed my body almost like I was drowning.

Voices surrounded me and I longed to open my eyes. The deeper voice spoke at a lower volume than the higher pitched one. Crusty goo stuck my eyelids together, making it impossible to see the face which I sensed near mine.

The hard floor had been replaced by something soft. Softer, anyway. A bed? Certainly, a pillow. *Why am I so tired?* I tried so hard to open my eyes and sit up as I pushed with one hand, but a stiff shell held the other one in place. Warm fingers gripped my bicep.

"Kennedy. You're okay. Honey, sit back. Stay still until the doctor comes." Soothing coos came from my right side. A faint odor of baby powder covered the smell of disinfectants.

Doctor? Jesus, what is going on? "What happened? Where's Cody?"

"He's at the police station, darlin'." A different

voice—an older male—came from the other side of the bed.

"Everything hurts." I swallowed hard; my mouth dry. After taking inventory of which areas of my body throbbed, I continued. "My head, face, neck, arm, ribs, stomach …"

"What do you remember, sweetie?" The nurse held my hand that wasn't in a cast.

"I fell down the stairs and must have been knocked out. When I woke up, I had horrible, excruciating pain in my stomach." My eyes flew open; I gasped. "The baby?"

The nurse shook her head and pursed her lips. "I'm sorry, honey."

Tears streaked down my cheek to my jaw. I didn't bother to wipe them away. "I guess it's probably better this way."

All I could think of was how I had made the biggest mistake of my life. Sure, there were warning signs and red flags. At first, I thought Cody's discipline had just been normal husbandly acts of "keeping me in line." But I never thought a few slaps here and there would turn into … this.

I wonder if he would have kicked me in the stomach if he knew I carried his child. I didn't tell him on purpose because I was afraid he would take the baby from me. In the end, that's exactly what he did anyway.

I had gained some weight but was still too early to show any physical signs. He couldn't have guessed, could he? Did he know? Did he do this on purpose?

After spending the night in the hospital, I was honestly scared; I knew he wasn't fucking around. My dumb ass didn't press charges.

Chapter 25

Jake, age twenty-three—June 2008

ANDREW AND Chad convinced me how using drugs and alcohol only masked the pain of my traumatic past. Self-medicating was not a practical way to resolve internal conflict—Chad's words, not mine. By removing fictitious cures, the truth would shine through.

With a clear mind, I would be able to find my way, to pave my way to an honest, respectable future. Somewhere in the back of my brain, I already understood what they said to be true; it was as if their words had been spoken in my voice for years.

I remember the last drink I had. It was the night before Andrew prayed for us. For me. He stood before me, offered his love, and read verses from his personal bible. It was a beautiful moment; I would never admit to the other guys in camp how it had changed me. Something clicked. I decided right then and there to get clean and make something of myself.

Before they left, Andrew handed me a bible, held my gaze, and said, "Have faith in yourself. I do." He had bookmarked some verses for me to refer to when I had doubts. The first one I had heard somewhere before but couldn't place where.

> *"The Lord is my shepherd, I lack nothing. He makes me lie down in green pastures, he leads me beside quiet waters, he refreshes my soul. He guides me along the right paths for his name's sake."—Psalm 23:1-3*

Could believing in the lord truly refresh my soul? Would he guide me down the right path if I gave myself to him? I sure hoped so. It sounded like a better plan than what I had been doing.

In addition to introducing me to the big guy, Andrew shared a tried-and-true way to get over things I have done in my past. Follow the four Rs of forgiveness: take Responsibility, show true Remorse, don't Repeat, and Repair damage I'd caused.

I've taken responsibility for my actions. I hate what I've done, but I can't change it. I've paid my dues, spent time in a juvenile detention center, and got beat down. I wanted to find a way to overpower others in the end.

I had remorse that I wasn't able to change how I reacted when Dad got mad; I would have protected my mom. I would have saved her. That was then, this is now.

Then came the hard part: don't repeat. *Was that even possible? Could I foresee the future? The situation may or may not present itself again. What would I do if someone threatened my life? Would I take theirs in return? Yes. I would.*

How could I know what my future looked like, though, unless I planned out every detail? Even then it was totally possible I may find myself in harm's way. But I shouldn't depend on it; I shouldn't plan for the worst. I needed to live my life one day at a time and make the safest space I could with the tools made available to me.

How could I repair what I had done? For my family, I couldn't. But to my own heart, I could. Doing things to help others was one way to heal my soul. In the past, it made me feel like I had a purpose when I made someone smile. Even helping someone carry groceries to their car or holding a door proved that I was worthy of life.

On the first day of my new life, I made a commitment to myself to do something that makes a difference for other people. Without any idea of what that entailed, I counted my money and planned my escape from Dallas.

My flight down here cost three hundred fifty

dollars; I only had three hundred; when I saved another hundred, I would take a bus to the airport and go home. I said a silent prayer asking for God to help me make a quick hundred so I could get on with my life.

Ready to start my plan, I opened the bible to the book of John, and something fell to the ground. A face in the middle of a two-and-a-half by six-inch piece of paper—green on a white background—stared up at me from between my feet. *Holy shit.* A one-hundred-dollar bill had been stuffed inside the bible. The verse behind it:

> *"Jesus answered, 'I am the way and the truth and the life. No one comes to the Father except through me.'"—John 14:6*

For the first time in ten years, I believed. I believed in a higher power, and I believed in myself. My prayers had been answered.

ANCHORAGE had called me for months, but I didn't know how to listen. The time I had spent in Dallas had been wasted, the desire to get home led me to the airport. Even if I had been afraid to be homeless in the frigid winter, I could surely find work in the city. Couldn't I?

Normal people followed a consistent hustle and bustle during their work week. Before, I felt like I was just in the way. Without anything to offer, there had been no purpose in my existence.

If I wanted to make a good life for myself, I needed to figure out how to be a productive member of society. First on the list, I needed to find a way to support myself; to make some money. I read another of Andrew's saved verses and knew I had to go.

> *"Trust in the Lord with all your heart and lean not on your own understanding; in all your ways submit to him, and he will make your paths straight."—Proverbs 3:5-6*

Flight 423—the cheapest flight I could book—occupied most of the day; with two layovers, I was in the tin can for over fourteen hours. As an afterthought, I wished I could have showered before getting on board.

On the first flight, the poor lady beside me wrinkled her nose when I plopped into the middle seat. Embarrassed, I held my breath most of the way in an attempt to hide my stench. At least my hair and face had been recently washed.

Hotels were a dime a dozen in the city, but not many of them were cheap enough for me to be able to stay for more than a few days. Familiar with one motel already, I decided to return. I was surprised that the owner remembered me. We exchanged a room key for a week's rent.

One of the men who had frequented the parking lot earlier this summer nodded as I followed the owner up the steps. Some things never change. I wondered how long he had been here and if his life had meaning.

I got settled in—which meant I sat my backpack on the bed—and jumped in the shower. Grime pooled at my feet; I felt the weight of the world wash off my body and swirl down the drain. This time, I had a good idea of what it looked like to start over. Get a job, keep my cool and work long enough to save the money needed to get an apartment. Work hard, enjoy freedom, find a way to give back. Maybe a church could use a strong young man to volunteer.

Not wanting to bother Pete and his lying brother, I had decided to find a way to support myself. My roommate at McLaughlin had mentioned which fishing boat crew regularly hired ex-cons. When I asked why they needed to hire so many, he shrugged. I figured I could give it a shot.

The two-mile walk through the downtown area of Anchorage and across railroad tracks seemed close and far at the same time. My mind wandered to the possibility of being tossed overboard, lost at sea; I shook the image away.

By the time I reached the dock, the sun had lessened, but wouldn't set. I didn't need to worry about walking around in the dark this time of year. The *Mystery of Alaska* had just pulled into dock, and I watched the crew tie off before they unloaded their catch. Taking note in my mind of how things worked, I knew this job would be for me. Andrew's voice rang in my ears: *Don't blow another opportunity when it comes around.*

"Hey, buddy." The first guy who jumped to the pier ignored me. Walked right by without even acknowledging I had addressed him. Heat rose up my chest, but I knew I needed to keep my anger under control until I had landed the job. Stench followed him and I wondered if they all smelled so bad. I hoped the glare I threw at him burned.

"Can I help you, friend?" The voice from behind startled me. *What's with everyone calling me friend?* "Yeah." I turned and almost gagged. *Yup, they all smell that bad.* "Looking for a gent called Rock."

"A gent? Dude." He leaned in close, his breath worse than the fish-gut stench. "If you're looking for a job, don't use that word. Rock hates that word." He lifted his chin toward the men staring at us from the ship.

I pursed my lips and nodded. "Noted."

The captain, hands deep in his front pockets, stood at the edge of the boat. "Only people who come down here lookin' for me are lookin' for work. You need a job?"

“Yes, sir.”

The barrel-chested man with salt and pepper hair descended the stairs and met me on the dock. “Name’s Rock.” He extended his hand, and I shook it. The other man still on deck crossed his arms over a button-up dress shirt.

Odd attire for a sailor.

“Not many men arrive on the same day as the boss man.” Rock lifted his chin toward the professional, who smirked. “Gus Miller owns this fleet. We’ve had some problems with the crew; he’s been helping me, let’s just say, ‘iron things out’.” A chuckle rumbled from Rock’s frame. “What’s your name, son?”

“Jake Knight, sir. People call me Moose, sir.”

“Look, kid, you can drop the sir. Where you from?” Rock asked.

“Moose Pass, originally.”

He lifted his eyebrow and nodded. “Makes sense. And now?”

I paused and glanced between the captain and the owner. I’d never had an actual interview and wondered if everyone sweated like this when they came to realize their livelihood was in one person’s hands. “Been living in Dallas for the past little while. Just got back today.”

“Lucky you. I just had a spot open up today. The pay is ten percent of the haul. I take forty, then split the rest between my men,” Rock said.

"What does that mean in dollars?"

He rocked on his heels and looked at the sky. "Let's see. This haul will be worth a hundred grand. That means ten thousand for all my men."

"What? You mean ten thousand dollars? How long is the hunt?"

"Yup. You know some terms already. Good for you." Close enough to see specks of gold in his brown eyes, Rock growled, "that means nothin' on the ship. We go out for six weeks at a time; sometimes more, sometimes less depending on when we can fill our quota. Most men only go out once because they can't stand to be away from their woman that long. Won't have to worry about that with you, will I? You hard working? Can I trust you?"

"No, yes, and yes."

With one hand, Rock pulled a cigar from the breast pocket of his shirt. He lifted the other one to block the sun as he raised his gaze to the top of the boat. A deckhand leaned on the railing and gave a thumbs-up, then flinched when Gus raised his eyebrows.

"We leave in one week. Need to give the boys a break. See you here Wednesday."

"But it's Friday. That's not a week."

"We stock the ship for two days before we push off, greenhorn."

I PUSHED MY glasses up my nose and took in my surroundings as I waited for the rest of the crew to arrive. On my way to the pier, I stopped by the secondhand store and picked up a couple of dirty sweatshirts and some rubber boots. I checked out of the motel and waved to the circle of men who shared a bottle.

No one knew my history, so I could be anyone I wanted to be if I remembered my lie this time. The crew wasn't aware of what had happened in my past life, and I didn't need to tell them. They had no idea I had spent four years in juvy, or that I had basically been homeless my entire adult life. They were leery anyway.

"I'm Freddie," the first to arrive had his hands full, so he nodded instead of offering one. "What's your name?"

"Jake, but my friends call me Moose."

"Nice to meet you, Jake." He shoved a box into my chest and nodded to the ladder. "Rock told me you're starting today. Got a good crew, now, so don't fuck this up." Freddie lowered his chin and studied me over the rim of his sunglasses. "Follow me."

Three more hands showed up to help and we spent the better part of the day lugging boxes and supplies up and down stairs.

Edward, Chuck, and Mac had all been dropped off by the same person. Chatter surrounded the men as they picked up supplies and helped load the boat. One after the other introduced himself as they passed, as if a new guy showed up on a regular basis.

"Where the fuck is Reggie? Is he a no-show again?"

My legs weren't as strong as I expected and I tired way faster than the rest of the guys. I sat on one of the boxes to rest and reached for a bottle of water.

"You already worn-out greenhorn? Fucking figures. We'll have to make up for Reggie as we're training a useless body. You just wait 'til we're in the thick of it."

I expected to get razzed and prepared for the insults before asking for the job. I blew off the comment. Being the new kid on the block, I had to earn respect and I intended to do just that.

Even though I'm from Alaska, I'm still a cheechako on this vessel. *Man, I hate that word, but it's true.* The crew didn't let me forget it, either. After the first week of name calling and stupid pranks, I kept my cool and pushed myself to focus on learning the craft.

Captain Rock complimented my ability to pick up quick and work fast, which angered one of the newer deckhands. Trapped on a boat with six other guys hadn't been ideal in the first place. Tension and jealousy drove Edward to throw insults every chance he got.

I just wanted to do a good job and have someone

act like they were proud of me. The other guys accepted me and laughed at my stupid jokes, but Edward had it in for me from the get-go. He glared at me each time I glanced his way and refused to answer any questions I had.

His usual response was: "Why don't you go ask Rock; you've already got your nose so far up his ass you can probably tell what he had for dinner."

"Stupid fuck." Frustrated, I turned away. It took him two weeks to break me.

One hard shove sent me sailing over the short deck wall into the freezing Arctic water.

"Man overboard!"

DURING DINNER below deck, the crew scarfed down the slop before them and reminisced about the incident. "Did you see him flailing his arms? What idiot goes out on a fishing boat without knowing how to swim?"

"Man, I wouldn't want to be in his shoes; he could have died. Do you know how many sharks I saw out here last month? Dude. He got lucky."

"No, Edward got lucky. No one wants a murder on their head."

"Who would have known? Fucker's homeless, from what I hear. Probably don't have no one to miss him."

I sat wrapped in a blanket; my teeth chattered no

matter how hard I tried to make them stop. Their words registered but my thoughts overpowered them. I *had* almost died. *Why didn't God let me go? What more could I do in this stupid life that would be worthwhile? Wouldn't everyone be better off?*

I hadn't ever been suicidal, never thought about taking my own life, but when even God wouldn't take it when he had the chance, I wondered why.

"If fuckin' Moose hadn't started shit, we wouldn't have lost four hours. Now we're not going to get to the prime spot with enough time to fill the hull. We're all out at least two grand," Edward said."

Pain in my hand registered before the sight of Edward laying on the ground. Blood seeped from his lip as he struggled to push himself to his feet. I learned to be the first one to act while at McLaughlin. If you didn't win, you'd lose big.

The minute Edward grumbled that I was to blame for not being able to make as much money as we wanted, anger radiated through me and warmed me enough to stand and swing.

Freddie pulled me into a choke hold. "The minute we dock, you're fired." Second nature took over and cost me a job.

The second I threw that punch; I heard God in my ear telling me I was wrong.

> *"If someone does you wrong, don't try to pay them back by hurting them. Try to do what everyone thinks is right. Do the best you can to live in peace with everyone."—Romans 12:17-18*

Without being able to take it back, I knew I had to suffer the consequences. Such is life. I put myself in these situations, and I had to take responsibility for what I had done. Again.

"I NEED MY STUFF." As the words came out of my mouth, my duffle landed beside my feet. Holding my bruised hand with my good one, I trudged to the city center and found a bench to rest.

Well, that was quite the experience. I pulled up some crab pods, got thrown overboard, and let my anger get the best of me. I sighed. *Stupid fuck made me so mad. Wait. That's not right.* I shook my head and closed my eyes. *God, why can't I get it through my thick skull that no one is to blame for my actions but me?*

The bible sat on top of my clothes zipped within my bag. I opened it to one of the bookmarks.

> *"If you are wise, you are wise for yourself; if you scoff, you alone will bear it."—Proverbs 9:12*

Amazed to find the exact verse I needed to hear—read—I closed the book and tucked it back into safety. *If I make it back to Talkeetna, if Pete allows me to stay, I promise I'll make up for my sins. I'll work hard, love my friends, stay sober, and volunteer. I need to do something good, not for me, but for someone else. I need to do some good deeds to repent. What's next?*

I need a vehicle. Thanks to my time on the ship, I had enough cash to last through the next few weeks and buy an old truck, if I could find one cheap enough.

Police sirens accompanied red and blue flashing lights. The car parked beside me, and an officer got out. Calm and cool, he sauntered over to the bench where I sat. "Heard you had a problem with one of Miller's crews." Sunglasses slid down his nose and he glared at me. "Moose."

Without any way to hide the incident, I admitted, "Dude called me a cheechako and tried to drown me. Pushed me overboard. Do you know how cold that ocean is?"

The cop smirked and put his hands on his hips. "I suggest you get lost before you end up in prison. I don't want to see you in this town again."

RUST ATE THROUGH the bottom of the doors of my

new truck, making it look much older than it really was. It ran, but barely. I used some of my cash to secure the Chevy from a makeshift dealership before I headed north.

Fingers crossed that Pete still worked with his brother in Talkeetna. *I hadn't thought about that. What if he's not even there anymore?* Spending time in the wild surrounding the cabins had been the only place besides home I had ever been happy. I needed to fill that space in my heart. Again. It seemed like the perfect time to start fresh. Again.

As I drove, I fantasized about owning a house on a nice piece of land like my dad had. At the moment, though, all I had to my name was a few changes of clothes, a flannel, parka, and work boots. *And this damn truck.* It seemed strange how the shortest moments in time could feel like an eternity.

Warm air poured from the vents even though I had the control turned to the lowest heat setting. Dirty floorboards masked the wrappers from a candy bar and a bag of potato chips.

The newest Godsmack song blared from the radio, and I smiled. One of the previous owners had broken the knob off the tuner, so I was stuck with heavy rock music. I wasn't mad about it.

I kept right at the fork. Red lights flashed as the railroad crossing sign warned of an oncoming train. I checked the clock and sighed. An empty energy drink can sat in the cup holder and I grumbled.

The safety arms lowered, and I wondered what it would feel like to get hit by a train. Would it hurt or kill me before I could feel any pain?

What is my purpose in life? Why am I here? I've never done anything to help anyone. I didn't help my mom; in fact, I let her die. I didn't help anyone in McLaughlin; I inflicted pain on other boys in the hopes of relieving my own. I didn't help Felix or Dennis. Hell, I didn't even help Kennedy. I didn't have a chance, she left before I could try. There's no meaning in my life. God, why did you save me from drowning?

A horn caught my attention, and I lifted my gaze only to realize my foot had come off the brake enough for my truck to inch forward. I was looking directly into the bright light of the train; I shifted into reverse and got out of the way just in time. I guess I didn't really want to know how much pain I would be in if the train didn't kill me.

Shaken, I tried to catch my breath. Through the partial darkness, a full moon illuminated picturesque mountains and still ponds of water. Sadness took over. Disbelief.

How did my life end up like this? I'm twenty-three years old and have nothing. Maybe I'd never live up to my mom's idea of a good man. Before I left Dallas,

Andrew had assured me that God has a reason for everything. "Dude, I sure could use a hint here."

Chapter 26

Kennedy, age twenty - June 2008

BLUEISH BLACK stretched from the corner of my eye to the edge of my cheek bone. It hurt to blink, let alone pat concealer over the area. When I smeared the creamy substance over the puffiest part, I winced and inhaled so I wouldn't cry out.

Applying makeup with my left hand proved more difficult than I imagined. A cast prevented me from using my dominant hand. "This must be a dream. Right?" If my entire body didn't hurt, I might have thought so.

Cody didn't want to see me without my makeup applied perfectly. I knew if I didn't follow his request—demand, really—punishment would be imminent.

Once skin is bruised, it hurts ten-fold when it's hit again. So, I endured the sharp pain behind my eye which pulsed with every beat of my heart. An

Oxy called to me from my top dresser drawer, who was I to ignore my dear friend?

I popped one pill and looked up to find a stranger reflected in the mirror above my dresser. New bruises dotted my skin, so I slid my dress to the floor and took inventory. I turned back and forth to capture the enormity of the beating.

Four purple fingerprints wrapped around the back of both of my upper arms; I didn't remember how he had shaken me like a ragdoll until that moment. *How had I missed those?*

Face, arms, neck. I turned. *Kidney?* The stairs left scrapes on my shins and the palms of my hands as I slid down them. I popped a second pill. I was surprised that my chin hadn't been damaged from falling down the concrete steps face first. My right arm snapped in the process. *That was a first. He'd never broken a bone in all the time …*

My thoughts stopped as I realized how ridiculous it had been to allow the abuse to keep happening. *Yes, allow. I did this to me just as much as he did. I stayed. But I can't leave; where would I go? Where* could *I go? Can I get away from him? Would he hunt me down if I just walked away? Yes.*

Definitely.

I lowered my chin, closed my eyes, and sat on the bed. *Shit.*

FOR A WEEK after my "tumble" as Cody called it, I didn't go to work. He treated the "incident" as if I had fallen down the steps because I hadn't figured out how to walk. My boss had been very understanding about the half-truth I spun about breaking my arm. When I did return to the bar, Brian welcomed me with open arms. Literally.

His hug struck me as genuine, even though I winced at the soreness of my torso; he truly cared about my well-being. "Do whatever you're comfortable doing. Don't lift anything with that hand, don't do dishes, don't put any stress on that bone. Can you write with your left hand?"

"My memory will have to carry me through; luckily, I don't really need to write much down. I'm sure I can use the cast as a way to cover if I forget." Getting back into the familiar groove gave me a sense of belonging. Regular customers made me smile as they waved on their way to a table they claimed as "theirs."

Something still felt off, though. Like someone was watching me all the time. I found myself looking over my shoulder and tried to hide my discomfort. A chill ran up my spine as I turned to greet a couple. "Hi there. So nice to see you again, Layla. Dan. What can I get you to start?"

"Kennedy. Oh my gosh, what happened to your arm?"

If they only knew, I'm positive they wouldn't have asked. "Oh, my clumsy ass tripped and slid down my stairs." I chuckled at Cody's explanation. "Apparently, I haven't figured out how to walk yet." A smirk and eyeroll made it believable.

The first day back passed faster than I thought it would. Customers kept me busy with chit-chat between running to and from the kitchen. Late in my shift, as I took an order from a tourist couple, I sensed someone looking at me. The hair stood up on the back of my neck.

When I turned to take the order to the cook, Cody grinned at me from a chair at the bar. His eyes were so void of emotion, I almost tripped over my own feet. Maybe he was right: I was just clumsy. A frown covered my face as I checked the time. The clock read seven fifteen; I still had two hours left in my shift. *Why is he here?*

Brian greeted Cody, who glared at him for no reason. On his way through the double doors to the kitchen, he lifted his chin in my direction.

I rounded the bar and smiled at my husband as if everything had been normal. "Hey, I didn't realize you had come in. You hungry?"

He nodded.

I kissed his cheek. "I need to put this order in real quick. Be back in a minute."

His stare burned a hole in my back as I walked away. Without making eye contact with any of the staff, I fulfilled my duties behind the counter, paused to take a deep breath, then joined Cody at the bar. "What would you like me to get for you?"

"I'll take you on the bathroom sink." Cody's eyes glistened. He was serious. "You're not wearing panties, are you?"

I responded the only way I knew would keep him from getting angry. I acted flirty. "Oh, Cody. You're so bad." With a smile and a pat on the knee, I rounded the bar and poured him a water. "I'll get you an olive burger. You wanna eat at the bar?"

"Sure, babe."

His eyes followed my every step. It was almost impossible to ignore, and I found myself changing my attitude with the customers. Happy-go-lucky and carefree, almost flirty, turned into carefully chosen words and minimal smiles. I had to be sure not to laugh, otherwise Cody would know how much I enjoyed being somewhere other than with him. God forbid I like to learn about other people's experiences.

On the few nights he showed up for dinner, I could

expect a ride home. Even if he did intend to surprise me and possibly catch me doing something wrong, the need to not have to walk home was a nice change. After he finished his meal, he let the silverware clank on the plate to get my attention. “You’re going to need to walk home tonight. Friends from Anchorage are coming over to welcome me back to Alaska.

“Oh.” I shrugged. “Okay.” Relieved he would be leaving soon so I could drop my charade, I offered my best fake smile. “Not a problem. It’s supposed to a little cold tonight, but I'm sure I’ll survive.” Wondering out loud, I asked, “Which friends?”

“None of your fucking business.” He stood and left without paying the bill.

Stunned, I looked from right to left hoping no one was within earshot. I stood in place long after he left not believing he would say such a thing in public. Usually, he waited until no one was around to be a complete asshole. What if someone had heard him? *What did I say?*

Brian called me from the kitchen. “Kennedy, would you please come here for a minute?” He led the way to his office and closed the door behind me.

I thought for sure I had just lost my job; my stomach sank.

“I’ve watched your interaction with customers today, and you seem to be nervous. Is that the right word? Like you're expecting something bad to happen." He paused, probably expecting me to respond. "Is everything okay?"

Refusing to meet his eyes, I played with my apron string. "I'm just getting back into the swing of things, is all."

His gentle touch on my shoulder made me jump and he pursed his lips. "I watched how you acted when Cody came in. I have to be honest, Kennedy. I don't know if I believe that you just fell down some stairs."

"I'm …" Pressured to tell the truth but terrified at the same time, I raised my eyes to meet his, hoping he would know. Just know.

"If you need help, Kennedy," he took a step closer and lowered his voice. "Please just ask."

I froze. *What if Cody found out? He'd kill me.* My heartbeat increased at the realization of how true those words rang. I had to catch my breath and forced tears from forming.

He could kill me, couldn't he? How can I get away from him? Would my mom help me? Probably not, Cody was right: she always told me I was just in the way. What am I going to do?

MUSIC BLARED from the inside of our trailer, and I cringed. I had not been in the mood for a party, but there

I was. Without a choice but to enter, I took a pill to chill my attitude.

Cody's welcome home party had started. His friends were strangers to me, and I didn't know what to expect. Smoke rolled out the door as I walked inside. Surrounded by a cloud, I waved my hands in front of my face as if walking through a spiderweb.

Two large men blocked my view as I took note of all the people in my house. Four men sat on the edge of the couch cushions, staring at something on the coffee table. One of them leaned forward and put a rolled-up dollar bill to his nose. *No way.* I had never seen anyone do coke. *Who the hell are these people?*

Four women danced in the small spaces between furniture, three of them smoking cigarettes and laughing. The other one held a bottle of vodka and looked wasted; she stumbled instead of moving as gracefully as her friends.

Unattended steak burned on the stove. I turned off the burner. Dishes littered the kitchen counter and spilled into the sink. Pizza boxes stacked on the floor beside the overflowing garbage can and pans filled with grease sat on top of the stove. I had just cleaned the house before my shift.

Disgusted by the filthy people inside my filthy home, I shuddered. "Cody?" He wasn't in sight, so I put my purse in the only open space on the kitchen counter and went to search for him in our bedroom. I found him.

When I opened the door, I covered my mouth with my hand to hide the gasp. A naked woman straddled my husband; her head was tilted back, and she moaned louder than I thought was necessary. Stunned, I just stood there and watched her grind her hips. I couldn't believe my eyes. "Cody?"

He pushed her off him and pulled on a pair of jeans. "How'd you get home so fast?"

That's his response? Not even some bullshit excuse like "it's not what you think"? The hallway seemed to never end, I just wanted to escape.

Cody snatched my arm before I could reach the door. My bicep ached under his grip. He spun me around, his nose almost touched mine. "Answer me." Spit hit my cheek; his breath smelled of sex. I almost gagged.

"Brian dropped me off." Embarrassed by how he talked to me in front of his friends, people I had never met, I could barely speak.

"I told you to walk."

I found a bit of courage through the pill I had taken and retorted. "I'm wearing a dress and heels." For the only time in my life, I fought back.

Chapter 27

Jake, age twenty-four—December 2009

JURORS REMAINED silent through my retelling of the incident. I knew my actions would equate to life in prison; somehow it didn't seem that scary anymore. As instructed, I gave my final account of exactly what had transpired the night I shot Cody Miller.

"It was raining so hard I could barely see fifty feet in front of me. It was late. So late it was early: around three in the morning. I had music blaring as loud as my speakers would go. I needed to stay awake long enough to make it to Talkeetna.

"I was already angry because I got turned around in some little town I'd never been to before. I was running low on gas, and I doubted any gas station would be open that late.

"I passed my exit at the cut-off before Susitna North and figured I'd catch the next one instead of backtracking. The rain hadn't stopped for hours; it poured hard enough for the road signs to blur. I took the next exit so I could turn back and that's when I saw her.

"There was something in the headlights—a dark figure—and I slammed on my brakes. At first, I thought it must be a dog, but it stood on two feet and was skinny. So skinny. I thought, 'Why would a person be out in this storm?'

"It was cold, too cold for a lady in a torn dress to be walking down the middle of the road. She turned and squinted at the bright light. I inched toward her, and she didn't even move out of the way."

The memory of blood running down her face and the sadness in her eyes took my voice. I cleared my throat and continued. "I couldn't believe my eyes. I recognized her through the bruises and blood. We crossed paths in Dallas. Miss Kennedy had been the waitress in a restaurant me and my friends used to eat at. She was nice to us. Unlike so many other people in the city.

"I got out of the truck, not caring about the storm; I just wanted to get to her. Blood ran down her face from a cut on her forehead. Mud covered her from the neck down. Her pretty dress was torn, she was drenched and shaking.

"When I realized someone had beat her, I almost puked. I remembered how she acted afraid of her husband when he came into the restaurant in Dallas. It must have been him. Our eyes met and I backed toward the truck. She followed me.

"I hopped back in the cab and leaned across the seat to push open the passenger door; it didn't open from the outside. She stood there for a minute, a mix of fright and relief crossed her face. Not sure if she would survive another ten minutes in this storm, I told her to climb in. She must have been exhausted enough to listen because in she climbed.

"The sight of her broke my heart. She was bruised and broke from head to toe. I could tell she hadn't slept in days. Dark circles surrounded her eyes, and she blinked so slow I thought she would fall asleep. A red "M" on her neck looked like someone had branded her. How sick do you have to be to stake your claim on a person as if she was something you owned, like a cow?

"I didn't load her down with questions; that girl had been through enough. She didn't have to explain why she was out in this storm in the middle of the night. I knew she had been trying to escape him. I simply looked in her eyes and asked where he was.

"The only words she spoke were when to turn. I followed her directions and pulled in the driveway beside a run-down trailer. There we were; no reason to turn back. No way she would survive a life with this guy. I reached under my seat and grabbed the nine I had bought from some shady dude in the city.

"I knocked and knocked, and no one came so I

kicked in the door. I don't know what I thought would happen; I know he wouldn't answer to a stranger, make a drink and discuss what he had done. The brand on her neck crossed my mind and something inside me broke.

"The house was dark; the storm probably knocked out the power. When the lightning flashed, I saw the state of the house—torn up from a party—and a man sitting in a chair directly across from me, eyes wide open. A twelve-gauge sat beside his chair.

"I stood frozen, the pistol aimed at his forehead, listening for any movement. My eyes adjusted to the darkness just enough to see an outline. The next flash of lightning lit up the room and I let the hammer drop before he could aim the twelve.

"I've never been a good shot with a handgun, but I was sure I must have hurt him bad; he didn't shoot back. With the next flash of light, I was able to confirm my suspicion. The bullet landed dead in the center of his forehead. I must have stood there forever looking at him; a surreal feeling overcame me, like I wasn't in my own body.

"The shot was loud enough for neighbors to hear; I knew someone would call the cops. As I walked out the door, I picked up his pack of cigarettes. I didn't try to run. I didn't try to hide my pistol; what was the use? I sat it on the hood of the truck and lit a smoke.

"The rain had stopped, so I just sat on the porch

smoking one of his cigarettes and waited for the cops to come. When they got there, one cop pushed me up against the truck, and I saw her through the windshield. Shaking. Scared. I could tell she was in shock, she barely blinked. As they cuffed me, I offered a little smile and shrugged. She mouthed, "Thank you," and they took me away."

Silence hung in the courtroom. I paused to survey the jury; not one of the people sitting in the box had a dry eye. I finished my testimony. "I get it, we're thrown into the cruel world alone—on our own—but damn, the sight of a lady who'd been beaten like my mom was my entire life flipped that switch for me. I couldn't just keep driving. I couldn't ignore her. The rage that overtook me was something I'd only felt once before. That time I was a scared fourteen-year-old kid."

Finished with my side of the story, I bowed my head and took a deep breath. When I faced the jury again, I spoke the final words in my defense. "Lord have mercy on me."

Chapter 28

Kennedy, age twenty-one–December 2009

JAKE'S ACCOUNT of what happened brought all the emotions of my years with Cody to the surface. The sound of Jake's voice soothed me, but the words were unsettling. I had cried for so long that I thought all my tears had dried up. I was wrong. My lawyer handed me her handkerchief and I dabbed my eyes.

After the judge called me to the stand and I was sworn in, I leaned my head back and sent up a silent prayer for strength.

"Mrs. Miller. May I call you Kennedy?"

I nodded. No one spoke, so I glanced at the Judge.

"You need to speak your answer so it can be recorded."

"Oh. Sorry." I responded to the judge, then focused on my lawyer. "Yes, you can call me Kennedy."

"Kennedy, would you please explain to the jury, in detail, the events which led you to walking down the middle of the road during a thunderstorm? Then please tell them why you got into a stranger's truck."

"Okay. Um." I had gone over where to start and what to include with my lawyer, but my nerves pushed the memory away. I had never been in a courtroom before, and the reality of the situation was overwhelming. It was hard to believe the direction my life had taken. My husband was dead, and I wasn't sorry.

"Kennedy?"

I must have paused for too long. "Oh. Sorry. Um. In detail, okay." I took a deep breath and glanced at the twelve men and women who stared at me.

"Cody, my husband, had some friends over to celebrate his coming back to Alaska." Simply speaking the words brought me back to that night. As I recounted the incident, as my lawyer called it, the scene played back in my mind.

ONE OF THE MEN grabbed me around the waist and lifted my skirt. His warm hand stroked my inner thigh. "Yeah, baby. I bet you paid for the ride home with this."

Fury filled my gut, and I picked up the first thing I could reach, twisted out of his grip, and hit him over the head. I lifted the heavy frying pan and held it like a baseball bat to defend myself. My broken arm throbbed inside the cast, and I knew I'd done more damage than good.

A vase flew from somewhere in the living room and hit me on the head. I dropped the pan and covered my forehead with one hand. Blood trickled down my face, but I didn't feel the pain.

It all happened so fast. I found Cody standing in front of me. Why I expected him to fight for me, I'll never know. A wicked grin crossed his lips, and he lifted the red-hot metal "M."

Shit. Where did that thing come from? I hadn't seen it in two years, since he used it to brand my forearm; thought we lost it in the moves.

"Have you forgotten that you're mine?"

I took a step back and slipped on the water from the vase. Pieces of broken ceramic pierced my hand as I fell to the floor. I screamed in pain, then in fear as Cody straddled me. I kicked and wriggled trying to get away, but his friends held my feet.

Another friend held my head still as Cody touched the "M" to the sensitive skin under my ear. Pain worse than any I'd felt before rippled through my body. My voice strained as I screamed, my entire body shook in pain.

There are no words to describe the overwhelming sensation on my neck as it burned from the metal tool. My stomach rolled at the smell of burning flesh. Then something broke inside of me and I stilled.

"There. Now everyone can see you belong to me." He rose up off me and the world stopped turning. The evil in his eyes reached my soul. "Including your fucking boss."

What seemed like an hour had only been seconds. Before he had a chance to stand straight, I lifted my foot and kicked as hard as I could, connecting directly with his groin. At that point, I didn't care if he killed me. Death would be better than this life.

"You bitch!" Through gritted teeth, Cody groaned. Bent at the waist, he held his family jewels and wreathed in pain.

I smiled. *Good. Now you know what it feels like, fucker.* Unfortunately, I hadn't thought far enough ahead to know what I would do after the scuffle.

At least I got him off me. If I called my mom to ask for help, it would take hours for her to get to me. I refused to bring anyone I worked with into my shit show. No one needed to feel sorry for me because I chose to marry an abuser.

Cody's friends all took off during the commotion and I stood before him prepared to take my punishment. More bruises were certainly in my future and for once, I wasn't afraid. For a brief second, I thought I might even try to fight him back. Sure, it would suck—pain always does.

I didn't expect him to push me out the door and

throw me in the truck. A new level of fear passed through me. Possibilities of what he planned to do raced through my mind. "Cody. Where are we going?" My voice was sturdy. *Would he drive off a cliff and kill us both?* "Come on, Cody. Don't do something stupid." *Would he take me in the middle of nowhere, dish out my punishment, and leave me for dead?*

He didn't even respond to me calling him stupid. I'd never seen him like this, and I knew I finally took it too far. Not speaking or trying to hit me as he drove, he just leaned forward, gripping the steering wheel with both hands. The way he stared straight ahead spooked me.

"What are you doing, Cody?" There's no way I was going to let him know how scared I was. *Maybe if I push him more, he'll snap out of it.* "You're being ridiculous, you know. I'm not scared of you," I lied.

Rain poured from the heavens, muddying the ground. The truck slid as he took a corner on the dirt road too fast. He slammed on the brakes and my body flew forward; my shoulder hit the windshield. *He is trying to kill me.*

Through slits in his eyes, his gaze made me shiver. A bottle of whiskey appeared in his hand; he sat it on the seat between us.

Shaking, I scooted closer to the door and hid my hand behind me as I felt for the handle. I don't know why; where would I go in the middle of a thunderstorm?

Cody grabbed my wrist, shook the pill bottle, but only one Oxy fell into my palm.

"Fuck," he spat and shoved the bottle of whiskey in my face.

"No. I don't want to take this."

"You'll do as I say."

The pain in my wrist shot all the way to my elbow as he squeezed harder and twisted. If I didn't take the pill, he would break my good arm; I knew it. *If this is the end, at least I won't remember anything.* I chased the Oxy with one quick swig, but he forced me to keep the bottle to my lips. I drank as quickly as I could but gagged and spit half of it down the front of me.

"Bitch, why you gotta be so fucking sloppy? Dammit, now my truck will smell like liquor for weeks."

His fist connected with my eye before I could blink. I gasped and my head hit the window behind me. Blood trickled down my face and my cheek pulsed.

"Get out." His voice coated in nonchalance. Lightning flashed and illuminated the inside of the truck. His silhouette was unrecognizable. For a split second, I wondered if it was one of his friends who had driven me to the wilderness.

"Out!" He screamed at the top of his lungs.

I shook my head, scared to leave and scared to stay.

The next second, Cody opened my door from the outside. The midnight thunderstorm crashed around him.

A flurry of flashing light and rolling thunder mixed with the calming effect of the Oxy and whiskey confused me; I wasn't sure which way was up.

In one swift move, he pulled me from the truck and threw me to the ground. I landed on my stomach; my hands sank into the mud and were scraped raw by the rocks underneath. By the time I looked over my shoulder, he was gone.

TO THE JURY, I finished recounting the story. "I know it sounds stupid, but I started walking home. What choice did I have? I had nothing to my name; I was one hundred percent dependent on Cody. In my fog, I was thinking of ways to apologize for what I had done.

"Then, headlights illuminated the road from behind me and when I turned, I thought I saw a halo. It was raining so hard, and I was only wearing a dress; I was soaked to the bone and freezing. My entire body hurt, especially my head, neck, and wrist.

"The man in the truck—Jake—wasn't a stranger, not really. But I didn't know it was him at the time. I was so scared and high that I didn't even bother to try to recognize whose truck I got into. All I saw was a man with kind eyes. I instantly felt safe. I knew that he wouldn't hurt me. His voice was low and calm and felt almost warm. I was so cold and tired. I just wanted to be warm and dry.

"It wasn't until I was talking with my lawyer, that I realized our paths had crossed before. His lawyer said that Jake knew me. My thoughts went back to my time in Dallas, and I did a double take. I asked her if his last name was Knight. She confirmed and I cried. He was quite literally my knight in shining armor. He saved me. He rescued me from my life of hell."

Jake stared at me from behind the lawyer's table. A faint smile touched his lips.

"I want to say thank you to my angel. Jake, you saved my life. I couldn't possibly find a way to express how much you mean to me. You gave me my best chance to live a normal, happy life. Without you, I may not have survived." I turned to address the jury directly. "I've told you what led up to Jake rescuing me, but please know that what he did proved how he is the most selfless person alive. He risked everything for someone he barely knew."

I took a deep breath and studied my pretty pink fingernail polish. "From my vantage point in the truck, I heard a gunshot, and I knew I would never be hurt again. Relief floated through me like a wave. My shoulders sagged and my head bowed as I cried. The tears that streamed down my cheeks were not because I was sad about my husband being dead, but because I knew I would never be forced to endure his abuse again."

My lawyer stood and pursed her lips. "You've explained a pretty horrific situation, Kennedy. I understand you were scared, but do you really believe your husband was so abusive that he deserved to die?"

We hadn't discussed this question in my preparations. My blood ran cold; I stared at her for thirty seconds too long. Unable to disguise the disgust in my voice, I said, "Every time I would walk towards him, my body grew tense because I knew I was headed straight for hell. I don't know how to explain how much his abuse killed me inside. I still can't sleep more than a few hours without waking from a nightmare. I see him on the road nearly every day. His voice rings in my ears." I paused and wiped away a tear. "Yes."

"I understand. Would you please show the nice people of the jury some of your other permanent reminders of your abusive life with Cody Miller?"

Starting at the top, I pointed to my head. "Multiple concussions which have left me with bad short-term memory. Broken cheekbone, nose, jaw, teeth. Branded with an "M" on my neck and arm. Scars from handcuffs, broken arm, broken ribs, bruises, and scrapes all over." I lowered my head and clenched my jaw to ward off more tears. "Two miscarriages."

After regaining my composure, I continued. "I spent a few peaceful days in the hospital when he broke my arm. At least I wasn't afraid of what he would do to me for those nights. I didn't press charges. I knew when he got out he would come after me and probably kill me.

"In addition to the beatings, he's raped me, drugged me, and sold my body to strangers, not to mention the years of mental abuse."

My lawyer turned toward the jury and studied the face of each person sitting in the box, one by one. "As you've heard straight from my client, she had been abused to the extreme and forced to endure the unimaginable, mentally and physically. People don't go around just deserving to die, but the world is sometimes a better place without certain people in it."

She addressed me again. "Is there anything else you'd like to add?"

"Yes. I'd held in the pain of others for over twenty years. I exhaled for the first time the night Jake saved my life. I guess maybe it was meant to be that I didn't recognize him. But God put him in my path for a reason. I don't know if he's an angel, 'cause angels don't do what he did. He was hellbent to find the man behind all the whiskey scars I hid."

The jury fixated on me; my case enthralled them. I bowed my head, embarrassed to even be in this position. "I didn't want to be a scared beat-down wife, it just happened. I didn't do anything to stop it when it started; that was my fault and I know it."

I took a deep breath and addressed my peers. "And

Jake saved me. I never thought my day of justice would come from a judge under his seat, but I knew right then I'd never get hit again when he said to me: 'Wait in the truck. Just wait in the truck.'"

Epilogue

Jake, age twenty-nine—December 2014

IT'S BEEN SIXTY months, and she still comes to see me from time to time. When she sits in the chair on the other side of the plastic barrier and picks up the phone, she nods for me to do the same.

It always takes me a minute to register why she comes to see me. She's the only person I ever did anything good for. Her bright smile makes my day, every time she says the only words I ever needed to hear: "Thank You."

The cadence of her voice warms my heart. She's happy. She gets together with her siblings. Her life has turned around completely.

Cody's dad tried to keep her from receiving any of the money she deserved. They had not signed a prenuptial agreement, so everything Cody owned became hers. Although she tells me money doesn't matter to her, it sure did help get her back on her feet.

"I hadn't told you this before because I didn't want to jinx the deal." Kennedy pauses and allows her smile to overtake her face. "Last year, I partnered with Brian, and we expanded his restaurant enterprise. Six months ago, we opened another location in Talkeetna, and next week, we're opening the third restaurant in Anchorage." Her excitement was contagious.

"That's fantastic. You'll have to bring me a burger next time you come see me."

Laughter fills the air. I think about how what I did changed both of our futures. I truly think Cody would have killed her sooner rather than later. Humbly, I know I saved her life.

After she leaves, the memory of that night and the years leading up to it marinade in my mind. It was worth the price to see a brighter side of the girl I picked up that night. I might be here forever; It ain't paradise, that's true. But it's a whole hell of a lot better than the place I sent him to.

Lord have mercy on me.

Wait in the Truck

Lyrics by HARDY
(feat. Lainey Wilson)

I got turned around in some little town
I'd never been to before
Working my way through a middle-of-June
Midnight thunderstorm

There was something in the headlights
It stopped me on a dime
Well, she was scared to death, so I said
"Climb in", and in she climbed
Oh, yeah

Well, she was bruised and broke from head to toe
With a tear in her blood-stained shirt
She didn't tell the whole truth but she didn't have to
I knew what had happened to her

I didn't load her down with questions
That girl had been through enough
I just threw it in drive, looked in those eyes
And I asked her where he was

I don't know if he's an angel
'Cause angels don't do what he did
He was hellbent to find the man behind
All the whiskey scars I hid

I never thought my day of justice
Would come from a judge under a seat
But I knew right then I'd never get hit again
When he said to me

Wait in the truck
Just wait in the truck

Well I knocked and knocked and no one came
So I kicked in his double-wide door
I let the hammer drop before he got
To that twelve he was reaching for

I didn't try to hide my pistol
I didn't even try to run
I just sat on the porch, smoking one of his cigarettes
And waited for the cops to come

I don't know if he's an angel
'Cause angels don't do what he did
He was hellbent to find the man behind
All the whiskey scars I hid

I never thought my day of justice
Would come from a judge under a seat
But I knew right then I'd never get hit again
When he said to me

Wait in the truck
Just wait in the truck
Whoa (whoa)

Have mercy on me, Lord
Have mercy on me
Have mercy on me (hey), Lord

It's been sixty months and she still comes
To see me from time to time
It was worth the price, to see a brighter side
Of the girl I picked up that night

And I might be here forever
It ain't paradise that's true
But it's whole hell of a lot better
Than the place I sent him to, yeah

(Have mercy, have mercy, have mercy on me)
Wait in the truck (have mercy on me)
Just wait in the truck

(Have mercy, have mercy, have mercy on me)
Wait in the truck (Lord, have mercy)
Just wait in the truck

(Have mercy, have mercy, have mercy on me)
Have mercy on me, Lord
Have mercy on me

(Have mercy, have mercy, have mercy on me)
Have mercy on me, Lord
Have mercy on me

(Have mercy, have mercy, have mercy on me)
Wait in the truck
Just wait in the truck

(Have mercy, have mercy, have mercy on me)
Wait in the truck
Just wait in the truck (have mercy)

Thank you for reading!

Please consider writing a short review wherever you purchased, rented, or borrowed this book or on your personal Goodreads and social media accounts. Reviews help readers find their new favorite stories and authors improve their craft.

Sign up for my newsletter to receive sneak peeks, deleted scenes, special pricing, early notice of the next book release, and for a chance to be on my ARC team. ARC readers are offered an advanced copy of a new release in exchange for an honest review. It's the best way to get one of my books for free!

www.kristicopelandwriter.com

Also by Kristi Copeland

TEXAS SUMMER NIGHTS Series – Romance

Somewhere Outside of Sunset - Book 1

Home in Paradise - Book 2

The Art of Loving - Book 3

OTHER WORKS

Oakdale – Rock Fiction

Heaven Scent – Rock Fiction

Uncle Eli – Paranormal Mystery

Lost in Uncertain – Ameture Sleuth Mystery

Scan the QR code to reach my author page:

SCAN ME

About the Author

KRISTI COPELAND is the author of contemporary and book club fiction. She lives in Texas with her husband and multiple critters on their ranch. When she's not writing, Kristi enjoys spending time with close friends, wine tasting, and cat collecting.

www.kristicopelandwriter.com

Let's get social :

Kristi Copeland (Instagram)
Kristi Copeland - Writer (Facebook)
Kristi Copeland (Goodreads)

Printed in Great Britain
by Amazon

57163697R00185